SOUTH BY SOUTHWEST

SOUTH BY SOUTHWEST

A Western Story

JOHNNY D. BOGGS

Skyhorse Publishing

Visit our website at www.skyhorsepublishing.com.

10 9 8 7 6 5 4 3 2 1

Library of Congress Cataloging-in-Publication Data is available on file.

Cover design by Brian Peterson

Print ISBN: 978-1-63450-432-4
Ebook ISBN: 978-1-5107-0042-0

Printed in the United States of America

For the Cub Scouts of Pack 414

Prologue

The wind blows hard in West Texas. Hard and, surprisingly, warm, reminding Zeb Hogan that it's spring, practically summer.

He's standing in a graveyard, overlooking a tombstone. Not much of one, really, just a wooden plank, with a name and year carved in it, already beginning to fade, to wither away.

Beside him stands the man he has sworn to kill, the man he has traveled across six war-ravaged states to murder.

Yet he turns away from the grave, away from the man, looks across the boneyard at a black boy. No, not a boy. No more. A black man, Ebenezer Chase, who is staring at Zeb Hogan, anxious, waiting. Ebenezer Chase's journey has ended here, too.

Young Zeb Hogan faces the grave marker again. Beside him, the man is saying something, but Hogan can't hear him. His mind has wandered, back to another graveyard, four months and more than a thousand long, arduous miles earlier, back to where the journey of Zeb Hogan and Ebenezer Chase began.

At the edge of the cemetery, Ebenezer Chase is also remembering . . .

Chapter One

The only way to escape the purgatory that was the Florence Stockade was to die. So on February 3, 1865, Zebulon Nathaniel Hogan, age fifteen years, four months, four days, died.

Corporal Favour and Private Gardenhire, the only two soldiers of the 16th Wisconsin healthy enough to tote Zeb's wasted-away ninety pounds, wrapped him in a dirty, stinking, damp blanket too holey to keep out the biting wind, and carried him to the Dead House.

"Got another corpse, Harry," a cracker voice said as Favour and Gardenhire laid Zeb on the floor. A weary sigh followed, and Zeb heard boots clopping on the wooden floor, knee joints popping, and heavy breathing. Zeb's heart pounded so hard, he felt sure that the Johnny Reb could see the blanket trembling. He tried to steady his nerves, but couldn't, when suddenly someone ripped the blanket off his face. The warmth of a lantern shone on him, and he did his best not to move his closed eyes.

"Land sakes," the Reb's voice said, "it's the kid."

"Yes. It is." Favour's voice cracked from nerves, but the Reb figured the Yankee corporal's voice broke because a pal, a kid at that, had died. "'Twas the typhoid pneumonia that got him."

From a corner of the room, another Secesh said, "Them Yanks been dyin' aplenty the past couple of weeks."

"Aye," the voice directly above Zeb said. "Though I'd prayed that would not be the case, now that the measles and mumps have run their course, and the smallpox has not increased."

"Must be the weather," the Reb across the room said.

1

A warm hand touched Zeb's cheek. "Feels cold," the Reb said.

Of course I'm cold, Zeb thought. *It ain't even forty degrees outside, been drizzling rain all morn, and the shelter you Rebs give us wouldn't keep a rat warm, or dry.*

"How's his shoes, Major?" another Reb asked.

Before the Confederate surgeon could answer, Gardenhire snapped: "You Secesh took any decent pairs of shoes we had when we checked into this hotel."

The cracker laughed.

A rough thumb and forefinger pried open Zeb's eyelid. Zeb saw the gray-bearded face of Major Harmon, eyes bloodshot, breath reeking of whiskey. Just like always. Zeb's eye began to water. He tried to keep still, wanting so badly to blink. Suspicion clouded the major's face, but at that moment, six men brought in two other bodies—one of which was Sergeant Major Engstrand's—and those men were really dead.

"Got two more Yanks that've been mustered out, Major."

The surgeon shook his head before releasing Zeb's eyelid, which snapped shut over his burning eye. The flap of the blanket fell back across Zeb's face, and Major Harmon asked in a haggard voice: "How many more must perish like this? I have pleaded and pleaded with Colonel Forno and General Winder." As his footsteps trailed away, Corporal Favour whispered: "*Adieu, mon ami. Bon voyage.*"

"Happy hunting, Zeb," Dave Gardenhire said before the Union prisoners were hustled out of the Dead House. A cracker voice began shouting out the back of the cabin for a burial detail.

The slaves came inside, and Zeb felt himself being lifted, then carried without the benefit of a stretcher or a coffin to the graveyard near the tall pines, away from the Stockade. His pallbearers dropped him roughly on the ground, and Zeb coughed as the air whooshed out of his lungs. Neither of the Negroes heard, however, because next Zeb felt the blanket being jerked from under him, and he rolled onto the cold, wet grass, face down.

"You go help them others back inside that house," a slow Negro voice said. "I'll take care of this one."

Zeb could breathe now. He heard the noise of a spade digging earth, smelled the foul odor of South Carolina's thick, black mud. Zeb's left hand gripped a reed, while his right fist clasped the last two brass buttons from his Army blouse, and he prayed, begged God as he had never begged Him before. Prayed for a shallow grave. Prayed that this slave wouldn't scream his head off when Zeb's eyes opened, when he told the Negro what to do. A shallow grave Zeb expected, for he had seen the graveyard while in stocks outside the palisade pine walls—punishment for an attempted escape—had seen razorbacks rooting out the dead bodies. Even now, the grunting of hogs made Zeb shiver as they moved about the graves. His gravedigger yelled, his shouts punctuated by his shoveling: "Get on, you swine! Get out of there! Go on! Y'all stop that! Lord have mercy."

His given name was Zebulon Nathaniel Hogan—after his father's great-uncle and an old Revolutionary War hero from his hometown, Madison, Wisconsin—but he answered to Zeb. Or Private Hogan these past eleven months, even though his parents had said plenty of times that Zeb was too young to be preserving the Union. *What am I doing here, pretending to be dead, about to be buried alive?* he wondered. As he listened to the slave digging a grave, humming some song that, at first, he couldn't make heads or tails of, he began pondering that himself.

* * * * *

January 31, 1862. Mustering day for the 16th Wisconsin Infantry. Zeb remembered that day all too well. So bitterly cold, tears froze on his cheeks. He was bundled up underneath coats, blankets, scarves, and gloves so that he could barely wave the flag his mother had stuck in his hand. Zeb happened to be standing next to Nathaniel Ames, a transplant from Rhode Island, better than one hundred years old, who had fought the British during the Revolution. Yet

Mr. Ames didn't sound a century old as he sang "Yankee Doodle" while young ladies paraded past, carrying the national flag, followed by all sorts of regiments as Wisconsin boys marched by proudly, steam rising from their mouths. They were bound for Union Corners, where Milwaukee, East Washington, North, and Winnebago Streets intersected. It was also where Randall Fitch ran a tavern, the last place those soldiers could fill their bellies with grog before they boarded the train and went off to fight the Secesh.

"There he is!" Zeb's mother began blowing kisses at James Madison Hogan, Zeb's older brother, who, Zeb grudgingly had to admit, looked dapper in his blue coat and kepi.

"I see him," Zeb's father said. Taylor Hogan was a brick mason, had helped build the Methodist church over on Mifflin and Pinckney Streets—and he had the hands to prove it—but on that morn he was just a proud father, watching his son march off to war.

Before Zeb knew it, it was all over. The last of the soldiers had gone, and his mother, now sniffling, took Zeb's flag, handed it to Mr. Ames, and led her son back home. His father said he was going to work, but Zeb figured that he'd likely head off to the Union Corners Tavern.

His parents had settled in Madison in 1836, shortly after Wisconsin Territory had been created. Now Wisconsin was a state, had been since the year before Zeb was born. His folks had told stories about when there was nothing to Madison, even after it became the state capital. Now it was a bona fide city, with a population of around seven thousand and a school and university, neither of which Zeb or James Madison ever went to. His mother, Kate, who sold eggs, and his father never saw the need for getting their children an education, since they'd never bothered to learn to read or write themselves. The Hogans were poor.

While the 16th drilled, James came by to see his family in their little shanty house till the soldiers boarded a Milwaukee & Mississippi Railroad car and went off to St. Louis. After that, the Hogans didn't hear one word from James till he came home

4

in the winter of '63 on a thirty-day furlough. James didn't look anything like he had when he'd left. He now limped something fierce, and sported a dirty beard. He had lost so much weight, if it hadn't been for his voice, Zeb might have pounded James's face with the rotten egg he was carrying to the trash heap.

Sobbing, his mother sent Zeb off to fetch home his father, and hurried James to the table. Hearing the news, his father stopped off at a dram shop and bought a jug of whiskey with his last coin. Said it was cause to celebrate, James being home and all.

Well, James had some stories to tell. He had seen the elephant at Pittsburg Landing on the banks of Tennessee River, where the 16th had suffered more than two hundred and fifty casualties. They'd lost more men at Corinth, Mississippi, where James had earned a limp and a wicked scar on his thigh. After that, the unit spent most of '63 in Mississippi and Louisiana before winding up at Vicksburg, where James caught a bad fever and almost died. Along about then, the Madison boys were seeing their enlistments run out, and the war wasn't going the way Uncle Sam ever figured it would. The Army didn't need any soldiers to go home, so they bribed James and all the other Wisconsin soldiers with a furlough. If they reenlisted, they could go home, or wherever they wanted to go, for a month. James told his brother and parents that every soldier signed his name or made his mark on those reenlistment papers, and here he was. Home.

He never left.

On account of he died.

It never occurred to Zeb that a soldier could just die. Sure, old Nathaniel Ames had been called to glory earlier that year, but Mr. Ames was one hundred and two years old, and Zeb's big brother was only twenty. Three days after he arrived, James began coughing, started running a fever, and went to bed. He never woke up.

Zeb's father fetched the jug he had bought for celebrating, and used it to forget. His mother just took to bed. They left everything else to Zeb—to find a preacher, to arrange the burying.

The Hogans had no money for a proper funeral, so James's corpse wound up at the potter's field.

His mother was too distraught to pull herself from underneath her blankets. His father was passed out. Zeb went to the funeral alone.

The way Zeb recalled it, when Captain Swanstrom's body came home after he'd been killed at Pittsburg Landing, Wisconsin's governor paid his respects and delivered the eulogy. Half of Madison had turned out for the brave captain's funeral, but nobody came to see James Madison Hogan buried excepting Zeb and the preacher. While the parson read from the Good Book, Zeb found himself looking down at that reenlistment paper James had brought home, and though Zeb couldn't read the words, he got the idea to take his brother's place. The way the war was progressing, he didn't think the 16th Wisconsin would mind which Hogan brother they got.

The preacher said to bow their heads, and that's when Zeb turned to see those gravediggers standing behind him, taking off their fur caps and slouch hats with their hands that weren't holding a pick or shovel. They listened to the parson's prayer, then he started singing "Asleep in Jesus."

* * * * *

Lying in a prisoner-of-war graveyard in South Carolina, Zeb thought about that while listening to his own gravedigger, realizing that he was singing that same old hymn.

> *Asleep in Jesus! Far from thee,*
> *Thy kindred and their graves may be;*
> *But thine is still a blessed sleep,*
> *From which none ever wakes to weep.*

The singing and digging stopped, and Zeb swallowed, held his breath, listening to the slave walk over, stop. Zeb could feel the Negro's presence, could almost picture him as the slave knelt beside Zeb's body, and then rolled him over. Zeb figured the slave meant to rob him, guessed the Negro to be some kind of fiend, but the slave lifted Zeb's left arm, and as Zeb let the reed slip out of his hand, the Negro did something Major Harmon hadn't thought to do. He felt Zeb's pulse.

"Glory," the voice said, astonished, "this soldier's alive."

Instantly Zeb's eyes opened as his hand shot out and clamped on the slave's wrist. The black face in front of Zeb started to pull back, started to scream, but Zeb jerked him forward, whispering harshly: "Not a word, boy. Not a word. Just do as I say. There's a couple of brass buttons in it for you." His right hand opened, letting the slave see the shiny buttons that served as currency in a prison camp.

This was the moment Zeb had feared. If this slave screamed, if he didn't help, at the least Zeb's head and arms would be locked again in the stocks outside the prison walls. At the worst, Zeb would be buried after the guards—South Carolina Reserves, as mean, as foul a lot as ever wore any uniform—killed him, and the plans made by the 16th Wisconsin's survivors would have been for naught. Zeb wouldn't escape. He'd never live to see Vicksburg. Never live to see Sergeant Ben DeVere's traitorous face again.

The gravedigger wasn't much older than Zeb Hogan, although he was bigger, taller, and his dark eyes showed a maturity, a sadness. The slave bit his lower lip, and he looked up past Zeb and toward the guards, the prison, and other slaves digging other graves.

Tightening his grip, Zeb pleaded: "Please!"

The slave looked down on the Union prisoner of war.

His clothes, Zeb noticed, were more wretched than his own. A tattered and patched muslin shirt stained tobacco brown. Frayed and thin calico bandanna, once red, now a faded pink. Butternut woolen britches with the ends ripped off, exposing his calves to the elements. Brogans, probably without laces, wrapped with the muddy remnants of his pants legs. Slouch hat, battered into some unrecognizable shape. And a vest made from a patchwork quilt.

Zeb shook the brass buttons.

The slave's Adam's apple bobbed. "What you want from me?" he asked in a low whisper.

Releasing his hold, Zeb picked up the reed. "Bury me," he said, "but shallow. When I'm in the grave, I'll put this reed in my mouth. I can breathe through it. Don't cover it with dirt. That's all you have to do. I'll dig out tonight, and be gone."

"I'll get whipped, maybe something worse, if they find out I've helped you," the Negro said.

"They'll never know I'm gone." Zeb spoke with more confidence that he actually felt. He rattled the buttons again.

"Ebenezer!" a voice cried out from across the graveyard. "What you doin'?"

The slave rose, shaking his head. "Nothin'." Gripping Zeb's shoulders, he dragged Zeb to the grave.

"You need some help, Ebenezer?" the voice called out.

"I'm fine, Zeke. I'm fine." He dropped Zeb into the muddy grave. A pig came over and peered at Zeb, snorting, sniffing, until the slave named Ebenezer poked him with the tip of the spade, and the hog ran off, squealing.

When Zeb put the reed in his mouth, Ebenezer dropped down, removing his bandanna. Zeb held out his hand, offering the buttons.

"You best keep them," the slave said, and covered Zeb's eyes and nose with his bandanna. Moments later, the first shovel full of muddy earth landed on Zeb's stomach.

* * * * *

Breathing with a load of mud on his chest proved much more difficult than Zeb had ever imagined. Being underneath the sod, buried alive, was even more frightening. Zeb almost began clawing out of the grave before an inch of dirt covered his body, as the slave was still filling the grave. He had to bite down that fear, stop himself from climbing out of his grave and running back to the Florence Stockade with his hands above his head, pleading with the Secesh not to shoot him down.

Zeb lost all sense of time, had no idea how long he lay buried, but when the rain began seeping mud onto his hair, and the hogs began digging, he started to claw out. His breathing turned ragged and, for the first time that winter, he felt hot. He dug until his right hand broke free, and icy rain numbed his fingers. A pig went screeching into the darkness, and Zeb stopped, hearing mumbles of guards at the Stockade. Ten minutes, maybe longer, passed before he resumed digging. His left hand broke through the sod, and then he was pulling himself out, spitting out the reed, filling his lungs with fresh, cold, wet air, letting the icy rain wash the grime off his face while he dragged the rest of his body free of the grave.

The rain stopped, but not the wind, and Zeb rolled over. He looked into the darkness toward the prison, but saw only the flaring lights of lanterns. A banjo strummed from inside those pine walls, and Zeb thought of Corporal Favour, of Private Gardenhire, and suddenly he recollected Sergeant Major Engstrand's chubby, bespectacled face, and he started to cry.

No, no tears. I know my duty, Sergeant.

Damming the tears, he began pushing the mud back over his grave. He had to make it look as if nothing had been here but foul, evil, corpse-eating hogs. When he had finished, he backed his way into the woods, still watching the Stockade as the moon peeked from beneath the clouds, until he determined it was safe to begin his flight.

Which is the exact moment that a hand gripped Zeb's shoulder.

Chapter Two

A cold rain, more mist than shower, fell for a spell, but as soon as the rain stopped, a quarter moon managed to peek out of the clouds, shining some light on the cemetery.

When Ebenezer Chase saw the shadowy figure of a hand clawing through the muddy dirt over that grave, like it was reaching to pull anybody nearby to the deepest parts of Hades, he thought he might be called to glory. It had been bad enough with those hogs rooting around, tugging on dead white men, hearing their teeth sink into rotting human flesh. Ebenezer thought he might scream, warn every man Jack in the Stockade, but nothing would come out of his throat.

He'd never been so scared.

Clouds swallowed the sliver of a moon, and rain drizzled again.

Backing into the woods, Ebenezer wondered if he should do what he had planned, or just hightail it back to Oliver Hall's plantation, and forget his dreams, forget his family.

For sixteen years, all Ebenezer had known was slavery. His daddy had been in bondage up till his death from fever two summers ago; his mama remained a slave, and their parents and even their parents' parents had been slaves. Ebenezer's wife and daughter were also slaves, but not in Florence, not even in South Carolina. Last summer, Master Hall had sold them both. Sent them down with Master Hall's brother to some far-off place called Dallas, Texas. Since that July day, Ebenezer had been dreaming of seeing them again. Dreaming of being free, of seeing sweet Lizzie and their baby, Tempie, free.

Without realizing it, while hiding in the woods beside the graveyard, Ebenezer had been playing with the wedding ring on his right pinky finger. Lizzie had given it to him, bawling, right before Master Hall's brother took her away, just took her and little Tempie. Ebenezer had given Lizzie the ring, which Uncle Cain had carved out of a big red button, the day they jumped the broom and got married.

That had been the day Uncle Cain had said that he was going away, as far away as Texas, maybe the Western Territories, or California, and that, if Ebenezer ever wanted to run off, get free, he should seek out a white couple on Lynches River, northwest of Cartersville pike. "Names of Patricia and Tres Hudgens . . . they help free slaves, but don't you never tells nobody about them," Uncle Cain had said. Well, that had been Ebenezer's wedding day, and he hadn't given much thought to running off, or ever being free. Fact is, he had forgotten about Patricia and Tres Hudgens, and Lynches River, a few days after Uncle Cain disappeared—the first of Master Hall's slaves to escape in twenty-two years, which infuriated Master Hall so much he made his overseer, Mr. Anderson, whip two field hands who had been close to Uncle Cain. They never told Hall or Anderson anything. Ebenezer doubted if those poor slaves knew anything to tell.

Uncle Cain was the last of the Hall Plantation slaves to run off.

Till now.

Certainly, since losing his wife and daughter, Ebenezer had often thought about taking to the swamps, heading north. It just had never struck him as how he could get free until he found himself burying a soldier boy who wasn't dead. Afterward, when Ebenezer had returned to Hall Plantation, the image of that young soldier burned into his mind, and Ebenezer kept thinking of how that soldier planned to run off. So, without any real plan, that night Ebenezer had sneaked away from the plantation.

Maybe, he figured, *this white boy, who looks no older than me, might help me. That's what brings these Bluecoats to the South, Mama says. To bring us the jubilee. He might help me find my Lizzie and my baby girl. Help me get free.*

Now, as the rain ceased once again and the moon reappeared, Ebenezer squatted, watching the Bluecoat fill up his grave with mud and grass as the hogs kept an eye on him from a distance. Ebenezer looked beyond the boneyard to the pine walls to make sure no soldier suspicioned that something peculiar was happening on this frigid night.

The boy started backing his way through the mud and dead grass and weeds, backed right up to where Ebenezer hid behind a sweet gum tree. Summoning up the courage, Ebenezer managed to get his right arm to work, and he gripped the young soldier's shoulder.

Zeb Hogan rolled over like a wet dog, feisty, tossed Ebenezer's arm off his body, and started kicking, giving the slave the what-for, but Ebenezer told him in a harsh whisper: "Easy there, Captain. Take it easy. You'll get us both killed if you keep this up."

That stopped Zeb. He stared, his face a mask of confusion, till the quarter moon hid behind rain clouds. Neither moved. Both too scared. Ebenezer looked off toward the Stockade, ears perked to catch the slightest noise, but all he could hear were branches rustling in the wind, and pigs snorting, grunting, rooting. The moon reappeared, and Ebenezer looked down at the soldier.

"What are you doing here?" Zeb Hogan asked.

"I was hoping to run off with you, Captain."

"I'm a private, not a captain, and the answer's no."

Zeb eased up to a sitting position, and started rubbing his legs, his feet, trying to get the blood to flowing again. Ebenezer could tell by the soldier's face that he was hurting bad, but Ebenezer could also see rugged determination in the boy.

"Captain," Ebenezer told him, "I know this country. I can get you back to where your Army is."

With a snort, Zeb Hogan looked the slave in the eye. "I'm not going to the 16th Wisconsin. I'm bound for Vicksburg, Mississippi."

"Mississippi?" Ebenezer said. "That's a Southern state."

"That's right. You best get gone, boy."

"Vicksburg," Ebenezer said. The Bluecoat didn't respond. Ebenezer had never been outside of Florence or Darlington Counties much, except for that one time Mrs. Hall took him and his grandmother to Columbia to see Mrs. Hall's sister get married. Once, however, before the Rebellion, an eternity ago, Mrs. Hall had shown Ebenezer a map of the United States. Ebenezer couldn't remember everything on that map, but he knew that Mississippi had been fairly close to Texas. Closer than Florence County, that was certain sure.

"Listen, Captain, please . . ." Ebenezer began, but Zeb shut him up with a look of his hard eyes.

Ebenezer swallowed, looked away. A hog ran right past them, unnerving them both. Then the soldier was pulling himself to his feet, leaning against the sweet gum tree for support.

"My wife and baby girl are in Dallas, Texas," Ebenezer begged. "I got to get to them."

"I don't care."

"But you're fighting to free us slaves."

Zeb's head shook. "I never joined the 16th to free slaves. I did it for James . . . I did it to preserve the Union. And I don't need nobody, especially with a bunch of Secesh on my trail."

"They won't be looking for you." Desperately Ebenezer pointed at the grave Zeb had covered over. "You're dead."

The Bluecoat pushed away from the tree, weaving a bit, but keeping his balance, and looked Ebenezer coldly in the eye.

"They'll look for *you*," he said, and Ebenezer knew the soldier was right.

His heart started sinking, and Ebenezer felt something running down his cheeks as the Bluecoat started walking away. Ebenezer stood there a bit, but soon turned to see the soldier's back, and he called out softly: "Captain."

The Bluecoat stopped, looked over his shoulder. The moon disappeared again, and Ebenezer couldn't see him, but he told the darkness: "You keep walking that way, you'll wind up right back here. You're heading straight to Florence Town. You need to be traveling west."

The moon broke free again for just a moment, and Ebenezer hooked a thumb in the right direction. Zeb stared at the slave the longest time, but finally turned and followed the direction the thumb was pointing. Ebenezer thought he heard the young soldier whisper—"Thanks"—yet he wasn't certain. Zeb kept walking through the woods, and Ebenezer stood there, wondering what he had gotten himself into. He felt all alone. It started raining again, harder this time, colder. He thought he might be able to make it back to Hall Plantation, if he were lucky, if those 'coon hounds were trying to keep out of the cold and wet. Even if he got caught sneaking back into his quarters, Mrs. Hall likely wouldn't let Mr. Anderson whip him too badly.

Hall Plantation lay northeast of the Stockade, and Ebenezer started walking in that direction, but after traveling a quarter mile, he stopped, let out a sigh, and remembered what Uncle Cain had told him. Again, Ebenezer found himself playing with his wife's wedding ring, and he pictured Lizzie and their baby. Before he knew it, Ebenezer had turned around, and started walking west.

* * * * *

Dawn found Ebenezer following the soldier boy a couple of miles from Florence. Maybe six or seven hours had passed since that Bluecoat had dug himself out of his grave, and he had traveled four or five miles. Ebenezer felt bitter. *Who's dumber, that captain*

15

who's been walking in circles, or me for following him? Ebenezer could have—should have—abandoned the Bluecoat, and struck out on his own, but for Ebenezer the thought of being alone, truly alone, petrified him. *This white boy's all I got,* he thought. For hours, Ebenezer had kept hoping the Bluecoat would wise up, and start heading west. After all, it could be downright tough to find your directions on a cloudy night. Maybe the soldier was waiting for sunrise, so he'd know which way he should start walking.

The Bluecoat did show enough smarts by staying in the woods. The boy had kept out of the clearings, the fields, the roads. Problem now was that he had wandered into the swamp country, but Ebenezer gave the soldier his due. The kid kept sloshing through mud and muck, through briars and brambles, the low-hanging Spanish moss, never once complaining. Never turning back.

A few minutes later, Ebenezer heard a little shriek, followed by a cuss. With a heavy sigh, Ebenezer ran deeper into the swamp to see what kind of trouble that soldier had gotten into. He found Zeb Hogan up past his stomach in a bog, thrashing around, sinking deeper and deeper, but savvy enough to latch his right hand around a vine. Grunting, gasping, he tried pulling himself up. The problem, Ebenezer could have told him, is that Carolina mud's not ordinary. It takes hold of you, just won't let go. The boy would try to climb on that vine, but the mud just sucked him back down.

"Hold still!" Ebenezer shouted, and the soldier's eyes widened, his face paling until he saw the slave. Then his eyes hardened, and his face showed anger, irritation, maybe a touch of embarrassment. Ebenezer cautiously felt his way around that bog, not wanting to get into a predicament like the soldier was in. "Don't let go of that vine," Ebenezer said.

Zeb Hogan's hands were black as tar from the mud, and he wiped the thick goo onto his long, dark hair, one hand at a

16

time, keeping the other hand on the vine, his eyes never leaving Ebenezer Chase.

The runaway slave pulled out the knife he had stolen from Mrs. Hall's kitchen the previous evening, and cut off about a six-foot vine. He tossed one end into the mud. "Pretend you're swimming," Ebenezer said.

Zeb Hogan just stared. His mouth opened, closed, without uttering a sound. At last, he shook his head and said, "I don't know how."

"You can't swim?" Ebenezer could hardly believe it. He had been swimming as far back as he could remember.

"No," Zeb snapped.

"Well." Ebenezer shook his head. "Just kick your feet after you take hold of that vine. I'll pull. You kick. We'll work together, and get you out of there."

Zeb stared at the end of the vine he had been tossed, but didn't reach for it. Instead, he kept both hands on the vine he'd been holding.

"You don't have enough strength to pull yourself out," Ebenezer told him. "You need me." He was thinking—*And I need you*—but wasn't about to tell him that.

"You been following me!" Zeb sounded angry.

"Yeah. I been following you around in circles, but Lord, don't ask me why. Because I don't know. I'm a fool, I guess. Biggest fool ever born, if you ask me. I could be nigh to Lynches River by now, but I figured I'd better stick close to you." Suddenly Ebenezer smiled. "Good thing, too, I reckon. For *you*." The smile vanished, and Ebenezer pointed a long finger at the vine. "You grab that vine, Captain, or I'll take my chances and leave you here. And that muddy grave you're in, it's not gonna be as shallow as the one I dug for you yesterday."

It took some doing, but Zeb managed to let go of the vine, and grab hold of the one Ebenezer had pitched to him.

"All right." Ebenezer pulled. With Zeb kicking, straining against the mud's suction, Ebenezer backed through ankle-deep muck, finally reached firmer ground, heard a loud slurping sound, and fell onto his backside. Quickly he rose, splashed a path to the soldier, and pulled him the rest of the way out of the bog, through the muck, until both fell onto the wet leaves, chests heaving, sweating despite the morning chill.

When Ebenezer thought he could talk, he rolled over on his back, and slowly sat up. Zeb kept his eyes closed, his heart pounding, drawing in every breath like he thought it would be his last. Finally he opened his eyes, and pushed himself up. He looked at the black boy, wet his lips with his tongue, and said, "Thanks."

"No need." Ebenezer looked through the dense forest, found the sunlight peeking through the timbers, and pointed. "Yonder's west."

Zeb thanked the slave again, but made no move to stand, to start walking.

"Listen," Ebenezer said. "If you don't mind . . . I was hoping I could follow you a little ways." Before Zeb could raise much of a protest, Ebenezer held out a palm and began explaining. "There's a white couple on Lynches River. That's twenty miles, or thereabouts, west of here. You're going west. I'm going that way, too. These whites, they're Southern, but they been helping runaway slaves. I figure they could help us both."

Adamant, Zeb shook his head. He said he didn't need any help.

Ebenezer just grinned. "You gonna walk all the way to Mississippi without any shoes or pants?" he asked, and enjoyed the look on that soldier's face when he realized that the bog had sucked off his trousers—what passed for his britches, anyway—and the remnants of the shoes he had been wearing.

Zeb jumped to his feet, started back toward the mud, but stopped, like he was scared to get too close to that bog. Ebenezer couldn't rightly blame him for that. Suddenly the soldier shook his head, balled his fingers into fists, and let out a little oath. His hands unclenched, and he buried his face into them. His shoulders shuddered, and Ebenezer, no longer smiling, heard the Bluecoat's sobs. Ebenezer walked up to the soldier, hesitantly put his hand on his shoulder, and whispered: "Them Hudgenses. I know where they live. Uncle Cain . . . he told me. They helped him get free. They'll help you, Captain. Help us both. We can work together, Captain." Ebenezer shuddered. "We got to work together, Captain."

The Bluecoat stepped away, and Ebenezer's hand dropped by his side. Turning, Zeb Hogan took in a deep breath, and let it out slowly. "It's not captain," he told the slave again. For the longest while he just stared, like he was trying to make up his mind. Finally he did.

"The name's Zeb," he said. "Zeb Hogan."

Chapter Three

"My name's Ebenezer Chase," the slave said. He started to say more, but before he could speak, they both heard the baying of hounds.

"Come on!" Ebenezer grabbed Zeb's left hand, jerking him into ankle-deep water. They started running, splashing, ducking underneath limbs, briars, vines, running so hard that their lungs felt as if they'd been set afire.

The thought of dogs chilled Zeb as he ran. The hounds might have belonged to the slave's plantation owner, but they could also have been the curs of the South Carolina Reserves. The commandant loved siccing dogs on any Union soldier who tried to escape the Stockade, and Zeb couldn't shake a grisly image from his mind—one of Colonel Forno's pets, more wolf than dog, ripping Sergeant Major Engstrand's legs to pieces, pulling him down from a tree, biting, slashing. Zeb had always thought those cuts and bites, and the infection that followed, wound up killing the sergeant major, not the typhoid pneumonia.

On the other hand, the dogs could be chasing the runaway slave. That was no good, either. Not for Zeb. But what could he do now? Other than run?

For two miles, the boys kept up that relentless pace, before Zeb stumbled, crashed into the wet leaves, and rolled over, chest about to explode, stomach turning over. He pulled himself to his knees and retched. Only there was nothing in his stomach to throw up. Beside him, the slave heaved too. Finally they just rolled on their backs, waiting till they could breathe right, waiting for their hearts to slow down. They stared up at those tall longleaf pines, listening.

"I . . . don't . . . can't hear . . . dogs," Zeb managed.

"Yeah." Ebenezer sat up. "But we got to keep running. 'Coon hounds can't track us through water, but this swamp doesn't go on forever, and Mister Anderson, Master Hall, or them Confederate guards, they'll guess which way we're both running."

"West?" Zeb said. "Why . . . how?"

"I heard Mister Anderson talking about it the other day, talking to one of those Confederate officers at the Stockade. Said that Bluecoat Army is pushing toward Columbia. Makes sense that a runaway slave or a Union soldier would be trying to meet up with that outfit, don't it?"

"Sherman," Zeb whispered, sitting up. From the guards at the Stockade, Zeb had heard a lot about Sherman's march, but you couldn't put much stock in anything those liars ever fed their prisoners. They had claimed that Yankee troops had been licked at Franklin and Nashville last winter, but later the prisoners had learned that those battles were disastrous Rebel losses. They had said that Uncle Billy himself had been killed at Savannah, but a preacher visiting the Stockade later told them the truth, that Savannah had been captured, practically without resistance, and that General Sherman was still alive, and burning and pillaging across South Carolina.

"He'd be able to help us," the slave said.

Zeb's head shook. "I don't need any help. And I certainly don't need to run into no Union . . ."

The dogs! Ebenezer and Zeb heard them again. Zeb looked down at his muddy, bloody, bare legs. "I can't go on like this," he said. Naked below the waist, he felt embarrassed. "If I'm gonna be kilt or caught, I want to be wearing pants."

"Here." The slave removed his vest, as gaudy a thing as Zeb had ever seen. "Wrap that around your waist." He pulled a lengthy piece of twine from his trousers pocket, and tossed that at Zeb as well.

He didn't want to do it, felt like a fool, but Zeb figured this quilt would at least keep his buttocks warm, so he secured the vest around his waist with the twine. He probably looked like one of those fool Scotsmen in a kilt he had seen at some of the Union camps while campaigning across Georgia.

"Come on," Ebenezer said, and they started footing it again.

* * * * *

Three full days passed before they reached Lynches River, but after the first night, Ebenezer and Zeb no longer heard any hounds. After they had cleared the swamp, the slave had pulled an onion out of his pocket. Zeb had figured he meant to eat it, and his stomach starting growling at the prospect of food, even a yellow onion, but Ebenezer just rubbed that vegetable on his shoes, then did the same to Zeb's bare feet, rubbing that onion till Zeb thought his poor, naked feet would turn raw. "That'll keep those dogs off our scent," Ebenezer had said, and the trick must have worked. Later, however, Zeb wished they had eaten that onion. The only thing they had eaten were a couple of raw eggs that Ebenezer swiped one evening from a chicken coop at a ramshackle farm.

At least it had stopped raining, and the sun reappeared to warm them. Zeb's feet began blistering, so Ebenezer cut off quilt patches from the vest serving as Zeb's kilt and wrapped those around Zeb's feet. That was good enough to carry him to Lynches River.

Ebenezer looked upstream and downstream. Zeb shook his head, and let out an exasperated sigh.

"You don't know which way to go, do you, boy?" he said.

Eyes blazing, Ebenezer whirled to face Zeb. Being wet, cold, and on the run had left his nerves as frayed and his fuse as short as Zeb Hogan's.

"How old are you?" he asked.

"I'm eighteen." Zeb tried to stand a little taller.

Ebenezer snorted. "Come on . . . truthful. How old?"

"Eighteen!" Zeb fired back. "Be nineteen in August."

"How old?" The ferocity of Ebenezer's tone caused Zeb to take an involuntary step or two backward.

Zeb's shoulders sagged. "I'm four months past fifteen."

"Well, I'm sixteen. So you watch who you're calling boy, boy. I've told you . . . the name is Ebenezer. Ebenezer Chase."

Zeb's own fuse was burning close to the powder. "All right," he said, his voice laced with sarcasm, "Mister Ebenezer Chase, which way is it to that family you say'll help us both?"

"This way!" Ebenezer barked, and took off upstream. Using a walking stick he had picked up in the woods, Zeb slowly followed.

It took them the rest of the day, but shortly before dusk, Ebenezer turned away from the river, and they entered a clearing. About sixty, maybe seventy rods from the river stood something that looked like a barn—actually, Ebenezer called it a pack house—that had been converted into a home. White smoke puffed out the chimney.

"Wait here." After filling his lungs with air, Ebenezer walked toward the door.

A dog, tied up to a pine on the other side of the house, began barking.

Ebenezer hadn't made it halfway across the field, when the door flung open, and Zeb flattened his body against wet pine needles. Ebenezer stood motionlessly, spreading his arms out at his side, palms open.

A blonde-haired woman in a green dress stepped outside, and she let out a mouthful of snuff. "Who are you?" she called out in a voice far from hospitable. "And what do you want?" Then—"Hush, Goliath"—and the dog not only quit barking, it dropped to its belly.

Silence followed, but something sharp and metallic clicked somewhere inside that pack house, and Zeb knew somebody had just cocked a musket. *If this ain't the Hudgenses' spread, and maybe even if it is,* Zeb figured, *I'd be wise to start backing my way to the river, and leave that runaway slave to his own devices.*

"Uncle Cain . . . !" Ebenezer's cracking voice called out. "Uncle Cain said you might help me."

"I don't know no Uncle Cain."

Quietly backing away, Zeb cursed himself for trusting a fool Negro.

"I'm just following the drinking gourd, ma'am," Ebenezer said. "Thought this might be a station."

The woman took a step from the pack house. For the longest while she just stared. Zeb had stopped backing. He didn't know what to do. Finally the woman said, "Come here, son."

Once Ebenezer Chase started walking, a man's voice boomed from inside the house: "And tell your friend to come out of those woods with you!"

* * * * *

They ate bacon and grits and drank buttermilk. Neither Ebenezer nor Zeb could recall when they'd ever eaten so well. Not at Hall Plantation. Not at the Stockade. Not with the 16th Wisconsin or back home in Madison. Not even on that wedding trip with Mrs. Hall to Columbia.

Tres Hudgens was a barrel-chested man, broad-shouldered, bald at the top of his head, with hands the size of the seat of Zeb's chair. His wife appeared to be practically all bones and snuff. Reformed Presbyterians, the Hudgenses had moved to South Carolina from Kentucky shortly after the war broke out. In Kentucky, Tres Hudgens said, they'd worked on the Underground Railroad, and hadn't quit doing their part to free slaves, even though, from what Zeb had heard, that operation pretty much ended when the war broke out, and had rarely operated this deep in the South.

While Zeb ate his third helping of grits, Patricia Hudgens applied a balm to his feet, and her husband brought in butternut wool britches and green flannel shirts for the two boys. Zeb pushed away the empty bowl, and ran his finger along the faded red stripe that ran down the legs of the pants. He looked up at Tres Hudgens.

"That's right, sonny. Them pants oncet belonged to a Johnny Reb cannon boy."

Zeb stared blankly, and Patricia Hudgens laughed as she wrapped a strip of linen around his right foot. "Don't worry, Zeb," she said. "Tres didn't kill any Reb for his pants. We's Reformed Presbyterians. God don't like killin'."

"No, ma'am," Ebenezer said. "He don't."

Zeb tried to swallow. He looked at the pants, at the kindly woman doctoring his blistered feet. He thought of Sergeant Ben DeVere. He remembered Sergeant Major Engstrand.

"Sherman will be in Columbia soon," Tres Hudgens said. "I've heard that McLaws had to retreat from the Salkehatchie River a few days ago to Branchville after the Federals flanked him. Victory is inevitable."

"Hold your horses, Tres," his wife told him, and splattered the side of a spittoon with tobacco juice. "Wade Hampton's cavalry's still in Columbia, and Hampton ain't no McLaws."

"He ain't no Sherman, neither."

"*Bah.*" Patricia waved her hand at her husband, then finished wrapping Zeb's other foot. "There. That should hold you. Fetch 'em some footwear, Tres."

Zeb stood, testing his feet, then grabbed the trousers that had once been worn by a Confederate artilleryman. Ebenezer Chase was already dressing in his new duds. Mr. Hudgens fetched him a pair of brogans, and gave Zeb a pair of boots that were a couple of sizes too big, but Zeb wasn't one to complain. He even handed Zeb a pair of linen underdrawers, and everyone turned their backs so Zeb could remove the slave's quilted vest and get dressed.

Ebenezer picked up the vest, and put it on.

"You sure you want to wear that, son?" Patricia Hudgens asked.

The runaway slave smiled. "Yes'm. It was . . . a gift." The smile died. Lizzie had made it for him, before they had been married. He steeled himself, refusing to cry, and sat down to pull on the brogans.

"It's about fifty, sixty miles from here to Columbia," Mrs. Hudgens said after the two boys were dressed. "You follow this little game trail out back, and it'll lead you straight to the Cartersville Road. At the crossroads, you turn west on the Camden Pike. Just stick to the woods, or close to them, and follow that road. When you get to near abouts Camden, the road forks. Go southwest, and that'll get you close to Columbia. You should be able to find the Union soldiers there, by then. But keep your eyes open for Rebs. I don't care what Tres says. This war ain't over. Not yet. South Carolina ain't got no quit in her."

"We're not going to Columbia," the slave blurted out, and Zeb ground his teeth. "I'm bound for Texas. Zeb here's going to Mississippi."

"What?" The couple's eyes clouded with suspicion.

"Thank you both," Zeb said, and started for the door, but Tres Hudgens fetched and cocked, his long rifle, and poked Zeb's stomach with the barrel.

"Not so fast, son," he said.

Zeb was ready to tear Ebenezer Chase's head clear off.

"Mississippi's a long way from South Carolina," Patricia said, "and Texas is even farther, and both are Confederate states. What you two boys want to go there for?"

Zeb didn't answer, but Ebenezer said, "My wife and daughter got sold to a planter in Dallas, Texas."

Patricia said something about him being a poor child, but Tres said, "You're too young to be a husband and a daddy."

"Well, I am both. And I'm going to Dallas."

"And you?" Tres still held that long rifle only inches from Zeb's belly button. "What business you got in Mississippi?"

"Personal. I got a fellow to see in Vicksburg."

"What a couple of young fools," Tres said, but didn't lower his musket. "You know how far it is to Dallas? Or even Vicksburg? Do you even know where your wife and child are? You'd never find them. You'd never get there. You'll both get killed, or captured."

Ebenezer's lips trembled, and tears welled in his eyes, but his voice never wavered. "I got to try."

"Tres," his wife pleaded, and her husband lowered the rifle, said, "Wait here," and disappeared into the loft. A few minutes later he climbed down with a rolled bit of parchment, which he spread out over the table between the empty bowls and glasses. It was a map, though not fancy, and not overly detailed. Tres Hudgens pointed to an empty spot. "Here's about where we are." He traced to a black star. "This is Columbia." Dragging his finger across the paper. "You just go south by southwest across Carolina, Georgia, Alabama, and Mississippi, and you might reach here, if the good Lord's willing." His finger stopped at a black circle next to a blue line. "Vicksburg." He sighed. "It's on the Mississippi River. Been under Union control since '63," Tres said. "But you know that."

Patricia told Ebenezer: "You'll be safe in Vicksburg, son."

"But I'm bound for Texas." Ebenezer looked at the map. "Where's Dallas?"

"I'm sorry, boy," Tres said. "This map ends at the Mississippi River. To get to Dallas, you have to cross that river, then go through Louisiana. Then you're in Texas, but honestly, I don't have any idea where Dallas is."

"Aye." Patricia Hudgens slowly traced her finger from the black star that marked Columbia to another dot that marked Vicksburg, Mississippi. "It's a long, long way to there. I'd go to Columbia. Your chances are much better of surviving than . . ." Her voice trailed off.

Zeb pointed to some lines on the map. "What are these?"

"Railroads," Tres replied. "You'll need to stay clear of railroads. Although this map is some five years old, I am not sure if those railroads are still running, or if they've been destroyed by Federal troops. The map's yours, boys, but that's about all we can do to help you. Other than tell you, again, to make for Columbia. Make for the Union troops. Save yourselves. Forget your wife and child till this war's over. Forget that man you need to see in Mississippi."

The two boys remained silent, stern.

"Moon's rising," Patricia said. "Best to travel at night. Hide in the daytime. You'll have a full moon to guide your way in a few days. That's good . . . and bad, as it'll be easier for y'all to be seen. Be careful. Remember what Tres said. South by southwest."

Tres rolled up the map and stuck it in a cloth haversack that Patricia had filled with scones, jerky, and a jar of molasses. He handed the haversack to Zeb. Zeb slung it over his shoulder and followed Ebenezer out the door.

Patricia Hudgens called at them to wait as she fetched a couple of onions out of a barrel. She dropped them into the haversack, and said, "These onions, they ain't to be et."

"I know what they're for," Ebenezer said, and Zeb knew that was the truth. His feet still ached from where Ebenezer had rubbed them to throw the hounds off their scent.

After thanking the couple, Ebenezer and Zeb hurried back toward the river.

* * * * *

Everybody, it seemed, was coming down the road from Camden, even in the dead of night. Zeb and Ebenezer didn't make good time.

"Where's everybody going?" Ebenezer asked.

"Running, I guess," Zeb replied. "Fleeing Uncle Billy's troops."

The weather didn't help. It would rain, hard at times, and the clouds kept that sun from heating up their bones. Both boys felt as if they'd never get warm again. Zeb and Ebenezer stuck to the woods, hardly daring to show their faces on the road. One time, they hid in a ditch as a troop of Rebel cavalry led a bunch of cannon and caisson down the road.

"Reckon those soldiers are running, too," Ebenezer said.

They passed farms, the poor affairs owned by the white trash Sergeant Major Engstrand called dirt-eaters, and spotted dingy tablecloths hanging from the windows, words painted on them.

"What's that say?" Zeb asked.

"You can read," Ebenezer said.

Zeb balled his hands into fist. "Got something in my eye." He uncurled his fist, and began wiping his eye.

Sighing, Ebenezer read the words to himself.

HAVE MERCY ON US

* * * * *

The road ended at a river. Crossing by ferry would take some explaining to the ferryboat captain. Besides, neither Zeb nor the slave had the $50, Confederate, they heard the ferryman charged folks to cross the Wateree. But that river ran high from all the rains, way too wide for Ebenezer to swim, and Zeb couldn't swim.

Instead, they crossed the road that night, sneaking downstream about a mile. Then Ebenezer dragged a big log out into the shallows, told Zeb to hold on, and they floated across to a big island in the center of the river. There they spent the night, eating the last of the scones, though they still had some jerky and about half the bottle of molasses.

All the next day, they rested on that island, hiding in the thickets as rain fell off and on. After sunset, the two hauled the log out and into the river, floating the rest of the way across the Wateree.

Then they walked.

Walked.

Hid.

Slept.

Walked some more.

Zeb couldn't remember how long they had been on the road, running, but hardly covering any distance. Ten days? Longer? Did time really matter any more?

"Let's get the lead out," he suddenly announced, and picked up the pace, but he couldn't keep it up. His legs, his feet hurt. In less than a hundred yards, he was limping again, walking through the woods near the road, then stopping, leaning against a pine, trying to catch his breath.

"We'd better rest a mite," Ebenezer said.

Zeb tried to say they didn't have time to rest. He had to get to Vicksburg. By the Eternal, he was used to marching from his tour with the 16th Wisconsin. But he couldn't. He slid down against the tree, lungs working, and dropped his head.

* * * * *

A thick fog settled upon them for a few days, so they decided to chance walking in the daylight, but after a day or two, traffic on the road got heavier, much heavier, and steadier. Then, suddenly, the traffic died again.

The day turned clear, and a rumbling came echoing from up the road.

"Thunder." Ebenezer sighed. "Lordy, I've seen enough rain."

"That ain't rain," Zeb told him. "Artillery."

* * * * *

They stopped to eat under a maple tree.

Ahead of them came the muffled reports of cannon fire.

"Is that Columbia?" Ebenezer asked.

"I reckon it is."

"What are we going to do?"

31

"Find a way around that city. After we eat."

They had only the jar of molasses left, and Zeb unscrewed the lid, reached inside, pulling out fingers full of the sweet goo. He passed the jar to Ebenezer.

They never heard anything until the soldiers were right on top of them.

Chapter Four

"Well, looky here." About a dozen muskets being cocked punctuated that statement.

Leaping to his feet, dropping the jar, Ebenezer reached for his knife. He would rather die than be captured and returned to Master Hall and Mr. Anderson's black-snake whip, but when he saw the soldiers, he froze. Dressed in blue uniforms and bummer caps, none of the soldiers had shaved in days, and their eyes were rimmed red. Union soldiers. *Dirty and miserable*, Ebenezer thought, *just like Zeb and me.*

"Hey, what you got in that jar?" One of the soldiers handed his musket to the man standing next to him and ran over, snatching the glass that had dropped beside Ebenezer's feet. Zeb sat there, not saying a word, just staring at those muskets pointed at him.

"Hey!" The soldier licked his fingers. "It's molasses."

A burly man with stripes on his sleeves hurried over and swiped the glass from the younger soldier's hand. "I'll take that, Harker," he said.

"Aww, Sergeant . . ."

"Back in line." The sergeant could scarcely get his thick fingers inside the lip of the jar. As he licked the last of the molasses, he looked down at Zeb Hogan and said, "I warrant the war's over for you, Reb."

"I'm no Reb," Zeb Hogan said.

The sergeant snorted. "No, I reckon you ain't. Not no more. You don't even have a gun."

"Must have lost his cannon, Sergeant," a red-bearded man said.

"Yeah, that's right, Hopkins," said another. "Rebs ain't got no fight left in them."

Another Federal picked up the haversack, tossed the map aside, and shook the empty haversack before dropping it to the dirt in disgust.

"I am an escaped prisoner of war from the Florence Stockade," Zeb said, but nobody seemed to hear or care what he said. "You with Sherman?"

The sergeant threw the empty jar away and fished a piece of jerky from the pocket of his light blue trousers. As the big sergeant bit into the jerked beef, he tapped Zeb Hogan's shoulder with the barrel of his musket. "On your feet, Reb."

Zeb grunted, but stood, still proclaiming that he wasn't a Rebel soldier.

"You're wearing Secesh britches," the red-bearded soldier named Hopkins said. "Artillery britches. And you're traveling with your chattel." He hooked his thumb at Ebenezer.

"I tell you," Zeb said, "I escaped from the Stockade. This slave . . . he's a runaway . . . helped me to escape." A sudden desperation appeared in his face, in his voice. "You've got to tell Sherman about the Stockade. It's in Florence, maybe seventy or so miles east of here. You've got to free our boys up there. It's wretched. It's terrible. Thousands of our men are there. Hardly any shelter. Disease. Our men are dying there every day."

"Uncle Billy knows all about that Florence prison," Hopkins said.

"It ain't no Andersonville," Harker said.

"It's worse!" Zeb snapped. Frustration accented his voice. "I tell you I'm with the 16th Wisconsin. I was captured after Atlanta. Who are you with?"

Hopkins said they were with the 123rd New York.

About that time, Ebenezer found his voice. "He's telling y'all the truth!"

They all studied the black then. Unable to match their stares, Ebenezer looked down at his muddy brogans.

"Where'd you enlist?" the sergeant asked.

"Madison," Zeb said.

"Where'd you fight?"

"My brother fought at Pittsburg Landing and Corinth," Zeb said. "He was furloughed, and . . . well, I taken his place after he caught some sickness and died. I took a steamer to Clifton, Tennessee, then marched to Georgia. Come on, guys . . . you gotta believe me. I was marching with you boys."

"Which brigade?" the sergeant asked.

"First. Under Force. Third Division. Seventeenth Corps."

Silence. Harker looked at the sergeant, his eyes full of questions.

"We might as well take him back to Columbia, Sarge," Hopkins said finally. "Tell the captain we didn't find no Rebs on this road. I mean, there ain't no sense in us missing all the fun that's gonna be had back in that town."

"Yeah," another one said. "We can lock him up in one of them churches."

"That big brick one we passed," Harker said.

"Fetch somebody from the 16th Wisconsin," Hopkins suggested. "They'll recognize him, or he'll be on his way to one of our prison camps."

"All right," the sergeant said. "Let's march."

When Ebenezer started to go with them, Redbeard pushed him aside. "Not you, boy."

Hopkins stared at the slave, no friendliness in his face. "We got enough slaves following our Army. Run along, boy, you're free. But you can't come with us."

Stunned, Ebenezer watched them march down the road, muskets still trained on Zeb. For a moment, he couldn't move, trying to let Hopkins's words sink in, not believing them, but fear struck him as the Federals, and Zeb Hogan, started to disappear. He fetched the map they'd left on the ground and stuck it in the haversack, which he tossed over his shoulder, and then he took off, following the soldiers and their prisoner at a distance.

* * * * *

Columbia was nothing like Ebenezer remembered. He recalled the state capital as elegant. Real pretty—hilly, blue skies, and rich gardens. What he saw that day sent a shiver up his spine. In the gloaming, one Federal soldier galloped right past him, dragging a pig behind him and brandishing a silver plate in his free hand, his haversack bulging with who knows what. Ebenezer hurried to catch up with those soldiers of the 123rd New York, but before he could get close, a bunch of Negroes caught him and threw him against a stack of smoldering cotton bales in the middle of the street.

"The jubilee!" cried a bald man whose breath reeked of rum.

"Massah Abraham, he made us free!" yelled a younger man.

"Let go of me," Ebenezer said. "I need to catch up to those soldiers!"

"You gonna j'in the fight?" a third person said, and Ebenezer realized this was a woman. She smiled and held out a brown jug. "This here boy's gonna j'in the fight. I reckons he needs some courage to celebrate."

About ten men—though to Ebenezer it felt like a dozen times that number—encircled him. The woman came closer, giggling, her breasts about to come loose from her blouse. Two men grabbed Ebenezer's arms, pinned them behind his back, while another took hold of his head and pried his mouth open. Ebenezer tried to shake his head, tried to scream, twist, bite. Yet that jug of rum came closer. They had let his legs free, however, so, as much as he hated to do it, Ebenezer kicked out at that smiling woman, spilling the rum, and her along with it.

That tore it. She let loose with a curse, and the big bald man sent his fist right into Ebenezer's face, splitting his lips. Rough hands threw him onto the cobblestone road. The heavy jug flew, caught him in the head as he tried to regain his feet. He saw a flash of colors—red, orange, white—as he fell on his face. The jug shattered, and he heard the freed, drunken slaves shouting, cursing, closing in. Biting back the pain, he rose on unwieldy legs and took off, weaving down an alley.

He quickly discovered the slaves weren't the only ones drinking, celebrating, becoming more and more unruly. Ebenezer hid when he spotted some Bluecoat soldiers coming out of a house. One of them waved a torch in his right hand and a quarter-full bottle in his left, singing:

Hail, Columbia,
Happy land.
If I don't burn you,
I'll be damned.

The man tossed the torch back inside the house, and Ebenezer took off running, his leg muscles now cooperating with the rest of his body. Everywhere he turned, he saw cotton bales aflame and the fires spreading as the wind kicked up. A girl, maybe six years old, stood on the corner, crying for her mama, her papa, holding a doll in her hand. No one stopped to help her. Ebenezer wanted to, but he knew better, knew his place. *A black boy helping a white child?* The citizens of Columbia would have killed him. Maybe the Union soldiers would have, too. Besides, he had to find Zeb.

He kept looking for a brick church. At one corner building, he saw a frightened man passing out pails. He thought those containers would be used to help fight the fires, but no. Instead, while two big slaves were being forced to hold whiskey barrels on their shoulders, the Bluecoats, singing and laughing, were using the pails to dipper out the whiskey.

Madness, Ebenezer thought. *Everyone here has gone mad.*

Finally Ebenezer saw the church steeple, ran up to the building, only to slide to a stop when he spied Union soldiers, carrying torches, surrounding a man on the doorsteps. It was a brick building, but these soldiers hadn't been the ones who had captured Zeb Hogan.

"We aim to burn the church where you traitors signed the articles of secession!" one soldier yelled at a man on the ground.

On his knees, shaking his head, the old man clasped his hands as in prayer. A Union soldier pressed a bayonet against the old man's throat, and the white-haired man in black broadcloth begged, not for his life, but for the church to be spared.

"This is not the church, men! The Baptist church you seek is on the next block. Please . . . for the love of God . . . I beseech you, don't do this! Don't burn our new church."

"Which church is this?" the Federal with the bayonet demanded.

"Methodist," the old man answered.

The soldier lowered the big blade. "Criminy," he said, "I'm Methodist myself."

The Bluecoats turned as one, pushing Ebenezer aside as they moved on. When they were out of sight, Ebenezer went up to the old man and helped him to his feet.

"I'm all right," the man said, angrily brushing Ebenezer's hands away. "Get out of here."

Backing away a few steps, Ebenezer stared at the church. This church had brick columns, and Ebenezer recalled it well, because this was where Mrs. Hall's sister had been married back in 1862. He could remember sitting with the other Negroes on the balcony—this church had more Negro members than white ones—admiring the gas chandeliers and wondering how many folks this church would seat.

"This *is* the Columbia Baptist Church," Ebenezer suddenly told the man, who gave the black teen a look that told him he had better keep quiet, and not tell those Federal troops how they had been fooled.

Quickly Ebenezer left.

The darkening skies were heavy with smoke now, the streets full of wagons, cannon, men, women. Bells clanged, but nobody lifted a finger to put out the fires. What's worse, Ebenezer had lost Zeb Hogan. A covered wagon almost ran him over, and he tripped over the root of a giant oak tree, scraping his knee so badly that he started limping. Lips split, pant leg torn, knee bleeding, eyes full of fright, he wandered through the bedlam.

A woman screamed as two Bluecoats dragged her from her house, then began throwing bricks through the windows.

Another soldier came by, wringing a chicken's neck.

Crazy. The whole world's turned upside down.

That's when he recognized the soldier with the chicken.

"Hey!" Ebenezer yelled, and the New Yorker named Hopkins turned around.

"Yeah. What you want, boy?"

"Where's Zeb Hogan?"

"I don't know anyone named Zeb Hogan." He started to walk away, but Ebenezer didn't stand a chance traveling by himself. He needed help, and Zeb Hogan was his only chance. Or so he thought.

Yanking Hopkins's left shoulder, Ebenezer spun him around. The infantryman dropped the dead chicken, scared by Ebenezer's bloodied face and the desperate look in his eyes.

"Remember me?" Ebenezer asked. Hopkins showed no recognition. "The Wisconsin boy you captured. You thought he was a Reb. Where'd y'all take him?"

"You're free. You don't . . ."

"Where is he?" Ebenezer drew back his fist as if he planned on pounding him. Later he realized he might have struck the soldier if Hopkins, cringing, hadn't cried out, "The church . . . over there! We locked him in the basement."

Ebenezer didn't thank him. He just took off running, leaving Hopkins to his dead chicken and soiled britches.

When Ebenezer rounded the corner, he saw the soldiers who had been about to torch the Baptist church leaving the Washington Street Methodist Church.

In flames. The fire turning the dusk into high noon.

"Oh, good Lord, help me and that soldier boy," prayed Ebenezer as he ran across Marion Street.

This church was brick, too, though not quite as palatial as the Baptist building the Federals had spared. Choking, thick, black smoke poured out the open door and busted windows. Brick might not burn, but the inside of God's place had been turned into the pit of hell. The heat was so intense, Ebenezer had to shield his face as he ran along the sides, looking for a cellar door. At last he found it, grabbed the handle, and then saw the padlock. Leaning against the wooden door, pounding on it, he yelled above the roaring conflagration: "Zeb Hogan! Zeb! You down there? You alive?"

Maybe he heard a reply. He couldn't tell. He stood back, searching, thinking, and then heard a commotion across the street. A white woman holding a crowbar was chasing some laughing soldiers, although she wasn't coming close since she ran with a limp.

Ebenezer sprinted as fast he could across the churchyard and back across Marion Street as the soldiers raced down Washington. The woman had stopped, but she screamed when she saw this bloody black boy coming toward her.

"Ma'am!" Ebenezer stopped a short distance from her. "Ma'am . . . please. There's a boy trapped inside that church's cellar. Ma'am . . . please, ma'am. I need that crowbar."

She stared at him, looked up and down the street, knowing the soldiers she had been chasing were gone, and then took off toward the burning building. Ebenezer followed her, watching in awe as she broke that padlock with the crowbar and pried open the door. She even scrambled into the pit, leaving Ebenezer holding the door open, while she dragged out poor Zeb Hogan.

As soon as the woman and Zeb were clear of the danger, Ebenezer let the door slam shut. He took Zeb's arms—him coughing, sweating, his face blackened by soot—then laid him down on Marion Street.

"You poor, brave soldier," the woman said, sitting on the ground next to Zeb. She was blue-eyed, auburn-haired, fairly plump, maybe in her late twenties. She kissed Zeb's cheek. "There, there," she said, "you brave Southern lad."

Southern! Ebenezer gave her an incredulous stare before he realized that she, like those soldiers from New York, had mistaken Zeb Hogan, wearing Confederate Army pants, for a Johnny Reb.

Slowly Zeb sat up, shaking his head.

The woman pressed her right hand on his shoulder and said, "Sir, it is not safe for you, or your boy here, to remain in Columbia." Her breasts heaved with a sad sigh. "Columbia belongs to the enemy. What's left of Columbia. You must run. Quickly." She stood, lifted her skirt, reached inside her boot, and pulled out a brass-framed revolver. No wonder she had been favoring her left leg, because this wasn't some hideaway gun, but a regular six-shot revolver. "My dearest Frank carried this with him till he fell at Kennesaw Mountain," she said, and placed the gun in Zeb's hand. "Be gone," she said. "Hurry now."

She didn't have to tell the two boys again.

Chapter Five

Shoving the revolver in his waistband, Zeb Hogan stood, and then he and Ebenezer ran down the street, away from the Southern lady, as fast as they could escape that inferno that had almost been Zeb's grave. *Would have been,* Zeb thought, *if not for Ebenezer Chase. That slave done saved my hide twice . . . no, three times, iffen you count him burying me outside the Florence Stockade.* That rankled. Zeb had always been prideful, and he had never cottoned to owing folks. Maybe that was the real reason he had run off after his brother had died, his family always being poor, his folks struggling to pay the rent for that miserable shanty they called home.

For certain, Zeb thought those Secesh trousers he wore would get him stopped, arrested, but nobody seemed to pay much mind to a couple of teenagers moving through the crowds. Columbia civilians and blue-coated Federals were too occupied. As they dodged among the people, Ebenezer clutched the haversack close to his chest. Church and fire bells rang out, and the sky turned blacker than midnight.

Feels like we is walking through Hades, Zeb thought, and then he thought of something else, something even more frightening. *Maybe we are.*

Newly freed slaves stood on one corner, listening to a white-haired Negro preach at them. Down the road, a bunch of white women and children stood crying, watching from a distance as giant flames consumed a three-story brick building.

"Oh, Mother," one of the younger girls asked, "why, oh, why did those Yankees burn our convent?"

"I don't know," a lady in a bonnet answered as she placed a handkerchief under her eyes.

It struck both boys how crowded Columbia was. From all the traffic they had seen on the Cartersville pike, they had half expected the capital to be deserted. Instead, Southerners had moved into the city, swelling its population by thousands. They had fled the war, just hadn't run far enough. Zeb felt sorry for them, watching their city burn.

Down the road, Zeb and Ebenezer heard a Union lieutenant arguing with a man in a bowler hat and sack suit. The officer was laying blame for all this on Wade Hampton's Rebels, saying how they'd set cotton and hay bales aflame before they'd fled the city, while the man in the sack suit was calling the lieutenant a blasted liar. Neither Zeb nor Ebenezer was sure who should be blamed for the inferno around them. Maybe the Rebs had started some blazes, but it had been Sherman's Army that had almost roasted Zeb alive.

The two boys just kept right on walking past the rubble, the ruins, the smoke, and flames. Walked right out of Columbia, South Carolina.

Union soldiers had constructed pontoon bridges for crossing the rivers, and Ebenezer and Zeb had no trouble getting across. After leaving what was once the downtown of Columbia, they saw only one family, white farmers on the side of the road who, so intent on staring at the flame-brightened night sky, didn't even notice the two wayfarers.

* * * * *

Sherman's Army had been forced to corduroy most of the roads. Ebenezer had never seen such a road, which made Zeb feel smarter.

"Road'd be too boggy to get an army through," Zeb explained. "We'd cut logs out of the forest . . . you-all got plenty of pines out here. We'd flatten one side of them, fit saplings between them, make a good road for the wagons and such."

"Sounds like hard work," Ebenezer said.

"Slave's work, iffen you ask me," Zeb said, without thinking, and watched Ebenezer's back stiffen, his fingers ball into fists. *You numbskull,* Zeb thought. *That was an ignorant thing to say.* Yet he didn't apologize, couldn't apologize. *I didn't ask this Negro to come with me,* he told himself. *He taken up that notion his ownself.* "Miserable work." Zeb decided that if he kept jawing, maybe Ebenezer would forget what he'd said. "Just plain vile. I felt I should have been fighting, not doing road work. I ain't no logger. And dangersome, too, that work was. I seen one man from the 16th nigh chop his foot off when he mis-swung his axe. Couple others got killed when them big pines fell on them. This was over in Georgia, before I got captured."

Remaining quiet, Ebenezer kept walking ahead of Zeb. Zeb's words, his poor choice of words, had riled the runaway.

Zeb frowned. He hadn't meant anything about *slave's work.* They had never owned slaves, not with Wisconsin being a free state, and especially with the Hogans being dirt poor. When he thought about it, Zeb realized that he had only seen a handful of Negroes in Wisconsin, and they'd all been free, naturally. His father had worked with a Negro while bricking up that Methodist church.

"That was a Methodist church I was locked in, wasn't it?"

Ebenezer grunted.

"My pa, he helped build one in Madison. He's a brick mason. Was." Zeb's eyes clouded. He wasn't even certain his parents were still alive. He hadn't got anyone to write them a letter, and he had been gone practically a year.

Ebenezer still kept quiet, just kept walking, till he came to a sign at a crossroad. He reached into the haversack, pulled out the map to study it.

"Which way we go?" Zeb asked when he'd caught up.

Ebenezer pointed at the sign's arms. "That way is Lexington." Then, pointing the other way, "That way . . . it's ten miles to Edmund."

Looking at the markings on that warped piece of wood nailed to a post, Zeb asked, "You read that?"

"I did."

"You can read?"

"I can." He gave Zeb a curious look. "Can't you?"

Zeb didn't answer. Instead, he said, "Corporal Favour, he once told me it was illegal for slaves to learn to read and write."

"It is." Ebenezer folded the map, put it back inside the haversack, and walked straight. "We keep this way," he said.

That was the most conversation they had for the next few days. They walked, neither of them limping now. They made good time, their minds focusing on just putting one foot ahead of the other, giving no thought to the rumbling in their stomachs.

Once Zeb spied a cottontail rabbit, and thought about shooting it with the revolver the woman had given him in Columbia, but he only had six shots and only five percussion caps, so didn't risk it. Besides, he had never fired a revolver before, just the rifled musket he had carried with the 16th.

Two days later, Ebenezer Chase still wasn't doing a whole lot of talking. When they came to a little river, Zeb had had enough. "Listen," he told him, "I'm sorry about what I said the other day, about me corduroying the road being slave's work. I didn't mean nothing by it."

"That didn't bother me any," Ebenezer said, but Zeb knew the slave was lying. "I've heard worse."

"Well, I mean, it ain't easy being a free man. I'm free. And I ain't never had nothing. My folks, they was born poor. Never had no money. My ma, she raised chickens, sold eggs. That's about all I ever had to eat. She'd kill a hen that wouldn't lay. Eggs for supper. Eggs for breakfast. Providing them chickens was laying good. If not, we'd just do without. Like I told you, my pa was a brick mason, but that work wasn't steady, and Pa, well, he had a thirst, so, when he'd make money, he'd just spend what he had at some groggery. Now you take your life. You had shelter. Knowed what was expected of you. Knowed you'd get fed every day. You had . . ."

"Zeb," Ebenezer said.

"Yeah?"

"Shut up."

Blood rushed to Zeb's head, but he fought down his anger.

Ebenezer studied the map. "I think this is the Edisto River," he said.

"Ain't much of a river," Zeb said.

"It's pretty deep. Water's up on account of all the rain. And that current, it can fool you. It must have taken out the bridge here, or you soldier boys tore it down after y'all crossed here." He looked toward the woods, considering. "There's some trees that have been felled. Probably from y'all corduroying this road. You think we could roll one of those logs, end over end, to here?"

Zeb shrugged.

"Those logs are big enough . . . should be able to reach 'cross the river." Ebenezer nodded, approving the plan as it came to his mind. "Then we just walk across it."

"Sounds good," Zeb said. "Only . . ."

"Only what?"

"Well, we ain't hardly et since before Columbia. I'm hungry, Ebenezer."

Zeb stared at Ebenezer, the black face a mask, but quickly a grin spread across it, and Ebenezer nodded. "Me too." Just like that, Ebenezer walked down the riverbank, into the woods, and Zeb followed. When Ebenezer came to a bend full of driftwood and rotten pine logs, he said, "This'll do." He started stripping naked. "You ever noodled for catfish?" he asked.

Zeb shook his head.

"Oh, that's right. You can't swim. Well, Zeb Hogan, you just wait here. I'll see if I can noodle us up a couple of big cats."

He waded into the river, face cringing at the cold. He was right. That water was deep, and Zeb could see how fast the current flowed past the slave's bare chest. Ebenezer winked, but it was Zeb who was holding his breath when the runaway slave disappeared under that black water. Mouth agape, Zeb stared at the dark water.

About a minute later, Ebenezer surfaced, and Zeb cried out when he saw a huge fish on his right hand, halfway up his forearm, like it was trying to eat him. It reminded Zeb of that Bible story about Jonah.

Ebenezer made his way to the shore, his face masked in pain, lungs heaving, and he stumbled out onto the bank, crying, "Help get this monster off me, Zeb!"

As Zeb tried to pry that slippery devil's mouth open, Ebenezer warned him, "Watch them fins. They'll cut you to ribbons."

Finally the boys managed to get the big catfish off Ebenezer's arm, and it dropped onto the bank, flopping.

"That's more like a whale," Zeb marveled. "Must weigh ten pounds." He backed away, looked up, and saw that Ebenezer's arm was bleeding as he headed back into the Edisto.

"Where you going?" Zeb called out.

"To get your supper," Ebenezer answered before the river swallowed him again.

He come up a few seconds later, shook his head, didn't say a word, and dived back. When he surfaced the next time, he had another fish that looked as if it had swallowed his hand. This one was even bigger than the one that had stopped flopping on the banks. As Zeb helped remove it from Ebenezer's hand, it sliced Zeb's finger with its fin. That hurt like the blazes, but Zeb gritted his teeth as he pried open the second catfish's mouth, keeping his hands clear of the fish's whiskers as the leviathan dropped at their feet. Blood streaked down Ebenezer's arm in rivulets, but he just toweled himself off with his butternut britches, and said, "Fetch me some of that moss, please, off that tree yonder, Zeb."

Zeb obeyed.

* * * * *

"How'd you catch them fish like that?" Zeb asked.

They lounged under an elm, and Zeb speared another hunk of meat and put it over the coals. They were eating well this eve, Ebenezer having skinned the two fish with the knife he carried in his left brogan, the knife he said he had stolen from his master. The catfish had been the dickens to clean, but Ebenezer had done it, even with his arm wrapped with moss. Zeb had mostly watched.

Leaning back, Ebenezer said, "Uncle Cain taught me." He shifted his legs, took a sip of water, and said, "Catfish are bottom feeders. So you got to find a hole, reach in, and let whatever's in that hole bite you."

Cringing, Zeb asked, "What if it ain't a catfish hole?"

Ebenezer laughed. "Might not be. Uncle Cain lost two fingers on his left hand noodling. Got bit off by a snapping turtle. And sometimes you'll find a snake. Guess you just pray to God that you'll be lucky. Like we were today."

Zeb turned the hunk of fish meat over.

Ebenezer kept right on talking. "Now once that catfish grabs your hand, you shove it deep inside the cat's mouth and grab the gill cover, and just pull that cat out of the hole." He shook his head, and sat up. "Got to be strong. A good swimmer. And mighty lucky."

Zeb could only nod. He thought it just short of a miracle that Ebenezer hadn't drowned trying to pull those fish out of their holes. He smiled and removed the sizzling meat from the fire, blew on it once, and let the hot chunk of fish fall on his tongue.

"Never seen fish that big," he said as he chewed.

Ebenezer laughed. "They're tiny compared to some cats me and Uncle Cain noodled out of the Pee Dee River or swamps around Hall Plantation."

"This is the life," Zeb said.

"That's the truth."

"How's your arm?"

"It'll be all right. Cats have razor sharp teeth, but they're tiny. This moss'll suck out any poison, prevent infection."

"Your Uncle Cain teach you that, too?"

"Yes, he did. How's your finger?"

Zeb looked at the moss Ebenezer had wrapped around where the cat fin had sliced it. "Don't hurt none," he said.

"Well, I reckon we'll be in Georgia sometime tomorrow or early the next day."

Means I'm that much closer to Sergeant Ben DeVere, Zeb thought.

They watched the moon rise. The skies were clear, and the temperature had warmed. The two boys just lay on their backs, gorging on catfish. Wind rustled the trees, and Ebenezer felt peaceful, content.

"Zeb, you mind if I ask you a question?"

"Go ahead." Zeb's reply was barely audible.

"How come you want to go to Mississippi?"

Zeb's body tensed. He remembered what had happened back in Atlanta, and later at the Florence Stockade. He recalled Sergeant Major Engstrand dying slowly, and Zeb's pledge echoed inside his head. His right hand reached up, resting on the walnut butt of the revolver.

"There's a man I got to see in Vicksburg."

"Southerner?"

"No. He was a Union soldier. Sergeant Ben DeVere."

"What you need to see him for?"

Chapter Six

"I aim to kill him," Zeb Hogan replied.

It was his voice, the way he said it that chilled Ebenezer, who pushed himself up, looking over at the Union soldier. Zeb lay on his back, head resting in his hands, but his body rigid. Ebenezer tried to form the words, but they proved hard to say.

"Why . . . why . . . you want . . . to do that?" he managed after a struggle.

Drawing a deep breath, Zeb slowly rose. Despite the darkness, Ebenezer imagined seeing his eyes, how hard they'd become, how cold, and when Zeb looked at Ebenezer, even though he was just a shadow, Ebenezer had to look away.

"He's a traitor," Zeb said. "He got Sergeant Major Engstrand killed. He deserves to die. And I'll kill him. That's why I escaped."

The catfish started swimming in Ebenezer's stomach. Bile rose in his throat, but he swallowed it down, shaking his head, saying, "You're too young to have murder in your heart."

"Seems I recall somebody telling you that you're too young to have a wife and a baby," he said. "You mind your affairs. I'll tend to my own." He leaned back down.

Ebenezer's eyes locked on the glowing coals. The wind picked up, and his whole body shook with cold.

"You wasn't in the Florence Stockade," Zeb said. His voice sounded far away, and Ebenezer realized that Zeb wasn't really talking to anyone. Just talking.

"They taken us to Andersonville first . . . after we got captured outside of Atlanta." Zeb let out a hollow laugh. "DeVere

51

was in tears when they caught us, begging them Rebs to let him go . . . Sergeant Major Engstrand yelling at him to buck up, to be a man, not to let them Secesh see him like that. Then DeVere begged them for whiskey. 'Course, they don't give him none.

"We'd been on the skirmish line. Got taken by some boys who said they was with the 11th Tennessee. They was nice boys, them Tennesseans. We traded them some tobacco and coffee for johnnycake. One of them warned us to hide any valuables we might have, but I figured them Rebs was just funning us. Wasn't till they deposited us behind the front lines that I understood what them Tennesseans had meant. Our new guards taken my canteen, my hat. Most of our shoes got stole from us, too. Guess mine was too worn out for even them sorry excuses for soldiers. They liberated . . . that's how they termed it, a Reb's idea of a joke . . . Dave Gardenhire's trousers. Oh, they give him a ratty old pair full of graybacks in return. Went on like that, with every change of guard. Even when there wasn't much left to steal from us, the guards taken something.

"They marched us that night six miles to some miserable little town, and there we waited for a couple of days. Gave us hardtack. Said that would have to last us, and they taken us off to Andersonville. We wasn't there but for a few months. By the Eternal, I never seen such horrors. Pray, Ebenezer Chase, that you never live to see nothing like what we saw at Andersonville, and then later at Florence.

"But them Rebs at that miserable prison in Georgia, oh, my, they had a sense of humor. Told us we was being paroled. Said the Yanks had decided to exchange prisoners again. Man, what a relief. So we marched out of them walls one afternoon in September. They taken us to the railroad, prodded us with their bayonets into boxcars. Stacked us in there like cordwood. Hot. Miserable. Couldn't hardly breathe. We waited two hours in Macon, and when a couple of the boys died that afternoon, them guards said they wasn't opening no doors. We made it to Charleston, and the Rebs said we was going to Richmond. We'd be exchanged there. Only they taken us to Florence, instead, made us sleep in the boxcars all night. Unloaded us that morn, and marched us to that prison. They said we could build cook fires, but they didn't give us no food to cook. By the next day, five of the boys had died. Starved to death.

"The prison wasn't finished. The Rebs had us put up some of them walls, and then one day a fellow from an Illinois outfit escaped. That's when the commander first used his dogs. We heard them 'coons and curs baying for a couple of days. They caught him the third day.

"By then, we was given three tablespoons of cornmeal. That's all we had till some citizens from Florence brung us a sorghum stalk.

"Finally the colonel of the Rebs makes us all stand in formation. He blames everything on Abe Lincoln, Grant, and Sherman . . . says if we'll join the Confederacy, help man his post, he'll give us each one hundred and sixty acres at the end of the war. Says he'll pay us. Feed us. And when he looks at Sergeant Major Engstrand, the sarge, he says . . . 'Colonel, thank you kindly, but I reckon me and the boys'll starve a little more before we accept your terms.'

"That riled the colonel. What the colonel didn't know, of course, was that we was digging a tunnel. We had to dig deep, too, because the Rebs had dug a trench around those pine walls to prevent a tunnel, but we did it, anyhow. A couple of nights later, we dug our way out. Hightailed it for the woods, but them dogs was on us immediately. I tripped, and the sarge, he come back, put me up in this sycamore tree, and them dogs was on him, pulling him down as he tried to climb up behind me. Sergeant Major Engstrand, he beat them back with a stick he'd fetched, and when the Carolina Reserves caught up with us, he screamed at them . . . 'All right, you've caught us. Now call off your wolves.'

"They didn't, though. One of them rascals taken that club from the sarge's hand, and let the dogs have at him. I jumped down from that tree, tried to help, but a red-mustached Secesh grabbed me. Didn't have hardly no strength in me by then. They let them dogs half eat the sarge before they finally called them off, hauled us back to the Stockade. Nary a one of us got far. Put us in stocks for a week."

Zeb Hogan was silent for a little while. The coals had died down. Ebenezer waited, wondering if Zeb would finish his story, or if it was indeed over.

A moment later, Zeb began talking again. "When we was back inside our shelter . . . if you could call what those Rebs give us shelter . . . we heard the news. Sergeant Ben DeVere had taken the Reb colonel's offer. He'd decided to quit the 16th Wisconsin Infantry and join the Rebs. And he had informed the guards that we was digging a tunnel. He was a traitor. So when Engstrand was lying there, dying, we all drew lots. I got the short one, meaning I was to go. I was to get out of the Stockade, somehow, and track down that murdering, drunken scum of the earth, Ben DeVere, and kill him. And that, Ebenezer Chase, is what I aim to do."

Nothing else was said that night. Ebenezer slept fitfully. Zeb Hogan didn't sleep at all.

* * * * *

The following morning, after eating the last of the catfish, they walked to the felled trees and found one that wasn't too rotted and seemed the right length. The boys took hold of one end, lifted, straining, grunting, heaving, got that log standing upright, and pushed it forward. The big timber crashed in the wet grass. They picked up the other end, muscles straining, practically tearing, and pushed it end over end. They had to do that five more times before it was close to the riverbank, after which they rolled it over a tad, lined it up, and gave it one more hard lift. For a moment Ebenezer thought that the bottom end would slip into the river, but it caught on a root, or a rock, or maybe it was just a bunch of mud, and held there. They pushed it over one last time, and the far end landed with a thud on the other bank.

Grinning at his companion, Ebenezer tested their bridge with his foot. It seemed sturdy and steady enough, so he walked over and got the haversack, and eased his way over that pine log, made it to the other side, and hopped onto the bank.

"Your turn," Ebenezer told Zeb.

The soldier hesitated, looking at that black river.

"Don't look down," Ebenezer warned. "You just walk, easy-like. Keep your hands out for balance. It's easy. I did it. You can."

"You can swim," Zeb said.

"You don't have to," Ebenezer said, "if you don't fall off that log."

Zeb smiled, but Ebenezer knew it was forced, knew the young Wisconsin boy was petrified. Still, Zeb stepped onto the log, moving a lot slower than Ebenezer had. Ebenezer wasn't sure if Zeb had even sucked in a breath since he had stepped onto the log. He was about halfway across, when Ebenezer noticed the other end of the log begin to slip.

"Hurry, Zeb!" Ebenezer cried.

Zeb felt the log's movement. A glob of mud splashed into the water, and the log began falling.

"Zeb!" the slave screamed.

Zeb practically flew across that log for three or four steps, leaped off, landing in the mud, Ebenezer's hand reaching out, gripping his forearm like a vise. Behind them, the log splashed in the water, the end shot up, fell, spraying the boys with muddy water, then sped down the river like some ironclad ready to do battle.

Ebenezer helped pull Zeb out of the mud, onto firmer ground. "Man," Ebenezer said, "that was close." He started to sink to the ground, felt he needed some time to recover, but Zeb Hogan was already walking away from the Edisto River, south by southwest, toward the Georgia state line.

* * * * *

They crossed the Savannah River—large, deep, rocky—on a railroad bridge, and were in Augusta, Georgia. The discovery of a railroad bridge intact had surprised Ebenezer. After all, most of the railroads he had seen since Columbia had been destroyed, but Zeb explained, "Sherman hasn't been here."

Ebenezer raided a corncrib in town, finding barely enough food for Zeb and him. They sneaked through the city that night and kept right on walking till dawn. As the sun began to rise, they walked deep into the woods along the road, covered themselves with straw, and tried to sleep.

Only Ebenezer wasn't sleepy. Zeb hadn't talked about Florence Stockade, or Ben DeVere, or anything much since that night on the Edisto River, but Ebenezer's curiosity had been nagging him. He chanced spoiling Zeb's mood with a question, but he just had to know.

"How'd this Sergeant DeVere wind up in Vicksburg?" Ebenezer asked.

"He deserted the South Carolina Reserves, too," Zeb answered easily, as though he had been expecting the inquiry, or mayhap he'd just been thinking about the man he had sworn to kill. "Man's a born traitor," he went on. "Turned his back on the Union. Turned his back on the Rebs. Anyhow, while the 16th was stationed in Vicksburg, after the city surrendered in '63, DeVere got hisself smitten with this Mississippi gal. Promised he'd marry her, and that was scandalous for her family. Yet for some reason, this gal was taken by DeVere. My brother James, he'd told me all about DeVere, his thirst for whiskey. James, he couldn't figure what this pretty Mississippi gal saw in a piece of trash like Ben DeVere. Anyhow, Sergeant Major Engstrand always reasoned that DeVere would make his way back to Vicksburg. He talked about that gal all the time, and it ain't like he had anywhere else to go. Couldn't go back home to Wisconsin. Couldn't rejoin the 16th. Somebody might escape the Stockade, or get out word about what he'd done. Only place left for him was Miss Elizabeth Gentry of Vicksburg. If DeVere ain't there, *she'll* know where he's gotten off to."

"Elizabeth." Ebenezer closed his eyes. "That's my wife's name. Call her Lizzie, though."

Zeb Hogan kept quiet. Maybe he was asleep. If that was the case, Ebenezer soon joined him.

* * * * *

Over the next few nights, they kept close to the road. Whenever they saw, heard, or thought they heard someone coming, they ducked into the woods and waited for the travelers to pass. The land had turned hillier, and after about six days, they arrived at a narrow river with steep banks, heavy with trees, heavier with yellow clay—no bridge or ferry to cross it—and the water roiling. Ebenezer didn't see how Zeb could get across. Truth be told, Ebenezer wasn't even sure he could get across this river.

It was past dawn, and Ebenezer knew they should hide, but Zeb didn't want to cross this river in the darkness. He hoped that maybe they could find a way across. They were only one or two days from Atlanta, and he was in a hurry to find Ben DeVere.

"All right," Ebenezer said. "You go downstream. I'll head upstream. Whistle like a bobwhite quail if you find something. I'll do the same."

"What's a bobwhite quail sound like?" he asked.

"You're fooling me," Ebenezer said. Zeb, however, straightened, stiffened, and Ebenezer knew he had angered his companion again. *I keep forgetting he was born in the city*, Ebenezer thought. *Some Northern city, too.* He whistled like a bobwhite, and smiled, remembering what Lizzie always said when she heard one of those quail.

"Bob-bob-white. Are your peas all ripe?" Ebenezer murmured to himself.

"Huh?"

Zeb shattered Ebenezer's vision of Lizzie. "Nothing." Ebenezer let out a weary sigh. "You can whistle, can't you?"

Zeb responded with a dead-on imitation of a bobwhite.

"That's real good."

"I'd heard those before," Zeb said. "Marching with Sherman across Tennessee and Georgia. First time I heard one, I thought it was some hermit in the woods. Never knowed it was a quail. We got quail in Wisconsin."

"They are plentiful in Carolina. Georgia, too."

"You should see the passenger pigeons we have in Wisconsin. Red breasts. Millions of them. Almost blacken out the sky when they take flight. You'd find maybe a hundred of them nesting in one tree."

"I've seen them," Ebenezer said. "We have pigeons down here, too."

"Oh."

Ebenezer knew he had disappointed Zeb again. He couldn't figure out that Union soldier, often acting like he was trying to prove something to Ebenezer, that he was smarter, maybe even better, than him. *That's something. A white boy trying to prove he's better than a slave. Most folks around here take that for a fact.*

Zeb went off upstream, instead of down, but Ebenezer didn't bother correcting him. Ebenezer headed downstream, above those treacherous, steep banks, until he finally found a tree that had fallen across the river. *Providence is looking after us*, he thought. He tested the old pine, felt sure that it could support his weight, and certainly Zeb's, and let out with a whistle.

A couple of minutes later, he heard someone running through the trees, and turned to chastise Zeb for making such a racket.

Only it wasn't Zeb. Ebenezer sharply inhaled, his eyes bulging at four black-bearded white men. Every mother's son of them aimed a musket at him.

Chapter Seven

Hearing all the commotion, Zeb knew there was trouble, so he stopped running. Crouching, he sneaked along the side of the steep bank, finally stopping behind some brush to see what was happening. He ground his teeth when he saw them—four big, burly men with thick beards. Only one of them held a rifle. The others had leaned their weapons against a tree. Two held Ebenezer by his arms, tying him to a big pine. They'd taken off his vest and let it fall to the ground, along with his haversack, which one of them had gone through. The last of the men unfolded a knife, and cut down the back of Ebenezer's shirt.

The one with the rifle let out a chuckle, and sprayed a carpet of pine needles with tobacco juice. All four men wore shabby pants of patched gray wool. Zeb figured them all for Confederate deserters.

Ebenezer didn't say a word. He just stood facing that tree, letting them tie him up. What could he do? Against four of them? *For that matter,* Zeb thought, *what can I do?* Four grown-up men, who looked tougher than cobs. It would be folly to stick his neck out. Realizing his palms were sweaty, Zeb wiped them on his trousers. Then he quietly began backing away. After a few rods, he turned around and walked down the edge of that yellow riverbank.

There's four of them, he told himself. *Nothing I can do. Besides, I never asked that slave to come with me. He got hisself in that fix. I'll travel alone. Be a mite faster, maybe. They'll just whip him, let him go. Maybe take him back to Florence for the reward his master has surely put up. It's Ebenezer's own fault, getting caught. He . . . He saved my life.*

That's when Zeb heard the wicked slap of a belt against flesh, and Ebenezer let out a wail. The birds had stopped chirping. As Ebenezer's cry trailed off from the bowels of the woods, Zeb heard mocking laughter. One of the Reb deserters said, "That's a shame, Luke. There wasn't a mark on that boy's back."

Already Zeb had turned, started creeping back, listening.

"Your master musta been treatin' you right, eh, boy? Well, I'm gonna peel your hide down to the bone."

"You feel like tellin' us where you run off from now, boy?"

No answer. The belt slashed again, and Ebenezer cried out.

"How 'bout now?"

"NO!" Ebenezer shouted out in defiance.

Zeb peered around a tree. One man brought a belt back over his shoulder. It was russet-colored, the brass buckle shaped like an oval with some letters stamped on it, the leather cap and cartridge pouches having bunched up against the buckle.

Before the man could let that belt fly again, Zeb stepped into view, thumbing back the hammer on the revolver the woman had given him in Columbia.

All four men turned, staring. One of them started inching his way to the rifle leaning against the elm tree, but Zeb said, "You best stay where you are." And, to his surprise, the Reb stopped moving, even began lifting his hands skyward. The one with the belt—who had been holding the rifle while the others strung Ebenezer up to that tree—dropped the belt and eyed his rifle, lying on the ground at his feet, then faced Zeb. His teeth, the few that he had, were black.

"This any of your affair, kid?" he asked.

"Yeah." Zeb pointed the pistol at his big belly. "It is." Zeb tilted his head at Ebenezer, and tried not to wince over how the slave's back was bleeding, with two big welts across his shoulder blades. "That's my manservant you boys been sporting on."

The four deserters looked at each other. The one closest to Ebenezer shuffled his feet. He'd been the one who had cut away Ebenezer's shirt.

The one with the belt, the biggest of the four, spit out more brown juice, and shifted the quid from one cheek to the other. "Manservant?" He chuckled without mirth. "You ain't nothin' but a pup. A runt at that."

"I'm a lieutenant," Zeb said, recalling the outfit that had captured him outside of Atlanta. "With the 11th Tennessee. Who were you-all with?"

When they didn't answer, Zeb let out a disgusted snort. "Deserters, eh?"

"What about you?" one of them off to the side said.

"Scouting mission for General Hood," he lied. "He's planning on coming back from Tennessee to liberate Georgia." Of course, from what Zeb had heard about John Bell Hood—he'd gotten his Army practically slaughtered at Franklin that winter—he'd be licking his wounds for the rest of eternity. What Zeb didn't know, but later learned, was that General Hood had resigned his command of the Army of the Tennessee about a month or so earlier. Lucky for him, those four deserters hadn't heard that news, either.

Zeb wagged the revolver barrel at the one holding the knife. "Cut him loose," he said.

When the Reb didn't move fast enough, Zeb drew a bead on the piece of trash's forehead, and that prompted him to do as he was told. Zeb was tempted to pull the trigger, but wasn't sure what would happen. He hadn't checked the loads of the revolver, and it might have misfired, or not fired at all.

The man quickly unfolded his knife, and cut the rawhide off from Ebenezer's wrists.

Face masked in pain, Ebenezer turned, facing Zeb, the remnants of his shirt hanging from his body.

"Ebenezer," Zeb said, "gather them weapons."

"Hey," the leader said, "you ain't about to arm no slave."

"Shut up," Zeb told him, "or I might just tell him to take target practice on you." Suddenly he felt greedy. "You boys owe me. How much you think I ought to charge you for whipping my manservant?"

"We ain't got no money," the one who hadn't spoken said in a rough whisper. He slipped his hands into his mule-ear pockets, and hung his head in shame.

Zeb turned to the knife man. "Take off your shirt," he told him.

"What?"

"You heard me. My servant lost his shirt. You'll pay him in kind." It was then Zeb spied the map stuck inside his waistband. "I'll take our map back, too."

The man pulled the map out, let it fall at his feet, then tugged the once-white shirt over his head, wadded it up in a ball, and tossed it over toward Ebenezer, who had gathered up all four rifles, and was walking toward Zeb.

"Now what?" the man who'd done the whipping said.

"Now you all best get out of my sight. Start walking, and don't stop. If I ever lay eyes on any one of you again, I'll kill you."

The biggest started to bend over to pick up the belt. "I reckon that belt can stay where it is," Zeb told him, and the man straightened.

"What about our long guns?" the shirtless man said.

"They've been confiscated by the Army of the Tennessee. You gents might as well take off your powder horns, too."

"That ain't right," the big one said.

"What ain't right," Zeb said, "is four men beating a slave that ain't their property. What ain't right are four men quitting the fight when the Confederacy needs men most."

As soon as they'd removed the powder horns, Zeb waved the revolver barrel one more time. "You best start walking. Now!"

Not speaking, the men turned, walking deeper into the woods. Zeb didn't lower the revolver until he couldn't hear them any longer. When Ebenezer dropped the four rifles and sank to his knees, Zeb shoved the revolver into his waistband, and knelt beside the slave.

"I'm all right," Ebenezer said tightly, but Zeb knew better. He pulled off the slave's tattered shirt, wet it down with water from his canteen, and began to bathe the two welts on Ebenezer's back. Although he stiffened and bit down hard, Ebenezer didn't let out a sound as Zeb finished the job. Recalling how Ebenezer had doctored their cuts from the catfish, Zeb hurried to gather moss, which he packed down with mud, then bandaged the welts with the slave's ripped-up shirt.

Ebenezer's head bobbed a bit, and Zeb could see he was crying silently. Not from pain, but shame. Bitterly Zeb wished he had killed those four men. They were trash. Nothing but trash. A new feeling pushed aside's Zeb anger at those deserters. He felt shame, too, because he'd almost deserted this brave lad. He fetched the deserter's shirt and the crazy-quilt vest, handed them to Ebenezer, and refilled the haversack with the map and other items.

"You found a way across?"

Zeb nodded at the log that crossed the river.

"Yeah." After pulling the shirt over his head and arms, Ebenezer slowly rose, stiffly pulling on the vest. Slinging the haversack over his shoulder, Zeb picked up two of the rifles, flung them into the river, and grabbed another and thrust it into Ebenezer's hand. The slave acted like he didn't want to take it.

"We might need this," Zeb said.

Ebenezer shook his head. "I can't take a rifle, Zeb. Slaves can't have guns."

"You ain't a slave no more," Zeb said. "Remember?" Awkwardly Ebenezer's left hand accepted the barrel. "That's an Enfield," Zeb told him. "Shoots a .58-caliber bullet. Enfields are right popular with both armies in this war." He picked up the remaining rifle, shorter and lighter than the Enfield. A carbine, but Zeb guessed that it was a .58-caliber, too. "Don't rightly know what this one is," he said to himself, then hurried over to the belt on the ground, slid the cartridge and cap pouches off, unfastened them, looked inside. Sure enough, there were some patches and balls inside the cartridge pouch, maybe a dozen or so percussion caps, and a powder measure. Not much, but more than they had, and Zeb felt a whole lot more comfortable with a rifle or carbine than a revolver. He put the two pouches in the haversack, gathered the four cow-horn flasks, and threw them all over his shoulder.

"Best get moving," he said. "Them big oafs might come back."

They crossed the makeshift bridge, which they pushed into the river. They ran about a mile through the woods before returning to the road. After drinking water, they walked the rest of the day and all the next night, finally stopping to get some shut-eye as dawn broke.

* * * * *

Around noon they woke, and Zeb worked on Ebenezer's back, cleaning it as best as he could, putting more moss on the wounds, then packing down the moss with mud, hoping that poultice would suck any poison out. The last thing they needed was for those cuts to become infected.

"Thanks," Ebenezer said.

"It ain't nothing," Zeb said.

Ebenezer's head shook. "Them four men . . . they would have killed me." He shuddered. "I never got a whipping before."

Zeb grinned. "I have. Ma and Pa tanned my hide many a time. Mostly I deserved it."

"With a belt?" Ebenezer asked.

Zeb nodded. "Belt, hands . . . and Pa, he had some hard-rock hands. Sometimes they'd make me or James cut down a switch, and they'd switch us. That was torture. Making a kid cut down a switch that they would use on us. And heaven help us if we tried to bring back some tiny little twig for them to whip us with."

"Mister Anderson, he was Master Hall's overseer, he'd use a whip."

Frowning, Zeb looked down. "Well, my folks never taken no whip to me, or James."

"He never used a whip on me."

Zeb managed to swallow down whatever was rising in his throat. "They shouldn't use a whip on nobody," he said, suddenly soft-spoken. "Them four had no right to beat you with that belt." It seemed best to change the subject. "You want to walk some this day? It's warmed up. We ain't seen nobody on this road all last night or yesterday. Might be we could cover more ground."

"I'm game," Ebenezer said. Hefting the rifle, he walked off.

Ignoring their empty stomachs, they walked along the edge of the road for a couple of hours. When they came to a cross-roads, they spotted a wagon coming from the west. Zeb started to dash for cover in the woods, but Ebenezer stopped him.

"They're Negroes," Ebenezer said, and sure enough, as they come closer, Zeb realized his companion was right.

A white-haired man and a younger man in his twenties— most likely the elder one's son—rode up cautiously in a buck-board loaded with firewood, pulled by a floppy-eared old mule that was blind in its left eye. They stopped the wagon and stared, focusing more on the weapons butted on the dirt than on the two boys holding them.

"Afternoon," the old man finally said.

"How are you this wonderful day?" Ebenezer said.

"Fine."

"We're traveling," Ebenezer said. "Wonder if we might ride in the back of the wagon . . . if you're going our direction."

"Going to Atlanta," the man said.

"We're bound that way ourselves, then on to Elyton," Ebenezer said.

"That road goes right to Elyton," the old man said. "'Bout a hundred and fifty miles west of Atlanta."

"How about after that? Say, Mississippi, maybe? Or Dallas, Texas?"

He shook his head. "Never been farther west than the iron-works at Roupes Creek, a few miles beyond Elyton."

"Is it all right if we travel with you?" Ebenezer asked.

Again, the eyes of both men trained on the rifles. The old man wet his lips, and looked at the younger man, who shrugged. "Hop aboard," his son said.

* * * * *

A little more than an hour later, the old man reined in the mule and turned, eying his passengers over the load of firewood. "If you don't mind, we's at the outskirts of Atlanta. Y'all might want to get off here."

Meaning, Zeb figured, that he expected trouble. He couldn't blame those two Negroes for that. He and Ebenezer looked like they'd attract trouble, certain sure. "Thanks for the ride." Zeb slid off the end, and tipped his hat. Ebenezer eased off, too, and gave the black men a nod of appreciation.

"I admired that bedroll you got there," Zeb said, pointing to a rolled-up piece of canvas between the seat and the wood. "Reckon you-all might be willing to sell it? Trade for it?" The old man looked at his son, who gave a little shrug. More than likely they figured Zeb would just take the bedroll anyway, or shoot them.

Ebenezer stared at Zeb, trying to figure out what on earth this Wisconsin soldier boy wanted with a ratty old bedroll.

Zeb handed the young man one of the powder horns, and fetched the bedroll. "Thanks again," he said.

They watched the wagon go on down the road. Finally Ebenezer found his voice. "Maybe it'd be smart for us to walk around this city."

Zeb shook his head. From where they stood, maybe a mile from the city limits, they had an unobstructed view of that burned-out wreck.

"Anybody who still lives in Atlanta's got a fair view of us already. We try sneaking around this burg, we'd just be inviting trouble. Besides, it ain't like there's a place we can hide."

A treeless plain stretched out from the city of rubble. Even from where the two boys stood, they could make out "Sherman's sentinels"—chimneys rising out of the ash from what once had been homes, businesses, churches.

Quickly Zeb placed the bedding on the ground and began unrolling it, saying, "Hand me your Enfield." Ebenezer obeyed, and Zeb put both rifles on the blanket, rolled them up in it, tied it off, picked it up, and tilted his head toward the wagon with the firewood making its way into the city. "We walk right through this city," Zeb said.

Ebenezer gave a pitiful look, like he didn't trust Zeb at all.

Pretending to ignore the slave's look, Zeb kept talking. "Might find something to eat. Besides, this road leads right to Elyton, and that's where we need to get to."

"Yeah, but . . ."

Ebenezer was scared. Zeb could see that clearly but, grinning, he placed his hand on the slave's shoulder.

"Ebenezer," he said, "you know all about swamps and noodling for catfish. You got us this far. I'll give you that. But this is a city. Was one, anyhow. I'm a city boy. I'll get us through Atlanta. This time, you just do like I say."

Chapter Eight

"You keep your head down." Zeb gave Ebenezer a friendly shove. "Head down, and keep walking. Don't look nobody in the eye. If somebody says something, just pretend you didn't hear, and keep right on walking. Walking with a purpose. Now, if it happens that somebody stops us, you let me do the talking. Let's go. Just walk like you know where you're going, what you're doing. We'll get through Atlanta in no time."

Only it proved impossible for Ebenezer to keep his head down. He walked and stared. Never had he seen such destruction, and maybe now he understood why white folks back home feared these Yankees so much.

Railroad tracks had been ripped apart. Nothing on them except heavy iron wheels and ash, a lot of ash. Many of the iron rails were twisted. Ebenezer stopped and looked at a pile of them, scarcely imagining how anyone had managed to turn that iron so crooked.

"Sherman's hairpins," Zeb told him. "That's what the Secesh call them. Uncle Billy ordered us to make sure the Rebs couldn't never use a rail or tie again, so we'd burn the ties, heat the rails over the coal, twist them like that. Look at them two there."

Some creative soldiers had bent two iron rails until they formed the letters **US**.

"May not be able to read and write," Zeb said, "but I know what that means."

"Golly." It sounded stupid, but it was all Ebenezer could say. Then it hit him, what his companion had just admitted: Zeb

Hogan couldn't read. Or write. Ebenezer had suspected that. Now he knew for sure. Maybe that's why Zeb was always trying to prove something to Ebenezer, show how smart he was.

That was the last bit of conversation for a spell.

They walked.

The first house they passed, one that had not been torched, was pockmarked with holes from cannonballs and musket fire, the glass in the windows all gone, and a whole chunk of wall blown out. The trees that had lined the driveway lay on their sides, riddled with bullets, dead. Nobody lived there any more. Ebenezer didn't think the owners would ever return.

Like tombstones in a graveyard, chimneys rose from the ash and débris, and Ebenezer guessed that was what Atlanta had become—a cemetery.

While the carnage seemingly had no effect on Zeb, it tore at Ebenezer's nerves. He imagined that this was how Columbia, South Carolina, looked now—a blackened wreck of a city. He wondered if any of those homeowners were rebuilding. At first he thought the lumberyards were making a healthy profit, but he quickly realized that he heard no saws and few hammers. The city was quiet. Like a graveyard.

They walked by more charred ruins, more eerie brick "sentinels," and a few poor whites, who just stared at the two boys. Men and women Negroes passed them, and they didn't say anything either. The only voices the boys heard came from children, Negro girls and boys, singing in the streets, playing.

Not all of the buildings had been destroyed. A two-story brick building still stood near the railroad tracks. The sign in the façade read: BILLIARDS and SALOON. It hadn't been burned, though the stone building next to it was a roofless wreck with the western side caved in. Yet even the saloon and billiards hall, with its windows intact, was deserted, its front door locked, the windows dark.

At the corner, a couple of men in sack suits walked by, and one of them glanced at the two strangers, but didn't stop, and offered no greeting.

It had been long time since Zeb and Ebenezer had eaten, but neither felt hungry. Zeb didn't think there were enough scraps left in Atlanta to feed a starving rat.

"Where are the Union soldiers?" Ebenezer asked. His own voice startled him, sounding so strange in a city of rubble.

"Ain't here," Zeb said. "A new prisoner at Florence told us that Uncle Billy led his entire Army out after burning the city." A wicked grin stretched across Zeb's face. "By the Eternal, I reckon there wasn't nothing left to occupy."

Now Ebenezer lowered his head, watching his feet, not the heaps of ash, charred timbers, toppled bricks, never daring to lift his eyes again. He feared he might see another face, a citizen of Atlanta, white or black, and feel those cold, hollow eyes staring at him. He realized that everyone he had seen in Atlanta looked like a corpse. Again, he was struck by the thought that the entire city was nothing but a cemetery.

They walked. After a while, Zeb let out a little oath.

Quickly Ebenezer looked up, and drew in a deep breath. Soldiers were marching toward them, led by a man in a dark blue coat, riding a black horse, holding a saber.

"Head down," Zeb whispered, "and just keep walking."

Ebenezer dropped his gaze, again watching his feet trod across the dirt. He could feel his heart beat. "I thought you said . . ." he began, but Zeb told him to shut up and keep walking. He heard the horse snort and paw the ground as the soldier stopped it, but Ebenezer never slowed his pace, not daring to lift his head, feeling Zeb alongside him, and the eyes of every one of those blue-coated troopers boring through his insides.

"You there," the soldier on the horse said.

The two boys kept walking.

"I said you there!"

Still walking, still not looking up.

"Halt!"

When Zeb stopped, so did Ebenezer. His eyes focused on his now motionless feet.

"Yes, sir?" Zeb said.

"What are you two young 'uns doing?"

"Going home," Zeb told him.

"You were in the Confederate artillery?"

"No, Lieutenant. My brother was. These were his britches. I grew into them."

The soldier considered this, and Zeb reached his right hand inside the bedroll he was carrying. Ebenezer caught his breath, knowing Zeb's hand was probably touching the trigger and hammer of one of those rifles he had wrapped inside that section of canvas. Now Ebenezer looked up, wetting his lips, wondering if Zeb was such a fool as to think he could shoot down fifteen Union soldiers. Thinking: *He'll get both of us killed!*

"Where's your brother now?" the man on the horse said.

"Dead," Zeb said. "Came home on furlough. Died of fever."

Ebenezer couldn't believe how well Zeb could tell such falsehoods. Zeb's voice never faltered, and he kept looking that black-mustached Bluecoat in the eye. Then Ebenezer recalled that some of what Zeb was saying was true. His brother *had* come home on furlough, and *had* died of fever.

"And what of you?" The officer's penetrating hazel eyes locked on Ebenezer.

Immediately Ebenezer's gaze fell back on his feet.

"You! Look at me."

Trembling, Ebenezer made himself obey.

"What are you doing?"

"Going home to my family," Ebenezer said.

Zeb cut in suddenly. "Lieutenant, we done explained our-selves to a Yankee colonel by some building still standing down-town . . . or what once was downtown."

The officer's eyes narrowed. His men started looking uncomfortable.

"A colonel?"

"Yes, sir. Had a bunch of Bluebellies. Reckon they come down from Tennessee."

"Where were they?"

Zeb pointed. "Just down the road a bit. They had pitched their tents. Horse soldiers." He winked. "Never seen a dead cav-alryman. How about you?"

The lieutenant stared down the rubble-lined road.

Ebenezer studied his feet again. Zeb began to tell another story. "My folks got a farm on the other side of the Chattahoochee River. I told that Yankee colonel the same thing. Said he wasn't interested in Confederates. His orders were to capture foragers."

"All right. You two boys get out of Atlanta." The lieutenant tapped the side of his horse with the flat of his saber. The soldiers moved on, turning off on the first road they passed, long before they reached downtown.

Zeb watched them a while, then started walking.

Quickly Ebenezer caught up with him. "How'd you manage to tell them such lies?" he asked.

Zeb shrugged.

"They weren't any Union soldiers back in town. Why'd you lie to that officer?"

"He's no officer," Zeb said. "He's a forager. Scavenger. Deserter. Those men he was leading came from different outfits. Didn't you notice the differences in their uniforms? One was a Zouave, by the Eternal. Another wore an artillery kepi. Reckon that lieutenant is the bull of the woods, or thinks he is. They ain't better than them sidewinders that flogged you."

Ebenezer let those words sink in. After a moment, he asked: "Well, how'd you know about the Chattahoochee River?"

"I was captured just northwest of here," Zeb said, smiling.

They didn't run into anyone else in Atlanta, and nor did they meet any travelers bound for that deserted city. Most folks, Ebenezer guessed, had been forced out during the battle, and hadn't bothered to return. Thinking: *What's left to come back to?*

Chapter Nine

Days dragged into weeks. Georgia blended into Alabama. They crossed so many creeks and rivers, ate so much fish, they felt as if they had become waterlogged. Cold rains didn't help. Now the boys seldom spoke, just walked. Ebenezer no longer felt frightened or feared capture. The prevailing mood was one of monotony. Walking, sleeping, hiding. Drudgery. None of which helped their tempers.

The country started changing. Trees still lined the little road they traveled, towering longleaf pines that often made it seem as if Ebenezer and Zeb were walking through a tunnel, but the terrain started rolling, and the boys found themselves in hills of black, glassy rocks.

By now they had stopped traveling at night, and rarely fled into the woods whenever they saw someone on the road. Once, they met a family riding in an old, rotting-out wagon, and traded two powder horns for pork, coffee, a mess kit, and stale corn pone. The man told them they were fifty miles from Elyton.

As soon as the family had disappeared around a bend, the boys scurried off the road into a clearing. Zeb began striking flint against stone till the char paper caught a spark. Shortly afterward they had a fire going, coffee boiling in the cup from the kit, while they ravenously devoured the pork and pone like it was Sunday dinner. For all either of them knew, it might indeed have been Sunday.

"How long we been on the road?" Zeb asked.

Ebenezer reached for the coffee cup. "I don't rightly know, but my feet tell me we've been walking for nigh a month. Maybe longer." He drank, the coffee warming his insides.

The sinking sun shone through four slits in the bluish-gray clouds.

"Looks like rain," Zeb said. "Again." The last word came out as a sigh.

Ebenezer nodded, and passed the coffee to Zeb.

Zeb took the cup, and absently wiped the lip with his sleeve before he drank.

"You afraid your lips will look like mine?" Ebenezer said, unable to control the trembling of his voice. "If you drink after a Negro."

Zeb stared, not comprehending. "Huh?"

"Nothing." Ebenezer swore under his breath, rose, and walked deeper into the woods.

The rain began falling ten minutes later, the temperature dropping, the wind picking up, but none of it managed to cool Ebenezer's anger.

* * * * *

Another damned river, Zeb thought.

The river looked like it was on fire. Fog steamed off the water on a chilly morning, lifting about a foot off the black water, like smoke. There was no fog anywhere, except on the water. Water and fog stretched for an eternity from one tree-lined bank to another. Wider than any river they had yet seen since Florence County.

"I don't think we can float a log across this one," Ebenezer said.

"We don't have to. Maybe." Zeb was already walking down the hill. "Come on."

They followed the road to a ferry, where Zeb traded the cartridge and cap boxes for passage. The ferryman, a red-bearded, toothless man who called himself Abel Lee, said the river was the

Coosa, and asked Zeb if he had heard anything about General Forrest.

"We ain't heard nothing about nobody," Zeb answered testily.

"I heard Sherman's arsonists burned Columbia, South Carolina," Abel Lee said, "to the ground."

Ebenezer's eyes looked at that fog twisting around the ferry as Abel Lee worked the tiller. "That's true," he whispered. "We seen that ourselves."

Lee spit a stream of tobacco juice into the river. "Atlanta. Columbia. We're lucky to still have Mobile in Confederate hands, though that Yankee blockade has pretty much shut us off." He shook his head. "Lord, I don't rightly know how much longer Alabama can hold out. I heard Gen'ral Canby has more than eighty thousand men ready to march out from Fort Morgan."

The boys said nothing.

"Where y'all headed?"

"Elyton," Zeb said.

"And y'all ain't had no word about Bedford Forrest?"

"No."

"Got a boy. All I got left. Not much older than either of you two. He j'ined up with Bedford. Last letter I got from him was in November. He was at Spring Hill, up in Tennessee."

Zeb kept quiet. To him, it seemed that Abel Lee didn't want to start up a conversation. He just wanted to talk. *Maybe*, Zeb thought, *it's easier for a fellow to talk to a stranger than to his pals.*

"Greg, he was my oldest. He fell at Gettysburg. I got a daughter, just two years younger than Greg, and her husband fell at Day's Gap. Samantha, that's my girl, she's still a-wearin' black, whenever she gets out of bed, and that ain't very often. She's just give up. Preacher McCall tried to tell her it was God's will, but she don't even hear him. Barely knows I'm around. This war . . ." Reaching up, Abel Lee wiped a tear from his eye. "Then there was Eli. Fever claimed him, just like it claimed his mama, whilst he was a-marchin' with Gen'ral Hood. Lucas, he fell at

Brice's Crossroads. Oh, he wasn't kilt quick, not like Greg and Orrin . . . Orrin bein' Samantha's husband. No, Lucas hung on for two months after that pill-roller sawed off both of his legs. He made it back home, for me to bury him beside his ma. I guess there's some comfort in that, don't you reckon? I mean, Greg, Orrin, and Eli . . . I got no notion where they's buried. Wouldn't know they was even dead if their officers or bunkies hadn't writ me. Melvin, he's all I got left. I sure hope he ain't dead, too."

The ferryboat struck the shore, and Zeb started to thank the man for the ride, to tell him he hoped his son Melvin would come home soon, but when he saw Abel Lee's face, there was nothing to say. Silently they left the smoking river, began climbing the road up the hill, while Abel Lee silently returned his ferry across the river. As he followed Zeb, Ebenezer kept looking back, staring at the ferry, until the fog covered it like a shroud.

* * * * *

Hills thickened with brush, and the rains fell that afternoon, and all the next day. Rain and fog. Fog and rain. The road got mud-dier. The road grew steeper.

Toward evening, when the rain had stopped, they found a carpetbag on the side of the road. Zeb quickly hurried to it, opening it, pulling out a woman's blouse, a scarf, tossing them into the woods.

"Zeb," Ebenezer said. "That's not your stuff. You shouldn't . . ."

"Shut up!" He tossed a book into the mud. "Maybe there's some food."

There wasn't, however, and after Zeb had emptied the satchel, he threw it angrily across the road with a vile curse. He shook his head and looked down at Ebenezer, saw him opening the pages of the book.

The slave looked up, smiling, and said, "It's *Gulliver's Travels.*" As he stood, he turned another page, and read: "'The author of these Travels, Mr. Lemuel Gulliver, is my ancient and . . .'" He had trouble with the next word. "'. . . intimate friend.'" Smiling, he repeated the word. "Intimate." Nodding with satisfaction, he started to read more, but Zeb ripped the book from his hands, and tossed it deep into the woods.

"Words," he snapped. "What good is a book? It ain't gonna feed us. If you're coming with me, come on."

Zeb kept walking, his boots making a squishing sound as he trod across a wooden bridge. Moving with a purpose. It was dusk. Ebenezer felt worn out, exhausted, but he made himself sprint until he caught up with Zeb a few rods after they had crossed the river.

"Let's rest a spell," he said.

Zeb strode on.

"Zeb!"

The soldier didn't stop.

"I bet we can find a cave," Ebenezer said. "In these hills. Get a fire going. Dry ourselves."

Zeb acted as if he hadn't heard.

Ebenezer raced after him. "Where you going, Zeb, in such an awful hurry?"

"Vicksburg," he said.

"Well, we're not going to get there today. We're not even in Elyton, yet, and Vicksburg's plumb on the other side of Mississippi, according to our map." Zeb was still walking. "Zeb, you're not making a lick of sense." He reached out, grabbed Zeb's shoulder.

Zeb spun, slashed out, knocking away Ebenezer's arm, almost knocking the runaway slave into the mud. "You keep your hands off me you black . . ."

Blood rushed to Ebenezer's head. "Why don't you," he roared, "*say it?* Say the word. It won't be the first time I've heard it."

"I ain't saying nothing." Zeb turned, started.

Ebenezer reached out again, jerked Zeb around. "Something's in your craw," Ebenezer said. "What is it?"

"You." Zeb's right fist caught Ebenezer in the cheek, and the slave dropped like a fifty-pound sack into the mud. Zeb stared, absently massaging the fingers on his hand, hardly believing the look on the slave's face as he pushed himself into a seated position, shaking his head, gingerly fingering the cut underneath his eye.

Slowly Zeb let out a sigh, and extended his left hand, mumbling: "I'm sorry, Ebenezer. I didn't mean . . ." He never finished.

With a primal scream, Ebenezer pushed himself up, lowered his shoulder, slammed into Zeb's stomach. Air whooshed from Zeb's lungs as the two boys fell hard against the black rocks on the side of the road.

Chapter Ten

E benezer rolled over, came up, swung, missed. Looking down, he caught a blur, then felt Zeb's shoulder ram his stomach, sprawling him into the woods. An oak tree met his back, and he grunted, watched Zeb slide off him and slip on the straw and leaves, wet from rain. Straightening, ignoring the pain in his back, chest, gut, hands, Ebenezer turned and kicked out at the boy on the ground. He couldn't believe what he was doing. He, a runaway slave, tried to smash Zeb Hogan's nose with his brogans. He would have done just that, too, if Zeb hadn't spotted him, and dived away at the last instant. Ebenezer's ears were ringing, his chest heaving.

Zeb scrambled to his feet, watching the slave catch his breath. Their eyes met, locked, but neither spoke. They circled each other, feeling their way around the trees, watching the evening grow darker. Zeb spat out a glob of blood, wiped his mouth with the back of his hand, then charged. A backhand slapped him across the face, and he slipped again. Rolled over. But Ebenezer was on top of him, straddling him, reaching down, locking his fingers around Zeb's throat.

This was no good. Zeb had spent too many months in a prison camp, wasting away, while Ebenezer had been eating real meals, or so he thought, working in the fields, digging graves. Zeb didn't have the strength in his arms to whip this boy. He reached for the revolver in his waistband, heard Ebenezer's gasp. Shaking his head, Zeb dropped the pistol in a bush. He couldn't use a gun on an unarmed man. Wouldn't . . . unless it was Sergeant Ben DeVere. Yet he couldn't whip Ebenezer Chase, not with his fists.

But his legs . . . Now that was different. He had been marching so long, during his time with the 16th Wisconsin and for the past month, walking across South Carolina, Georgia, and into Alabama, that his legs were as strong as springall. He arched his back, moved his hips to his left, then shot out with his legs to the right, and Ebenezer fell to his side. Zeb came up first, kicked out, felt his boot graze the slave's shoulder. The slave leaped up, and Zeb shot out with his right fist, but the boy ducked, and his hand smashed a tree, bark gouging his flesh, jamming two knuckles.

Zeb swore. Shook the pain from his hand. Ebenezer's fist found Zeb's jaw, and Zeb was down, spitting out blood, shaking his head, trying to get his eyes to focus. The slave's fist felt like an anvil.

"You miserable little darky!"

Zeb felt confused. He hadn't said that. Had he?

"I'll teach you to strike a white man, boy."

Zeb tried to place the voice. A scream cut through the cool air, and Zeb reached out, felt hands gripping his arms, felt himself being jerked to his feet. His vision cleared, and he stared into hard faces.

Ebenezer cried out, and as the hands let him go, Zeb pushed a path through the people, saw a man in duck trousers and a butternut jacket placing a knife against Ebenezer's throat.

"You leave him be!" Zeb demanded, and the man with the knife spun around.

"No coon ever touches a white man, boy. Not in this here part of Alabama."

"It's none of your affair. Leave him alone." *Odd,* Zeb thought, spitting out more blood. *A minute ago, I was trying to kill that slave, and now I'm defending him. Why? I wonder . . .* "I said leave him alone."

He knew he needed Ebenezer. Zeb couldn't read, couldn't write, didn't know this country. He'd feel lost without the slave. What's more, he'd be dead if not for Ebenezer Chase.

"And who the blazes are you?" The stentorian voice turned Zeb around, and Zeb looked at a big man holding a Dragoon Colt.

"He's a Yankee spy!" another man shouted.

Zeb swallowed. Eight, no, nine men. All armed. Two of them carrying torches. Other sounds drew his attention out of the woods and onto the road. He couldn't see that well, but he knew more men, wagons, and horses were out there. *By the Eternal,* Zeb thought, *an entire army sneaked up on us while we were fighting each other.*

"You heard Hank," one of the men with a torch said. "What you doin' in these woods?" He extended the flame toward Ebenezer. "Brawlin' with the likes of him?"

"Who are you with?" the man with the Dragoon demanded. "Canby or Wilson?"

"I'm with Bedford Forrest," Zeb said, his voice cracking from the pain, "you blasted idiot."

The man lowered the Colt. He seemed at a loss for words.

Another man, much older, calmer, and not toting a huge six-shooter, pulled a handkerchief out of his coat pocket, and offered it to Zeb, who took it and used it to stanch the flow of blood.

"Who are you?" the man asked. This one didn't seem as rough, as unkempt as the others. He wore a broadcloth coat, tall black boots, and a wide-brimmed straw hat. He turned to the one with the knife. "Put the blade away, Conn. Leave the darky alone." Facing Zeb again. "I'll ask you again . . . who are you?"

"I'm Melvin Lee," Zeb said. "I'm a scout for General Forrest." Lying had always come easy to Zeb. He just prayed the fool Ebenezer Chase wouldn't do anything to give him away.

A pleasant grin stretched across the Alabaman's face as he pointed at Zeb's trousers. "Last report I got was that Lieutenant General Forrest commanded the cavalry corps of the Department of Alabama, Mississippi, and East Louisiana. You're wearing the britches of an artillery soldier."

"And the boots of a horse soldier," Zeb shot right back at him. "Maybe you don't know how it is . . . you being safe in your homes while us young men are off fighting, and dying, for you. We wear whatever we can get our hands on, these days."

The man's smile transformed into an angry frown. "Mind your manners, son," he said tightly. "I'm old enough to be your father, maybe your grandfather, and I'll tan your hide if I've a mind to. And we haven't shirked our duty. We're the Jones Valley Militia . . . skirmished a Yank patrol two days back. Now you say you're riding with Forrest. That's well and good, but I don't see a horse for you or your pal here." He hooked his thumb at Ebenezer.

"Remounts," Zeb answered. "We're looking for remounts. Lost my horse a couple of days ago."

"He don't sound like he's from Jones Valley," the man with the Dragoon Colt said, picking up Zeb's revolver, "but he's got a Spiller and Burr .36, and that's a Rebel gun."

"My pa captains the ferry on the Coosa River," Zeb said, and pointed east. "Abel Lee."

"I know Abel Lee," said a man in the back. He limped forward, and Zeb and Ebenezer saw he was on crutches, and that his left leg was gone below the knee. "Big fellow, gray beard, walks with a limp."

"Mister," Zeb said, "you don't know my pa at all. He ain't much bigger than me, his hair is red, or looks red when he washes it, and if he ever limps, it must be because he ain't found his land legs, riding that rocking river all day and half the night."

The man gave a little smile, and shook his head. He'd been trying to catch Zeb in a lie. "I know your brother, Greg."

"Knew him," Zeb said. "Greg was killed by Yankees in Pennsylvania. All my brothers is dead."

"He's Melvin Lee, I reckon," the man said, and moved back on his crutches.

"Whose the colored boy?" the older man asked.

"His name's Ebenezer," Zeb answered, pulling away the bloody handkerchief for inspection, returning it as he kept on with his lies. "General Forrest loaned him out to me. Now what brings you fellows out in the middle of this wet night?"

"Why were you fighting? Conn's right. No Negro ever strikes a white man, even a white boy. Not without serious repercussions."

Zeb wasn't sure what *repercussions* meant. "We weren't fighting."

The one with the Dragoon chuckled. "What do you call it then?" The smile disappeared as quickly as it had come, and he turned, thumbing back the hammer, pressing the barrel at Ebenezer's heart. "What do you call it, boy?"

"A . . . lesson." Ebenezer swallowed down his fear. "He . . ." For the life of him, he couldn't remember what name Zeb had used. "He . . . was teaching me what to do . . . in case . . . we got captured . . . by . . ."

"By Yankees," Zeb said.

The one in the broadcloth coat laughed. "I don't know who was teaching who what, but you both have a lot to learn about fisticuffs."

"And how to carry on during a war," Dragoon Colt added.

Broadcloth Coat introduced himself as Captain Andrew Whitaker, commander of the Jones Valley Militia.

"You know how it's been," Captain Whitaker told Zeb, nodding at him, calling him Melvin. "We're feeling the life squeezed out of us from the Yankee tyrants who have controlled Huntsville since practically the war began . . ."

"Don't forget all them Yankee-lovin' scalawags from up there, neither," Dragoon Colt said. "Ask me, we should ride up there and hang every mother's son of them. They's traitors. Traitors to Alabama. Traitors to the South."

Captain Whitaker let him finish, then tugged down on the brim of his hat and shook his head. "And from the south, down around Mobile. We're caught between the Yankees to the north and south. Squeezing us tighter and tighter. From what we hear, General Canby's preparing to assault Fort Blakely and Spanish Fort, and we hear that Wilson is preparing some type of assault from up north from the Tennessee River. We've been sheltered in Elyton, where I live, and Jonesboro, where Hank has a farm." Here he tilted his head at the man with the Dragoon. "This valley has always been sheltered. Soil's too rocky for cotton, the land too hard to clear. We don't have much here but iron. Iron has been our savior, helped us keep this fight going, providing material for the Confederacy. Yet now, I fear, iron might spell our doom. If the Yankees attack us . . . destroy our ironworks."

One man handed Zeb his revolver, and he slipped it into his waistband. "What are you doing?" he asked Captain Whitaker.

"That bridge," Captain Whitaker said. "We have to destroy that bridge. Keep the Yanks from crossing the Cahaba. That's what we came to do. You've seen the signs, Melvin. You know there are Yankee patrols all across the valley. We had a set-to with some Bluebellies two days ago. Those rains, flooded streams, quagmires for roads, they might keep Wilson from leading any campaign of any strength for a while, but that hasn't stopped him from sending out patrols."

"If they get control of this bridge," the man named Hank said, "they'll be able to capture, or burn down, the iron furnaces at Oxmoor, maybe Irondale."

Captain Whitaker nodded.

"We're here to destroy the bridge," Captain Whitaker said. "We'd planned to burn it, but . . ." He sighed, and gestured at the falling rain.

"We have powder. Plenty of powder." This came from Hank. "Brought it up from Selma."

A sudden pop drew their attention to the road. Another. Then the cannonade of musketry, followed by the screams of horses, the ripping of bullets into woods, into men.

"Capt'n! Capt'n Whitaker!" a voice cried from the road. "Yankees are upon us."

Muskets roared. From where he stood, Zeb could see the flashes.

The men turned, ran, drawing their weapons. Zeb felt himself being pushed, heard one of the Alabamans say he had a pistol and he'd better use it. Looking over his shoulder, Zeb saw Ebenezer running with the others.

On the Elyton road, those pops had become steady, and a whole lot louder, echoed by screams, shouts, curses. Zeb stopped at the side of the road, ducked behind a tree, reached out and grabbed Ebenezer's arm, pulled him down into a ditch. Twenty or thirty men stood on the road, ramming rods down muskets, lifting their weapons, aiming, firing at will. Flashes pockmarked the blackness on the other side of the Cahaba River, and somewhere in the darkness a trumpet blared. A bullet buzzed past Ebenezer's ear. Eyes widening with fear, Ebenezer flattened his face against the dead weeds.

"Steady men!" Captain Whitaker called. "Steady!"

Firing became general. A geyser of mud shot up over Zeb's head.

"Hank!" Whitaker called out. "We need those barrels of powder. We have to blow that bridge. Now!"

"I'll fetch 'em, Capt'n," Hank said, and he climbed out of the hole he'd taken cover in, started running down the road. Two other militiamen followed, but one fell down immediately, and he didn't get up. Another, carrying a torch, ran on.

"Come on." Zeb grabbed Ebenezer's hand, practically dragged him out of the ditch before he let go. He took off after Hank and the other soldier, and Ebenezer figured that he had no choice but to run right after him. Bullets sang past them, clipping trees, digging in the mud, or striking flesh. Never had Ebenezer been in a battle, but he couldn't mistake when a ball hit a man. He knew he would keep hearing that sound for the next month when trying to sleep. Now, maybe, he understood how Zeb Hogan could be such a hard-rock for a boy a few months younger than Ebenezer was.

They reached two covered wagons parked on the edge of the road. Behind those wagons, by the flames of campfires, Ebenezer spotted several horses picketed to the ground. About half a dozen soldiers raced from those fires, shouting, trying to get their muskets or shotguns—one held just a pitchfork—into the ready position.

Hank had climbed into the back of the wagon, and now he reappeared with a barrel in his arms. He handed it to the other militiaman, who dropped it into the mud.

"Careful with that torch, Thaddeus," Hank said. "The grand ladies of Selma donated their chamber-lye to help make the salt-peter needed to produce this powder for our boys."

"Huh?" The militiaman jammed the torch into the mud, away from the wagon.

Hank laughed. "Their pee, lad. My brother took a wagon around Selma, emptying ladies' chamber pots into barrels. He'll have a fine story to tell his grandkids when they asked him what he did durin' the War for Southern Independence."

Hank disappeared, and when Thaddeus bent over to pick up the barrel, Zeb pulled the .36-caliber revolver from his waistband and slammed the butt against the soldier's skull. His face sank into the mud next to the barrel, and he didn't move. From inside the wagon came Hank's cackles. "Yes, sir, Thaddeus, when this war is won, we should all thank the ladies of Selma for donating their pee and . . ."

His face froze when it reappeared beneath the canvas, his eyes trained on the Spiller & Burr in Zeb's hand.

"I knowed you wasn't no Alabama boy," Hank said.

"16th Wisconsin," Zeb said, his voice surprisingly steady. "I can't let you blow up that bridge." He waved the revolver a tad. "First, drop that barrel over the side."

Hank did as instructed.

"Now, with your left-hand finger and thumb, pull out that big horse pistol of yours and let it fall, too."

Again, Hank proved he was really good at following orders.

"All right," Zeb started, and then came that sickening sound, the sound of a bullet striking flesh, and Hank's face contorted, and he choked out a scream before toppling out of the wagon.

Zeb dropped to his knees, inched over, and put his hand on Hank's neck.

"Is he . . .?" Ebenezer couldn't finish.

"I can't tell," Zeb said. "Took a Minié ball in his back." He shoved the .36 in his waistband. "You get the small guy." Zeb nodded at Thaddeus's unconscious body. "Drag him away from this wagon." Already Zeb was standing, taking hold of Hank's arms, pulling him toward the fires.

"Hank!" Gunshots accented Captain Whitaker's voice. "Hank! We need that powder now!"

Ebenezer deposited Thaddeus by Hank's body.

"Hank! Hank, we've got . . . !"

A deafening explosion lit up a good chunk of the eastern sky, followed by screams and the sound of metal slicing through the night air.

"Grapeshot," Zeb said. He was back beside the wagon, busting open a barrel top with the butt of the Dragoon. "I want you to go fetch us a couple of horses." He tossed Ebenezer the giant pistol, which the slave barely managed to snag.

"Man," Ebenezer began, "I can't steal somebody's . . ."

"Do it!" Zeb barked, and Ebenezer turned, and ran toward the horses.

He found a couple of mounts already saddled, grabbed the reins, unfastened the tethers, and held them. Another bullet whizzed over his head. He kept expecting some guard, or maybe a bunch of Yankee soldiers, to come charging out of the blackness. Toward the bridge, flashes lit up the sky, and then Ebenezer spied sparks sizzling along the ground, a shadow running ahead of it. That shadow was Zeb.

"Can you ride?" Zeb asked as he grabbed the reins.

"Yeah," Ebenezer said.

Zeb was trying to put his boot in the stirrup, but the horse kept twisting.

"Good. 'Cause I ain't never been on a horse before."

Chapter Eleven

That horse wouldn't quit spinning. Ebenezer kept hollering at Zeb, spouting out something about how Zeb was pulling on the reins, but Zeb couldn't really hear. Although Ebenezer had already mounted his horse, he dropped out of the saddle to help Zeb. Later, both boys realized just how lucky Ebenezer was, because at that second the wagon blew up and a chunk of wood flew right over Ebenezer's head, just above the saddle. Had he been on that horse, Ebenezer would have been killed.

The concussion of the blast knocked the legs out from underneath the horse Zeb had desperately been trying to mount. The gelding rolled over, and Zeb couldn't get out of the way, feeling the crushing weight of the horse as it rolled over his right leg. He let out a fearful wail that seemed to rise over the din of battle. Miraculously the horse scrambled to its feet, kicking Zeb's thigh, but missing his skull, and took off running away from the battle, the flames, the carnage.

"Zeb! Zeb! You all right?" Ebenezer dropped beside Zeb, who had shut his eyes tightly, grinding his teeth, trying to choke down the pain.

"No," he replied, rolling over, watching the flames consume what was left of that covered wagon. Beyond it he could make out the forms of a bunch of Jones Valley Militia men hurrying their way. Zeb was hurting, but knew he'd be dead if he didn't get out of there. If the Secesh caught him wearing the pants of a Reb soldier and having claimed to have ridden with Nathan Bedford Forrest, Zeb would be shot or hanged as a spy. And Ebenezer . . . ? Likely

91

the same. Zeb tried to get to his feet, but his right leg refused to cooperate.

"Here." Zeb felt Ebenezer's arms under his shoulders, hoisting him to his feet. Hopping around on his left leg, Zeb fell against the side of a horse, realized that Ebenezer still held the reins to his mount. "Get on!" Ebenezer cried.

"I can't!" Zeb said.

"Hold onto these!" Ebenezer yelled as he placed the reins in Zeb's hand, then he squatted, lifted Zeb's left leg, shoved it into the stirrup. As the slave boosted the soldier into the saddle, Zeb howled. He could hardly bend his right knee, but somehow swung the injured leg over the horse's back.

"Hey! You there! What's in tarnation is y'all doin'?"

The Jones Valley soldiers had reached the inferno of the wagon. One of them started to raise his musket.

Zeb pulled the Spiller & Burr from his waistband, aimed, cocked, pulled the trigger. Nothing sounded but a dull click. He eared back the hammer, which took a lot of effort because that pistol wasn't easy to cock, when the musket flashed, roared, and a bullet ripped through Zeb's shirt, just underneath his armpit. The horse started twisting, turning, pawing, and spoiled Zeb's aim. Not that it mattered. The .36 just snapped again.

"They's stealin' our hosses!" another Secesh yelled. Something roared off to Zeb's right, and a Reb dropped his musket and let out a little yell as he fell to the ground. Zeb just barely made out the Reb scrambling to his knees, searching for the weapon he had dropped.

Another bullet ripped through the night, and Zeb heard the clopping of hoofs, and then he realized Ebenezer had mounted another horse and was right beside him. The runaway slave raised his right arm. A flash blinded Zeb, the roar leaving his ears ringing, his horse almost bucking him off. Only then did Zeb realize that Ebenezer was shooting the .44 Dragoon.

"Grab hold of the mane!" Ebenezer took the reins from Zeb's hand and kicked his horse while whipping its haunches with the hot barrel of the Dragoon. They loped into the night, Zeb bouncing every which way, gripping the mane for dear life.

Another shot roared, but the ball didn't come near the fleeing boys. After that the Rebs just sent curses after the fleeing saboteurs.

* * * * *

"Why'd you do it?"

Zeb wasn't sure he heard. Leaning in the saddle, gripping the horn, feeling light-headed, he weakly pushed himself up. His gaze settled on Ebenezer sitting on his horse in the middle of a stream — both of their horses slaking their thirst—staring at him.

Shaking his head, Zeb tried to clear his mind. It was mid-morning. They must have ridden all night. He couldn't remember much at all, but slowly he recalled what he had done the previous night. A flash of pain shooting up his right leg from the horse kick made everything clearer.

"Done what?" he said through gritted teeth.

"Why'd you blow up that wagon? You could have gotten us both killed."

"I'm a Union soldier." Zeb shrugged.

"I thought you were done with this war."

That made Zeb think. Gently he touched his right leg, which hung on the side, his boot out of the stirrup. He looked at the leg, and grimaced. It had swollen so much, it strained against his pant leg. Ebenezer nudged his horse closer, and offered Zeb his canteen. He took it and drank greedily, not bothering to wipe the spout before drinking after a black man, not noticing the smile that crept across the slave's face.

"Well?" Ebenezer asked again.

"I ain't no deserter," Zeb said.

Ebenezer gave him a questioning, doubtful stare.

"Well, they were gonna blow up that bridge," Zeb said. "Our boys needed that bridge to get to them ironworks, them furnaces, stop the Rebs from making iron and such, help end this war. Seemed to me that it was my duty to stop them."

That wasn't it, though. Zeb knew that. He wasn't any hero. Far from it. He had just seen a chance to do something, to prove to that slave that he was every bit as good as he was. Sure, Zeb couldn't read, not *Gulliver's Travels*, not even his own name, couldn't noodle for catfish, didn't know his way through these thick forests, couldn't even swim. Yet he could fight. He knew his duty. If anything, Sergeant Major Engstrand had taught him that much.

"You came this close to getting the both of us killed."

Ebenezer held his forefinger about an inch from his thumb. He was shaking, and had to squeeze his fingers into a fist. Zeb had seen that before, among the boys of the 16th Wisconsin, and other outfits. Last night, Ebenezer hadn't showed much fear after the initial shock of battle. He had fired that Dragoon, helped Zeb into the saddle, carried them both out of that storm, but now his nerves pricked him without mercy. Yeah, Zeb had seen that happen to many troops after a battle. He could recall shaking himself once or twice after he had seen the elephant.

"You're just upset," Zeb said.

"You're damned right I'm upset!" Ebenezer barked.

"Well, I feel sorry for them, too," Zeb said.

The slave's face contorted. "Feel sorry for who?" he asked.

"Them ladies of Selma," Zeb said. "All the pee they'd donated to the Confederacy got blowed up for nothing."

Ebenezer stared at Zeb the longest while before shaking his head.

Zeb had hoped Ebenezer might smile, but that would have been asking too much.

* * * * *

When they rested shortly after noon, Ebenezer opened the saddlebags on Zeb's horse. Lying on the ground, his head propped up against a pine, Zeb watched as the slave pulled out a Bible and a pair of binoculars, which he slid back into the bag. The other side held a shirt, a pair of socks, a clasp knife, and a wallet. Ebenezer pulled out a wad of money, looked to be counting it, and then shoved the greenbacks and yellowbacks back into the billfold, which he dropped back into the bag, and buckled it shut.

Zeb closed his eyes, listening to the wind rustling through the pine tops. It should have been cool, but he felt so hot. Suddenly he stiffened, let out a little cry and, opening his eyes, found Ebenezer pressing his hand on his right leg.

"How bad is it?" the slave asked.

Zeb shook his head, relieved when Ebenezer stopped pushing down on the swollen limb. "I don't know."

"Can you bend it?"

"No. Swole up too much."

"You think it's busted?"

"Don't think so, but it might as well be."

"Can you ride a little more?" he asked.

"If you can get me back in the saddle."

"Good. Map says there's a big river up ahead. I'd like to get across it, in case those Jones Valley men are chasing us."

Zeb figured those Rebs had their hands full in that little skirmish for the bridge over the Cahaba, but Ebenezer was right. They needed to press on. He prayed his leg would hold out.

* * * * *

No bridge spanned the Black Warrior River. No ferry, either.

"We'll have to swim our horses across," Ebenezer said.

"That don't hold no appeal to me." Zeb swallowed, looking across the river, deep, wide, foaming from the current. He had waded through streams, floated across rivers on logs, walked across creeks over fallen trees, crossed bridges, ridden ferries, everything, it seemed, but swum across one. Or swum a horse across one. "By the Eternal, that's the problem with the South," Zeb snapped. "There's too many rivers."

"Horses are good swimmers," Ebenezer said.

"I ain't."

"You get into trouble," Ebenezer said, "you just slide off the back of the saddle, latch tight to the tail. That horse'll pull you across." He didn't give Zeb time to argue, just kicked his horse's sides and plunged into the deep, dark, churning water.

Zeb wet his lips. He could stay here for all of eternity, or follow. With a curse and a shudder, he coaxed the horse into the river. Frigid water took his breath away. The horse lunged after the mare Ebenezer was riding. Almost immediately the water was up to the saddle, filling Zeb's boot tops. He fought off the panic trying to seize him and gripped the horse's mane, bracing as they went deeper and deeper, the current carrying them downstream. Pretty soon, Zeb had no choice but to slip off the saddle. He grabbed the tail, held on, kicking with his good leg, somehow managing to keep his head above the water, although he thought he might have swallowed a couple of gallons of river water and mud.

He closed his eyes and tried to recall some prayer. He heard the splashing, the sound of the river in his ears, his own short gasps for breath. Then Ebenezer hollering, "Let go! Let go!" Zeb's eyes shot open, and he realized the horse was on the bank. He released the tail, sinking into the muddy bottom, watching his mount climb up, water streaming off its body. Forgetting his bum leg, Zeb tried to stand, couldn't, and when he looked down, he saw the current had pulled off his boots and his left sock.

"Great," he said angrily, and Ebenezer laughed.

"You're mad because you lost your boots." Ebenezer shook his head. "Zeb, you could have lost your life. That's no small feat, pal, what we just did." Ebenezer pointed to four crooked wooden crosses on the banks. A mud-splattered gray kepi hung from one.

"Appears that a few soldiers swimming the Black Warrior didn't fare as well as you did."

* * * * *

When they made camp that evening, Ebenezer helped Zeb off the horse and on over to a pine tree. Zeb felt helpless, but he couldn't do any chores, couldn't walk, wasn't sure how he had managed to ride. He lay there, helpless, while Ebenezer got a fire going before sneaking off to a nearby creek to noodle for catfish. After they had eaten supper, Ebenezer pulled out the Bible and sat by the fire, reading it.

Zeb watched him for a while, finally asking: "How'd you learn to read?"

Slowly Ebenezer closed the Bible. "Master Hall's wife taught me."

"But that's against the law."

Ebenezer nodded. For a moment, Zeb thought that was going to be Ebenezer's only answer, but he cleared his throat, and started talking.

"Master Hall, he was gone to Charleston, and his wife . . . she's a good woman, a real fine lady . . . she started teaching me. Just the ABCs to begin with. She said I was a real fast learner, but I think she was a real fine teacher. Still, I guess I picked up the letters really fast, learning the sounds each letter makes. She was real proud of me, and when Master Hall came back home, she proudly showed him what all I'd learned, what all she'd managed to teach me."

Ebenezer stopped and for the longest time stared into the remains of the fire. They could have added a few twigs to it, but they didn't want some traveler to investigate the smoke, so usually—on those rare nights when they risked a cook fire—they would let the fire burn itself out, and do with a cold camp the rest of the night. At last, Ebenezer cleared his throat and continued.

"Master Hall beat her. He beat her bad . . . screaming, cursing. I was just a boy, and I feared he'd start whipping me, but he just slapped her, kept slapping her . . . her crying on her knees, him pulling her hair to keep her head up . . . slapping her. Her nose was busted . . . blood just pouring down her face . . . her lips smashed. It was horrible, Zeb. I just stood there, too scared to do anything, even to yell at him to stop. He just kept hitting her, telling her what a fool she was, that they could both go to prison for what she'd done. 'How dare she?' That's what he yelled.

"I guess he would have killed her that evening, and maybe he would have whipped or killed me after he'd finished, but Mister Anderson, the overseer, he come running into the parlor . . . that's where we were . . . revolver in his hand. He thought we slaves were revolting, killing Master Hall's wife, and when he saw what Master Hall was doing, he pulled him off her. She just toppled to the floor and curled up in a ball. Master Hall, he stood like he was in a daze, like he was a thousand miles away. Then he walked over to the cabinet and poured a glass of brandy, drank it down in one or two gulps, thanked Mister Anderson, and retired for the night. Mister Anderson fetched a couple of the house servants, and they took Missus Hall to a settee, started bathing her wounds. And Mister Anderson, I won't ever forget the look on his face . . . like I was to blame for what had just happened. He came over to me, whipping my arm like he was snapping a chicken's neck, and I knew I was in for a whipping, but Missus Hall, she cried out to him, told him not to hurt me. He shoved me outside, told me to get to my quarters. I run off, run to Uncle Cain, crying on his shoulder the rest of the night."

The fire burned out, and still Ebenezer said nothing.

"That ended your schoolin', I take it," Zeb said.

He looked up with a sudden grin. "No," he said. "That made me eager to learn. Uncle Cain, he told me that if reading and writing were so important, could scare white folks that much, maybe I'd better keep at it. Improve myself. He didn't say it, but I knew he was thinking that it could make me an equal to any white man." He laughed. "I've seen that look before, Zeb."

Zeb didn't know what Ebenezer saw in his face, but he desperately tried to change whatever expression it was.

"That's all right, Zeb. It doesn't bother me. There were no more lessons from Missus Hall. She recovered from that beating, even apologized to me a week or so later . . . like it was her fault! But she sneaked me a *McGuffey's Eclectic First Reader*, would even leave a newspaper or book out on the counter whenever I was in the house. I'd sneak a peek at those, keep right on practicing. Once I was in the parlor, reading, or trying to, some book about a boy named Oliver Twist, written by some fellow from England, and I happened to look up and caught her reflection in the mirror. She looked like she was proud. So I kept right on learning. Now, I'm not the best reader or writer, but . . ." He shrugged.

Leg throbbing, Zeb rolled onto his back, staring at the night sky.

"Zeb," Ebenezer said after a while.

"Yeah?"

"I could teach you."

Shame overcame Zeb, who closed his eyes, balled his hands into fists, tried not to cry.

"I mean," Ebenezer said apologetically, "if I can learn, anybody can. I mean . . . I didn't mean that. I meant . . ."

"I make out fine without reading or writing." Defiant on the outside, Zeb tried to hide the envy he felt toward Ebenezer Chase, a slave. "I'm going to sleep."

He knew, however, that sleep would not come easy on this night.

Chapter Twelve

"James! James! Come back, James! Don't leave me! James!"

Zeb's shouts brought Ebenezer out of a deep sleep, and he yelled at him to shut up, told him he was dreaming, but Zeb kept right on yelling, twisting, turning. Grumbling, Ebenezer tossed off his blanket and went over to his companion.

Dawn hadn't broken, but the eastern skies were turning gray. One of the horses snorted. Ebenezer placed a hand on Zeb's shoulder, and the soldier stopped fretting. Ebenezer could feel how warm Zeb was even before the back of the slave's right hand touched his companion's cheek.

"Zeb," Ebenezer whispered, more to himself, "you're burning up."

Zeb wasn't awake, but his eyes darted beneath his lids. His curly hair was pasted to his brow, soaked with sweat.

"I'm cold, James," Zeb said, and Ebenezer hurriedly fetched his blanket, covered Zeb with it, and then started saddling the horses.

They had covered a lot of territory since leaving the Cahaba River, had to be getting close to Mississippi. What Ebenezer wanted to do was leave Zeb Hogan here, make his way to Texas alone. Zeb would live or he would die, but that he was sick was his own fault. He shouldn't have blown up that powder back on the Cahaba River.

If I get him a doctor, Ebenezer thought while cinching a saddle, *that'll just slow me down, keep me that much farther from*

101

Lizzie and little Tempie. Zeb Hogan isn't my affair. He . . . He saved my life.

Ebenezer rose, gripping the saddle horn, staring into the woods, remembering those four deserters back in Georgia. Zeb could have let those men whip him. Zeb had gotten him through Atlanta, and there's no telling what those Jones Valley militia men would have done if Zeb hadn't spoken up. Besides, no matter what Zeb Hogan said, Federal soldiers were fighting to free the slaves, and Zeb had done his part blowing up that gunpowder. He had risked his life, been injured.

No, I can't . . . won't . . . leave Zeb Hogan alone.

Silently he returned to Zeb, knelt, and tugged on his shoulder, telling him to wake up.

"Let me sleep, Pa," he whimpered, and Ebenezer let out a sigh, then jerked Zeb up.

"Come on, Zeb," he said. "Lean on me."

It reminded Ebenezer of dragging cotton and tobacco sacks back at Oliver Hall's plantation, but he managed to get Zeb to his horse and shove him in the saddle. Zeb wasn't quite awake, but he had enough sense to grip the mane. Ebenezer then mounted his mare, took the reins to Zeb's gelding, and rode out of the woods and onto the road, praying they wouldn't pass any white folks while making their way southwest down the pike. There was no telling what a white man would think if he saw a Negro leading a sick white boy on a stolen Confederate militia horse.

Come noon, their luck had held. They hadn't passed anybody on the road, but Ebenezer hadn't found a doctor or even a town for Zeb, who was awake now, no longer delirious, but still sweating, feverish, chilled.

Ebenezer swung from his horse, uncorked the canteen, let Zeb drink a bit. As Zeb handed back the canteen, he leaned over and threw up all over the gelding's withers.

"God, Ebenezer," Zeb moaned as he straightened in the saddle, wiping his mouth with the back of his hand. He was paler than a whitewashed fence. He started weaving and leaned forward, head bent low. "I don't want to die," he muttered.

"You aren't dying," Ebenezer said, but he knew if he didn't find someone soon, be it a doctor or a grown-up, Zeb Hogan would likely die. Ebenezer stuck the Dragoon in the saddlebag, knowing he couldn't let anybody in Alabama see a Negro boy carrying a revolver, but he fetched the wallet and pulled out some money. That might take some explaining, too, Ebenezer knew, but maybe, he thought, he had learned a thing or two from Zeb over the past month.

About lying.

Again, Ebenezer led Zeb's horse. He kept glancing back, not sure how long Zeb could stay in the saddle. Zeb Hogan was game. Anybody else would never have gotten on that horse in the morning, let alone stayed on for all the miles they had covered.

Two hours later, they came upon a dirt trail that led off from the main road to a farm house about a mile away. Muttering a prayer, Ebenezer turned onto the trail, and headed toward the little shack.

He heard voices before he saw the people and reined up in the yard, already realizing what a terrible choice he had made coming to this farm.

A gangling man with a week's worth of beard stubble on his face held a cotton sack over the well, and something was moving, kicking, screaming inside that sack. Off to the side, a white girl, maybe sixteen years old or so, in a homely dress and no shoes, had dropped to her knees, tears streaming down her face. She clasped her hands as she begged her father not to do it, not to kill little Petey, saying that it had all been her fault.

"Boy was eatin' dirt," the man said.

Ebenezer could smell the corn liquor on his breath from where he sat in the saddle.

"I'm a-gonna drop him in the well. That'll teach him."

"No, Papa. Please, Papa! He'll drown."

"Serve him right. Eatin' dirt. No boy o' mine . . ." He stopped, having noticed the strangers, and slung the sack away from the well and dropped it with a thud. As the farmer stepped away from the well, a boy, no more than four years old, dirty face streaked from tears, crawled out of the bag's opening and kept right on crawling, away from his father, toward a fallow field. He stopped when he saw the two strangers and sat up, quietly staring while the farmer shouted, "Who is you? What you want? This any of your affair, boy?"

Ebenezer hooked a thumb at Zeb. "My master," he said, thickening his accent. "We's bound for Vicksburg, but he taken sick. Bad fever, and his horse rolled over his leg. Needs some attention, and I just don't knows what to do."

The farmer spit. "I ain't no doctor."

"Papa," the girl said.

"Shut up, Luansy." The man wiped his mouth with the back of his hand. "Nearest town's Livingston," he said, staring at Zeb. "'Bout ten, twelve miles that way." He pointed behind the barn. "It's the county seat. Doc Truluck might . . ."

Angrily Ebenezer pointed at Zeb. "He can't make it ten more yards, so how's he goin' to make ten miles?"

"Ain't my concern."

Ebenezer gestured again. "If he could just rest here some. Maybe . . . maybe you . . ."

"Get out of here!" the man barked.

Reaching into his vest pocket, Ebenezer withdrew a few greenbacks, letting the farmer see them: $100 banknotes from the State of Alabama, with a picture of Indians in the center of each bill. "We's willing to pay."

The man stared at the money. His Adam's apple bobbed. "What if what he's got's catchin'?" he asked. "I don't want my kids to get sick."

"A horse rolled over on him." Ebenezer felt like adding— *Last I heard, that wasn't contagious.*—but he stopped himself, not wanting to infuriate this man, who obviously had a wicked temper. He realized that the farmer wanted to know if he had even more money, but Ebenezer knew better than to show him the wallet.

Their eyes remained locked until the farmer looked over at his daughter, who had pulled herself to her feet. She was walking over toward the two riders, wiping her face, trying to make herself look presentable.

"Luansy, what you doin'?" the man snapped.

"He needs help, Papa."

The man took a step toward his daughter, but stopped as if his legs refused to cooperate as his eyes went back to the $300 in Ebenezer's hand. Again he wet his lips, and after a moment's pause, he strode over, snatching the money, pointing to a rickety old barn. "Put him in the barn. Luansy, don't you spend much time frettin' over that boy. Make sure you got supper cooked. I'll be back."

His long legs carried him down the road, and Ebenezer was watching him when he heard the girl's voice. "Help me get him off that horse." That brought Ebenezer's attention back to her and Zeb. The slave slid out of the saddle and, with Luansy's help, eased Zeb to the ground.

"Is your pa going to fetch that doctor?" Ebenezer asked

"No. He's going to Cutch's still. Now help me get him to the house." She pointed.

"But your pa . . ."

"Never mind Papa. Just do as I say."

＊ ＊ ＊ ＊ ＊

Her name was Luansy Taylor. With her father and little brother, she lived on this farm that was bordered on the west by the Tombigbee River. Her mother had died giving birth to Petey. Her older brother, Russ, was fighting with Holtzclaw's Brigade, or had been last she'd heard, back in October.

She told Ebenezer this while she tended to Zeb, laying him on her cot in the corner of the one-room cabin. She put a wet rag on his forehead, then cut off his trousers with a butcher's knife. When she looked at his leg, she grimaced and gave Ebenezer a look of pure disgust.

"Looks like he got kicked."

The slave's head bobbed slightly. "Might have. Horse rolled over him." He figured it best not to go into details.

"The shoe cut him," she explained. "It's infected. Knee and ankle are likely sprained, but I don't think he broke any bones."

She had blonde hair, dirty and stringy. Calluses covered her hands, which were rough and filthy, yet somehow she managed to be gentle with Zeb.

"What's his name?"

"Zeb Hogan."

"And yours?"

"Ebenezer Chase."

"He a deserter?"

Ebenezer started to answer, but didn't know how. He wasn't so good at lying, after all. Luansy turned away from Zeb and stared at Ebenezer with the clearest, coldest blue eyes he had ever seen. He knew he couldn't lie to her, not convincingly, and swallowing he turned his head to stare at Zeb, who was sleeping.

"Is he going to die?"

"I don't know. He will if I don't fix up his leg."

"Will he keep it? His leg, his limb, I mean."

"*I* ain't hacking it off. Now you answer my question, Ebenezer Chase. Is he a deserter?"

"He escaped from a prison camp in Florence. In South Carolina. He's from Wisconsin. I can't remember what city. He's bound for Vicksburg." Zeb let out a long sigh. *Now I've done it*, he thought.

Yet Luansy Taylor chuckled. "A Yankee soldier. Don't that beat all." She straightened Zeb's leg, and he let out a little moan, winced, but didn't wake up. "And what about you?"

Ebenezer wet his lips. "I ran off from Master Hall. Bound for Dallas, Texas, to try to find my wife and daughter."

She gave him the longest stare. "You got a wife?"

Ebenezer nodded.

"And a child?"

"About fifteen months old now, I guess. Her name's Tempie."

"How old are you, Ebenezer Chase?"

"Sixteen." He stiffened. "Don't say a word about me being too young to be a daddy."

She laughed again, musically. "Bosh," she said, gesturing with her hand before looking down at Zeb. "I got cousins younger than me, and I'm your age, and they got young 'uns older than your Tempie. Besides, I'd say you act a whole lot more growed up than many moms and dads I know." She frowned, whispering tightly, "Includin' my daddy."

Ebenezer looked down and realized he was rubbing the button ring on his finger.

"How old's your wife?" asked Luansy.

"She was eighteen, we reckon, when we jumped the broom and got married. But we love each other." Suddenly he laughed. It felt good to talk about Lizzie, about Tempie, even with a stranger, a white girl at that. Strange, but Ebenezer trusted this poor farm girl, and he wanted to talk. "Master Hall, he figured that slaves weren't apt to run off if they were married. Lizzie and I just fell in love, and Uncle Cain, he spoke up for me, asked Master Hall to let us marry. Master Hall, he said that would be fine. Didn't have a preacher, so Uncle Cain married us, and Missus Hall, she came to watch. Made her smile. Afterward, Uncle Cain laid down the broom on the floor, and Lizzie and me jumped backward over it. We didn't touch the broom. That was supposed to mean good luck. But . . ." He didn't want to think about the selling of Lizzie and their baby to Master Hall's brother. He tried to think of pleasant memories, and one came to him.

"When Lizzie gave birth to Tempie, and Master Hall was away, Missus Hall had her house servants bring Lizzie to the big house. I was nervous, let me tell you . . . just paced up and down outside. They wouldn't let me in the house. I felt about to pull my arms out of their sockets, hearing Lizzie shouting so. Birthing must be the hardest thing anybody can go through, I'll tell you that. And then I don't hear my wife screaming any more, and I'm worried sick, fearing she died, but the door swings open a few minutes later, and there's Missus Hall, and she's beaming. She tells me . . . 'Congratulations, Ebenezer, you have a strong, and quite vocal, little daughter.'"

He stopped, praying that Miss Luansy wouldn't ask anything else, because emotions had overcome him. He just stood by the cot, tears rolling down his face, as he tried to recall all those good times he had enjoyed with his wife and daughter.

* * * * *

For nigh a week, they stayed at the ramshackle Taylor farm. Ebenezer kept expecting Mr. Taylor to come back, maybe bring a bunch of men with him, but Luansy laughed at his fears, assuring him that her father wouldn't return in a 'coon's age, not with $300 to spend at Cutch's still.

"Your pa'd spend that much money?" Ebenezer shook his head in disbelief. "On John Barleycorn?"

Luansy waved her hand. "Oh, it ain't that much money, not in these hard times. Three hundred dollars'll buy a barrel of flour over at Johnston's Trading Post. Bushel of cornmeal . . . which often don't look fit to eat . . . costs twenty bucks. A pound of coffee, fifty. That's the price of things. But with Cutch, that three hundred dollars'll look like pure gold to him. Give him a reason to drink, and give him somebody to drink with. Nope, I daresay Pa'll be gone a spell."

She had lanced the cut the horseshoe had made on Zeb's thigh, drained it, put a poultice on it, and the swelling had gone down. She fed him a broth, mostly water, while the rest ate bacon and cornmeal boiled into something far from tasty. Cush, Petey called it.

Resting did Zeb a world of good, and Ebenezer too. Ebenezer hadn't realized how tired he was. Walking every day, seven days a week, hiding—at least trying to—from soldiers wearing both blue and gray. It wasn't just the physical strain of walking twenty miles a day, but how it all played on the mind, the nerves. Since Ebenezer wasn't confined to a cot, like Zeb, he found himself doing chores—chopping wood, milking the goat because either Yankees or deserters had stolen the Taylor cow, watering and graining the horses and the Taylors' mule. Petey stayed right by Ebenezer's side, talking about nothing, pretending to be helping, when in fact he was mostly in the way. Ebenezer didn't mind. He liked the boy. Maybe he took his mind off Tempie.

While they worked the farm, Luansy remained at Zeb's side, day and night, irritating him immensely because he didn't take to being an invalid, didn't like anybody, especially a pretty girl, tending to his needs. It was Ebenezer who had decided that, underneath all that dirt and grime, Luansy Taylor was real pretty.

By the fifth day, Zeb was on his feet again, just piddling around, getting his strength back. Luansy had given him some clothes that had belonged to her older brother. The pant legs were way too long, but Zeb rolled them up and pulled on a worn pair of brogans that belonged to Mr. Taylor. Ebenezer cringed, imagining what Luansy's father would do if he came home to find Zeb sleeping in the house, and wearing his shoes.

Zeb didn't care a whit. All he wanted to do was get back in the saddle, make his way to Vicksburg, find Sergeant Ben DeVere, and kill him.

By the end of the sixth day, Zeb announced that they would be riding out at first light. Luansy didn't try to argue him out of it. She merely said, "That's for the best, I suppose. Papa's likely out of money, or near abouts, and he'll be comin' home soon."

"I don't want them to go, Lu." Petey started crying, and Luansy picked him up and took him to the kitchen, where she made supper.

There wasn't much conversation that evening, or the next morning. Zeb just thanked them both. Ebenezer led the horses out of the barn, helped boost Zeb into the saddle, said his farewell, and thanked them again. The two headed down the trail to the main road. By the time they reached the pike, they heard hoof beats, and turned to see Luansy riding the mule, with Petey clutching her from behind.

"By the Eternal, what do you think you're doing?" Zeb snapped.

Before she answered, he saw the smoke.

Chapter Thirteen

"We're coming with you," Luansy Taylor said. "Oh, no, you ain't!" Zeb barked right back. He let out a weary sigh, staring beyond the girl and her brother, watching smoke pour out of the barn and house. His head started spinning, and he thought he might reel out of the saddle.

Ebenezer shouted, "What did y'all do?"

"I set everything afire," Luansy said matter-of-factly. "Now we best ride before the McCutcheons or the Becketts come to investigate."

Zeb refused to budge.

"You listen to me, Zeb Hogan," she said. "The Mississippi River's blocked, so the Confederate Army has been using the Tombigbee to send supplies and troops down to Mobile. Bedford Forrest is around these parts, and I don't think you want to run into him, being a fugitive Yankee soldier and all."

Turning savagely, Zeb glared at that big-mouthed Ebenezer Chase.

Ebenezer returned the look meekly before dropping his head down in shame.

"I know this country," the girl continued. "I can get you across that river. I can get you to Meridian, just over the border in Mississippi. You're bound for Vicksburg, and that sounds like a good spot for Petey and me."

"What about your pa?" Zeb asked.

"What about him?" Never had he heard such venom in a female's voice. "If the devil had a brother, it'd be our daddy. I

111

want to get Petey as far away from him as I can, before he kills him . . . or the both of us. Now, you want to sit here and argue, or do you want to ride?"

* * * * *

After watching a dozen hard-riding Confederates thunder past, galloping too hard even to notice the riders hidden in the trees, Zeb, Ebenezer, and the Taylors forded the Tombigbee. The river was swollen, but they swam their horses across it easily and trotted a few miles before slowing to a walk.

Later they rode through Livingston, a little burg of mostly frame buildings and a few old cabins, stopping to water their mounts at an artesian well in the center of town that Luansy said they called the Bored Well. Ebenezer filled their canteens, and they moved on. Nobody paid them any mind.

On the road to York, they saw two boys fishing underneath a covered bridge that crossed the Sucarnoochee River. Petey squealed with delight over the sounds the horses and mule made when they went through that bridge. Zeb found himself smiling. Little Petey acted like they were just going for a ride, and that took Zeb's mind off the war going on all around them. Later, they skirted around York, and by dusk, Luansy told them that they had to be in Mississippi. By then Petey was worn out, so they pulled off into the woods, and made camp for the night.

When Luansy pulled salt pork and scones from her cantle bag, Ebenezer clapped his hands in delight. "Aren't you glad you brought her along now, Zeb?" he asked.

They all think they're on some joyous ride! Zeb spit. "I didn't bring her," he said stiffly. He ate two scones and a hunk of salt pork, however, and enjoyed it.

Yet any fondness he was feeling for Luansy Taylor died after supper when she approached him, and said, her voice plain bossy and full of gumption, "Take off your pants."

"I ain't doing no such thing."

"I want to look at that leg."

"You ain't seeing my . . . You just get gone, Luansy Taylor."

Shaking her head, she let out a laugh. "If it hadn't been for me, you wouldn't have that leg, Zeb Hogan. It was about to mortify, would have had to come off . . . though I don't know how we'd have managed that task. More than likely, we'd just have had let you rot and die. Now, I've seen your leg plenty of times when you were delirious."

"I ain't delirious now."

"Come on, Zeb. I practically raised Petey, changed his diapers after Mama was called to glory, given him baths more times that I can count. I got another brother, and a worthless daddy. No need to be bashful."

With that, her bony fingers latched onto the waistband and started yanking down his pants that slipped off easily, being too big in the waist. He tried to fight her off, but he remained weak, especially after that long ride. He kept yelling: "Help me, Ebenezer! Help me!" But the slave just laughed, slapping his thighs. Then those pants were down.

She pulled back the bandage she'd wrapped around Zeb's leg, studied the healing wound, and at last announced: "You're mending."

"You done?" Zeb demanded.

She shrugged. "I don't know. I'm just admiring the view."

That caused Ebenezer to howl even louder, and Petey, he started laughing, too, though he didn't know why.

Zeb jerked up his pants, calling Luansy Taylor "a brazen little harlot," but she didn't seem to mind that one bit. *By the Eternal,* Zeb thought, *I don't reckon she would.*

"You're blushing, Zeb Hogan," she said as she walked away.

* * * * *

Zeb knew what they would find in Meridian. Same as they had seen in Atlanta. He dreaded it.

He hadn't taken part in that fight. When Meridian had burned, Zeb was still in Wisconsin, or maybe on his way down the Tennessee River, but some of Sherman's bummers had later told him how they'd laid waste to that town. It was a fairly new city, founded only five years earlier, where the Mobile & Ohio Railroad intersected with the Southern Railway. A corporal named Allison with the 15th Iowa, whom Zeb had befriended on the march to Atlanta, had informed him how Sherman had given the orders to wipe Meridian off the map. "And that's what we done," Allison had said. Federals spent about five days in February of '64 in the town after the battle, turning railroad tracks into Sherman's hairpins, tearing down bridges, burning locomotives and cars and buildings—both businesses and people's homes. Corporal Allison said the troops got paid in full for what they did, too: salted meat, fresh pork, fresh beef, flour, and salt. They took all that grub with them when they marched back to Vicksburg.

Riding into the remains of Meridian, Zeb thought: *From the looks of this city, I don't think many people have had much to eat since Sherman come along.*

"My word," Luansy said as they passed a burned-out shell of a home, nothing left but the white marble columns in front of what once had been a mansion. A tent was pitched in the front yard, and from inside came a baby's bawling and a mother's frantic words for the child to "hush, please, hush."

One man wearing the shell jacket of a Confederate infantry captain hobbled off a freshly built boardwalk, using his hands as crutches because his legs were gone right below the hips. He begged for money, but they rode right past him, unable to answer his pleas, unable to look him in the eye.

* * * * *

Traffic on the road became heavier with civilians, their wagons loaded down with supplies, fighting the mud, all of them heading west. Once Zeb asked a gent in dungarees how much farther it was to Vicksburg. The man just shrugged, saying, "Never been out of Newton County since they carved it out of the Choctaw lands after the Treaty of Dancin' Rabbit Creek."

Several wagons had bogged down to their axles, and Zeb could feel those travelers staring at them as they rode on, envious of their mounts. Nobody said much.

The forests here seemed practically solid, the lumber thicker and taller than anything Zeb or Ebenezer had seen since South Carolina. *Like we're traveling in a cave,* Zeb thought. *Can't hardly even see the sun.*

They came out of the woods abruptly the next morning. Trees had been cut down, splintered, about five to eight feet from the ground.

"What happened here?" Luansy asked.

"Battle," Zeb replied.

They kept riding and eventually came to a little clearing. Two cannons lay at the edge of the road, spiked, the spokes of the wheels hacked away. Beyond that, wild hogs rooted in the mounds, and Zeb's stomach turned queasy. A big razorback stood on top of a mound of dirt, snarling, daring the riders to get a closer look. Zeb shuddered, picturing Sergeant Major Engstrand's body lying in some shallow grave back in Florence, wondering if the wild hogs had unearthed his body, ripped his dead flesh. That thought made him want to ride on, find Sergeant Ben DeVere in Vicksburg.

And kill him.

"Dearest God!" Luansy tried to cover Petey's eyes, but Petey wouldn't have any of that.

Tears streamed down Luansy's face. Ebenezer slapped the mule's rump, hurried them out of that clearing, away from the battlefield, back into the woods.

Luansy was still crying. "Couldn't they have buried them properly?" she demanded, and slid from the saddle, depositing

Petey on the banks of a bar ditch, while she leaned over, gagging, coughing, spitting up.

"You . . ." Zeb stopped. He was about to tell her that she should have stayed back on their farm. He couldn't tell her that. Nor could he explain to her what she'd just seen.

"They were soldiers," she said, still crying.

"They were men," he told her, and dismounted.

"Rebs or Yanks?" Petey asked, still looking at the mounds, at the feral pigs.

"I don't reckon it much matters," Zeb said, and repeated, "They were men. They deserve better, but in war . . ." He shook his head, and squatted beside Luansy. "We need to keep riding," he said, and gently gripped her arm. "Can you keep going?"

She shook free, staring at Zeb as if he were to blame for what they'd just seen. She rose, stumbling, snatched up Petey and shoved him in the saddle, then climbed aboard the mule behind him.

That night, they didn't eat, just rode off into the woods and made a cold camp. Nobody was hungry.

* * * * *

The weather had warmed as they bypassed Jackson. By afternoon, they were sweating. When they stopped to water their horses at a creek flowing through the forest, Ebenezer shed his quilt vest, securing it behind the saddle, and fished out the map from his haversack. He studied it for a minute before looking at Zeb.

"We'll be splitting up soon, Zeb."

Zeb answered with a nod.

"You sure you want to do what you got planned?"

"It's my duty. I'm honor bound."

Ebenezer studied him, wanting to say something—argue, Zeb suspected—but he kept quiet.

"What are y'all taking about?" Luansy asked.

"I'm going to Vicksburg," Zeb told her. "Got to see a fellow. You and Petey can go along with Ebenezer. He's going to Dallas."

"Dallas." Luansy spit out the word like it left a bad taste in her mouth.

"That's where Lizzie and Tempie are," Ebenezer told her. "My wife and daughter."

"Who's waiting for you in Vicksburg?" she asked Zeb.

Zeb didn't answer, just kicked his horse into a walk.

* * * * *

The land turned hillier, and they kept passing more and more people. Families in wagons. Slaves. Men riding alone. All bound west. Trying to flee this war. Zeb had stopped looking at the faces, seeing how sad they were, how heartbroken, miserable. Some of them were sickly looking. The only person he wanted to see was Ben DeVere, and he knew his trail was coming to an end. Vicksburg was less than a day's ride away.

Ebenezer rode right alongside Zeb. Luansy and Petey trailed behind a few rods. Zeb would never make it as a cavalry trooper, but despite how stiff his legs and backside were, despite how much his back ached, he kicked his horse into a little trot. He was desperate to reach Vicksburg.

"Slow down." Ebenezer's words rang out behind Zeb. "Zeb Hogan, slow down! You hear me?"

Reluctantly Zeb reined up, shot Ebenezer a menacing look, and said, "What do you want, Ebenezer?"

The slave pointed a long arm down the road at Petey and Luansy, about two hundred yards behind, urging their mule, trying to catch up.

"I didn't ask them to come!" Zeb snapped.

Ebenezer started to say something, words he would probably live to regret, but it was then that he spotted the wagon on the side of the road, with the red lettering stenciled onto the canvas tarp.

Chapter Fourteen

Without thinking, licking his lips, Ebenezer swung from the horse and stared at the wagon. Behind him, Zeb Hogan muttered a curse and started to ride on, but something stopped him. Breathing heavily, he wheeled the horse around and headed back to Ebenezer.

"What is it?" Zeb asked.

The slave pointed at the wagon.

"I can't read," Zeb griped.

"Says Hall Farms and Plantation. Dallas County, Texas."

Another mule-drawn wagon churned up mud in the road, the driver cursing, so Zeb and Ebenezer eased their mounts out of the way. By that time, Luansy and Petey had caught up with them.

A white man crawled from underneath the wagon and, pulling himself up, said, "What you young 'uns want?"

He was broad-shouldered, wearing trousers and shirt caked with mud and grease, holding a wrench in his right hand, a porkpie hat resting beside the wheel. He had hazel eyes, a receding hairline, and a flamboyant black mustache that matched what hair remained on his head.

"What you want, I say? What you doin' here?"

"Looks like you need a hand," Ebenezer said, handing the reins to Luansy.

Grumbling, Zeb also dismounted. He wrapped the reins around a bush and nodded at the white man. For the life of him, he couldn't figure out why he had come back. He should have just ridden on, left Ebenezer and the Taylors. The name Hall, however, rang a bell, and he knew Dallas, Texas, was where Ebenezer hoped to find his wife and daughter.

"Wheel's busted," Zeb said.

Distrust showed on the white man's face. "What you want?" he asked again.

"Just helping," Zeb said.

"Why?"

"It's called Christian charity." Luansy had answered the question, and now the man looked away from Zeb and at the girl on horseback.

He stared at her longer than he should have, and Zeb didn't like the look on the man's face.

"Wheel won't fix itself," Zeb said.

The man's eyes left Luansy and locked on Zeb. "Why ain't you in the war?" the man asked.

Zeb laughed. "Mister, I ain't but fifteen years old. Not a full-growed man . . . like you."

The man lifted his wrench. "Watch how you speak to me, boy."

"No offense meant," Zeb said, smiling, lying again, because he certainly had meant to offend this ornery cuss.

"We just wanting to help, sir," Ebenezer said, thickening his accent.

The man stared at him for a moment. He jutted his jaw at the slave. "He yourn?" he asked Zeb.

"My manservant," Zeb answered. Another wagon lumbered by. Zeb gestured at Luansy and her brother. "This is my sister, Luansy, and my brother, Petey." *By the Eternal*, Zeb realized, *they look nothing like me.* "Half-sister, half-brother, I mean."

They waited. The man didn't move, just watched them.

"You can't fix that wheel by yourself," Zeb said.

"Can't pay you nothin'," the man said.

"We're not asking for anything," Zeb said. "You've had some trouble."

"Little bit." The man lowered his wrench.

Zeb held out his right hand. "Name's Zeb Hogan."

"Charley Prescott. Bound for Dallas, Texas." Reluctantly he moved the wrench to his left hand, and shook Zeb's hand.

"Let's get to it," Zeb said.

"Can't your darky fix it?" Charley Prescott asked.

Zeb stopped. His fingers balled into fists. For a second, he considered taking a swing at Charley Prescott's nose. It would not have been the first time that nose had been punched, but a half-dozen Confederate cavalry troopers trotted past, and Zeb smiled at Charley Prescott. "He can't do by himself."

Ebenezer stepped forward. "We's all gonna have to do some work, Mister Prescott."

* * * * *

Fate, providence, divine intervention, God's plan, just plain luck. Whatever one called it, Ebenezer didn't know how to explain it. They had been riding along, probably would have ridden right past Charley Prescott's wagon. *It was as though God stopped us, right there. He directed my eyes to that wagon tarp. He . . .* Ebenezer shook his head.

"I work for Major Clyde Hall," Charley Prescott told them that evening, after the spare wheel had replaced the busted one. "He lives in Dallas most times, but he also got himself a cotton plantation on the Pearl River in Hancock County, way down south on the Louisiana border. That's where I'm comin' from."

Charley Prescott had found his voice, and had loosened it considerably with the liquor he was drinking from a jug.

"Yanks control the Mississippi River these days." Prescott burped. "Rebs tried to recapture Natchez back . . . oh, I reckon it was early winter in '63 . . . but couldn't do it. Anyway, the major sent me back to fetch some of his valuables from his Pearl River Plantation." He had another long pull, swallowed, and wiped his mouth. "Sent me alone. Didn't mind that so much, 'cause

I got me a woman in Hancock County. That's where I used to spend all my time . . . workin' on the Pearl River Plantation . . . till Yankees took over most of Mississippi." Another drink. "But I tell you, it ain't no easy trip, taking a wagon from Dallas to Hancock County, and back again."

"I reckon not," Ebenezer said. "What with Yankees all over the place."

Prescott snorted, tried to push himself up, but his legs wouldn't cooperate. "Yanks ain't half of it. You's got to keep your eyes peeled for scavengers."

"What are they?" Luansy asked.

"Deserters mostly. Quit the Confederate cause. Now they's just fightin' for themselves. Road agents, they is, preyin' on wayfarers from Mississippi to Texas."

"Great!" Petey shouted, and his sister told him to hush.

"Maybe we should tag along with you then," Ebenezer said. "Could help each other out. After all, we're bound for Texas, too."

Zeb glared at Ebenezer. *He* wasn't going to Texas. *He* had an appointment with Sergeant Ben DeVere in Vicksburg, and after that . . . *After that . . . what?* Well, it didn't matter. First he had to find that traitor, and kill him. But Texas? Texas sounded a million miles away. Texas was full of wild Indians, burned-over desert, poisonous plants, killing water, vicious rattlesnakes, and savage renegades. Or so he'd heard. He felt the blood rushing to his ears, his anger at Ebenezer Chase rising, but Charley Prescott's grunt got his attention.

"That'd suit me right down to the ground."

Ebenezer had figured Prescott would agree. He was no fighter. While they had been fixing the wagon's wheel, Prescott had told Zeb how he had paid a kid about Zeb's age to fight for him after Prescott had been conscripted.

"Them scavengers . . . vermin they are . . . they ain't nothin' to trifle at, 'specially with y'all travelin' with that good-lookin' thing," Prescott advised. "Criminy, it's taken all my willpower not to try to steal a kiss already."

Zeb rose, his anger moving from Ebenezer Chase to Charley Prescott, but Luansy said out to him, "It's all right, Zeb. He don't mean nothing. He's just drunk."

He stopped, but not because of Luansy's pleading. Charley Prescott was snoring like a chugging locomotive. That drunkard could wait, so Zeb whirled on Ebenezer.

"You got a big mouth."

"I just figured it'd be safer if we travel with him. We don't need to meet up with scavengers."

"You seem to forget, Ebenezer Chase, that I ain't going to Dallas. My trail ends in Vicksburg."

"I guess that's as far as Petey and me'll go, too," Luansy said.

"No, you ain't. You ain't gonna watch me kill . . ." Zeb bit off the words. "You and your little brother'll be safer in Dallas than in Vicksburg. Trust me. You'll be that much farther from your pa, and Vicksburg ain't no place for no young 'un. City's full of sickness. Always full of sickness. My brother told me that, so did Sergeant Major . . . well, it don't matter none. Fever. Yellow fever. Folks dying all the time there. You go on to Dallas."

"What about Comanche Indians?" Petey said.

Ebenezer chuckled. "Ain't no Indians in Dallas, Petey. It's civilized." At least, that's what he hoped.

Charley Prescott had awakened, somehow managing to pull himself to a seated position. He snorted and spit, then said, "What's that you's sayin'?" He picked up his jug and shook it, only to find it empty. "Dallas? Civilized?" He chuckled. "Texicans don't like to be called that, no, sir. Ain't no Indians there. Well, no wild and savage ones, but them Texicans, they be wilder and more savage than Nathan Bedford Forrest hisself. Major Hall, he told us what the folks in Dallas done back when the war had just started, maybe a bit before. He said there was a fire. Burned up a lot of the town, and folks just natural-like said the slaves was behind it all. So they hung three of 'em. And whipped every slave in the city." He spit again. "Wish I could have been there to see that." Somehow, he managed to find his feet and, unbuttoning his trousers, staggered off into the woods.

"Won't be no civilization for colored folks till Master Abraham brings the jubilee," Ebenezer whispered.

For a couple of minutes, until Charley Prescott stumbled back, and fell onto his bedroll, they just stared at the fire, listening to the flames crackle. Even little Petey kept quiet.

* * * * *

The road became even more congested. The temperature kept rising until the air became muggy as they churned through the muddy road, Prescott whipping and cursing the span of mules, Zeb and Ebenezer riding in front, Petey and Luansy following the wagon.

When they reached the cut-off to Vicksburg, Ebenezer reined up, and pointed to the sign. "This is it. Sign says Vicksburg's that way."

Zeb stopped his horse.

Prescott halted the wagon. "What's the matter?" Charley yelled from his seat.

"You can't do this," Ebenezer whispered.

"Yes, I can," Zeb said. "You ride on with Prescott. You find your wife, your baby girl." He pointed toward Luansy and her brother. "You look after them."

"But I'm supposed to be your slave."

Zeb wheeled his horse, and walked it back to the wagon, drawing a handful of script from the saddlebag, offering them to Charley Prescott. "Mister Prescott," he said, "I have business in Vicksburg. I reckon that's enough money to cover passage across the Mississippi River."

"Don't know why you want to go to that city, boy," Prescott said.

"I'm honor bound," Zeb told him. "Need to pay a call on an old comrade. It's my duty." He looked over at Ebenezer, sitting his horse in the middle of the road, and called out: "You mind Mister Prescott, Ebenezer!"

Prescott shoved the money in his pocket, and shifted a quid of tobacco from one cheek to the other. He didn't say a word, just stared at Zeb.

"I'll catch up." Zeb thought to add, "Might be a while."

Another wagon was coming up the road, the driver yelling for them to move on or get off the road.

Prescott spit at a fly on one of the mule's rumps, grumbled—"Suit yourself"—and whipped the lines. The wagon moved on.

Luansy Taylor didn't. "Will you?" she asked.

"Huh?" Zeb twisted in the saddle.

"Will you catch up with us?"

"Sure." With a wink, Zeb hooked a thumb at Ebenezer. "Me and Ebenezer's traveled so much together, I don't know how I could get along without him." He smiled, but it was a sad smile. The driver of the wagon behind them cursed again, and Zeb swallowed down something in his throat, or maybe it was his heart. He turned the horse and loped down the Vicksburg cut-off, never looking back.

For half a mile, Ebenezer rode alongside the wagon, but his heart was sagging, and his lip trembled. "Mister Prescott," he blurted out, "I gots to tell Mister Zeb something." He turned his mount, kicking it into a furious lope, and rode toward the cut-off, hearing Prescott curse him as lazy, worthless, and disobedient.

* * * * *

"What are you doing?" Zeb demanded. He had reined in his mare, and he was sounding meaner than a cottonmouth just out of hibernation.

"Figured you might need some help," Ebenezer said.

"I don't. Get on back with them others."

Bells started ringing all through town.

"How you going to find that woman that Sergeant DeVere was courting? You can't read any street signs. You need me."

"You need your wife and daughter, Ebenezer."

Gunshots popped, keeping time with the bells. Both boys looked down the road, curious. Bells pealed. More now. More shots, too.

"Must be a fire," Ebenezer offered.

"That don't explain the musket fire," Zeb said.

"Zeb," Ebenezer said, "you don't have to kill that man."

Zeb took a deep breath. "Yeah, I do, Ebenezer. Go on back to your family." He kicked his horse into a walk. Ebenezer caught up with him, but Zeb wouldn't even look at the runaway slave. They rode down the road, which soon became a street of busted-up red bricks. Their horses had to pick their way around vicious holes.

As they rode into the city, the ringing bells grew louder. In front of a brick church, a preacher and a woman sat on the door-steps, crying. Inside, blue-coated soldiers kept pulling the bell rope, cheering. Another soldier, a white-mustached officer, staggered down the street, a bottle in his left hand, a revolver in his right. He would stop, take a pull from the bottle, point the pistol in the air, jerk the trigger, and let out a loud hurrah. Other soldiers came trotting down the street.

Zeb and Ebenezer reined their horses to a stop.

"Mister Quirk!" the man leading the trotting soldiers, a thin man in a bummer cap, called out. "What is the meaning of this?"

The white-mustached man drained the bottle, threw it against the church's brick wall, pointed the pistol, cocked it, pulled the trigger, but only the percussion cap fired. The man dropped the revolver to his side, and slurred: "Celebrating, Colonel."

"You can celebrate in the guardhouse, Mister Quirk." Two wiry men with the colonel suddenly yanked Quirk by the arms, and dragged him down the road, while the colonel, who didn't look much older than Zeb or Ebenezer, went to the church. He swept off his hat, apologized to the preacher and the woman, and yelled and yelled until the bells stopped pealing. Finally three soldiers came shuffling out onto the church landing.

"General Lee may have surrendered in Virginia, gentlemen," the colonel said, "but until we receive word that General Taylor has turned in his saber, the war in Mississippi continues. To your posts, soldiers, or to the guardhouse to share a cell with Lieutenant Quirk. Now!" He apologized again to the elderly couple, and marched off behind the three reluctant troopers.

"Colonel . . ." Zeb said, his voice breaking, as the soldiers marched past.

The officer stopped, and stared at Zeb.

"What's all this about General Lee, sir?"

The colonel studied the two boys a long while before answering. "General Lee surrendered the Army of Northern Virginia to General Grant at some courthouse in Virginia last week." He started off, but Zeb called at him again. The colonel turned, again staring sharply.

"I'm looking for a soldier named Ben DeVere."

"What business do you have with him?"

"Personal. Do you know him?"

"No. What unit?"

"16th Wisconsin."

The colonel shook his head. "They haven't been in Vicksburg for months. They got to fight . . . unlike me." Bitterness laced his words.

"How about an Elizabeth Gentry? Comes from a fine family somewhere in this cesspool of a city."

"The name is not familiar to me. Good day," he said, and walked off.

Chapter Fifteen

His entire body trembled in the saddle. Zeb knew Ebenezer was saying something, but he couldn't, or wouldn't, hear him. Instead, Zeb jerked his head savagely toward that old couple sobbing and clutching themselves on the church's steps, and barked out some command. He had to shout twice before the old woman looked up.

"The Gentry family!" Zeb repeated. "Know where they live? Elizabeth Gentry. Her and her folks."

The woman stared as if struck dumb.

"Elizabeth Gentry. She'd be . . . I don't know . . . nineteen years old or thereabouts. You heard of her?"

Her head slowly shook.

"Heard of any Gentrys?"

"No," the old man croaked. "Leave us be. Our nation has been torn asunder."

Zeb swore.

The old woman spoke like she was living a nightmare. "Our two sons died for naught."

Yanking the reins, the mare fighting the bit, Zeb managed to turn his horse, and headed down the road.

Ebenezer called his name, and pulled up beside him. "Zeb, what the Sam Hill are you doing?" he asked.

"Hunting Ben DeVere."

"But Zeb." Ebenezer's voice sounded bewildered. "General Lee surrendered."

"So what?"

"The war's over."

"You heard that colonel. Said until General Taylor gives up, the war's still going on in Mississippi."

Spotting a young black man, head shaved clean, carrying a bucket of milk out of a barn, Zeb kicked the mare into a trot. That got him away from Ebenezer, but not for long, because he quickly caught up, and continued his argument.

"You know better than that, Zeb Hogan," he said. "The war's over. Or will be."

"Good for you. You're free, I reckon. Now leave me be."

"But, Zeb. You don't have to go through with this. You don't have to find Ben DeVere."

"Yeah, I do." He had caught up with the young Negro with the milk bucket. "Hey! You there!" The startled man almost dropped the bucket. Zeb said, "I'm looking for the Gentry family. Girl about nineteen. Named Elizabeth. She was smitten by a sorry excuse for a Union sergeant named Ben DeVere . . . a drunkard, a traitor, a disgrace to his uniform. You know where the Gentrys live?"

"No, boss. No, sir, I ain't heard of 'em folks afore." He hurried on down the street, milk splashing over the brim of the bucket.

"Zeb!" Ebenezer again.

Starting to sound like my conscience, Zeb thought to himself, but slowed, tugging on the reins. "What?" He felt as though he would begin sobbing at any second. He had come this close, this far. All he had to do was find Ben DeVere, and kill him. That louse had to be somewhere in this city.

"Zeb," Ebenezer said. "The war's over. All but over. You don't have to kill . . ."

"I done told you, I *do*. Sergeant Major Engstrand ordered me. We drawed lots."

"But the war's over. They'll hang you if . . ."

"Go on, Ebenezer!" Tears streamed down Zeb's face. "The war's over, you say. Don't that mean nothing to you? You're free. Your wife and baby's free. Go on to Texas. Go on. Leave me be . . ."

He didn't hear Ebenezer's words, but later, much later, Zeb Hogan would recall what the slave had said, and he would picture Ebenezer's face clearly, the sadness in his eyes, would hear that voice so haunting, the words Ebenezer told him before turning his horse and loping off, leaving Zeb to his vengeance.

I'm sorry for you, Zeb Hogan. I'll pray for you.

No longer could Zeb see, he was crying so hard. He gripped the horn, leaned forward. He neither saw nor heard Ebenezer ride off, but when Zeb finally managed to regain his composure, he was sitting in the saddle, alone on a rough street, surrounded by the ruins of what once had been a prosperous city.

* * * * *

Four hours passed before Zeb located the Gentry home. Two carpenters had given him directions to Grove Street, and he found the place as church bells rang out and gunshots echoed across the city. That colonel, Zeb reasoned, must have given up trying to keep his troops from celebrating. Zeb should have been celebrating, too, but couldn't bring himself to feel any joy. Not until he had killed Ben DeVere. Now, getting closer to fulfilling his orders, Zeb's stomach twisted into a hundred knots as he climbed the brick steps, found the knocker, and gave it five solid raps.

The house was made of red brick, the top windows busted out, the upper story checkerboarded with missing shingles. In the sprawling front yard, only two of a dozen oak trees hadn't been chopped down, blown up, or uprooted. He had spotted smoke rising from two of ten chimneys, so somebody must be home, yet no one answered. He knocked again.

Still nothing, but Zeb heard something behind the big brick mansion, so he walked down the steps and headed toward the carriage house. A Negro man carried a bucket toward the well house. Spying each other at the same time, they both stopped. The Negro lowered the bucket, waited.

"This the Gentry home?" Zeb asked.

"Yes, sir."

"Elizabeth Gentry?"

He just stared.

"Does Elizabeth Gentry live here?" Zeb raised his voice. He felt his body trembling again.

"Miss Beth? She's . . . she's dead."

Zeb took a step back, unbelieving.

"You all right, sir?"

The Negro's voice snapped Zeb out of his trance. He must have nodded, perhaps even said something, because the Negro resumed his walk toward the well house, leaving Zeb standing like an oaf, not knowing what to do. Quickly Zeb recovered his senses and chased down the servant about the time he reached the outbuilding.

"There was a Federal soldier she had taken to . . . Sergeant Ben DeVere. You remember him?"

Now the Negro looked nervous. His head bobbed slightly, but he didn't speak.

"Is he in Vicksburg? When did this Gentry girl die? Is Ben DeVere in town? Speak up, man." Zeb realized that he had grabbed the Negro's muslin shirt, was shaking him. Releasing his grip, Zeb stepped away. The black man just picked up the bucket and hurried back toward the carriage house. Zeb started after him, but another voice stopped him, and he turned.

Standing in front of the back door to the main house stood a woman in her forties, maybe older, a white woman, her black hair pinned up, wearing a tea gown of copper taffeta trimmed in black. A black ribbon was tied around each arm. When Zeb walked toward her, she took a step back, using the screen door she held open as sort of a shield. Something about Zeb frightened her, and he stopped, tried to control his voice as he said, "Ma'am, I'm looking for Sergeant Ben DeVere."

"What do you want with him?"

Maybe Zeb detected something in her voice, because he decided this time not to lie. Instead he spoke matter-of-factly. "I mean to kill him."

She stepped back inside the house, but held the door open. "Come inside," she said.

* * * * *

"I don't know what Beth ever saw in that wretched, wretched man." Mrs. Gentry placed her china cup in the saucer and dabbed her eyes with a silk handkerchief. Her voice was rich, sweeter than molasses and just as thick, but her eyes alternated between a dark sadness and a deeper anger. "I'm glad my Windermere, my late husband, Beth's father, did not live to see her disgrace the Gentry name so." Her eyes found Zeb's. "Windermere died during the siege. Yellow fever."

"I'm sorry for your loss." He didn't really mean it. He just wanted her to say where Ben DeVere might be found.

"Why do you want to kill him, young man?"

Zeb told her, leaving nothing out, keeping his account plain and truthful, and she never once blinked while Zeb laid out everything Ben DeVere had done. How he'd betrayed both the uniform of the 16th Wisconsin and the South Carolina Reserves after the Rebs had galvanized him out of the Florence Stockade. How he'd gotten Sergeant Major Engstrand killed. How it was up to him, Zeb Hogan, to seek out retribution. Why he told her everything, he had no idea. She was a fine Southern lady, and Southern ladies didn't hold much truck with Union soldiers, and Zeb was one. Had been one, at least.

"I see," she finally said.

Zeb's head bobbed. He wet his cracked lips. He asked her, "Where might I find him, ma'am?"

She sipped her tea like they were talking about their parson's Sunday sermon.

"He came back here last November," she eventually told him. "Stole my Beth away from me. I begged her not to go, but she wouldn't hear of it. I warned her . . . God love her . . . that this beau of hers was no good." She lowered her voice to a dark whisper. "He pulled many a cork, young man, many a cork. Windermere never touched intoxicating spirits."

"Yes, ma'am. Ben DeVere was a drunk."

She coughed, polished off her tea, and held her head high. "He was bound for Franklin, a city on the Mexican border, far away in the state of Texas."

"Franklin." Zeb tested the name. "Texas."

"It might as well be China," she said, and let out a heavy sigh.

"I'd track Ben DeVere to China, ma'am, if that's what it takes."

She gave him the oddest little smile, like she was telling him—*Yes, I know you would, young man*—but the smile died on her face as she fumbled for the handkerchief again, tears running down her face.

"Beth left with him. Did not even marry him. I warned her that Almighty God would frown upon how she was acting." She fell silent for a long while, and her lips quivered as she sadly shook her head. "But I did not know our Lord's vengeance would be so . . ." Here she broke down, and cried again.

The screen door opened, and footsteps told Zeb that the Negro had come inside to check on this lady. Zeb felt the servant's presence, but didn't look at him, just kept his eyes on the woman, waiting for her to regain her composure.

"Miz Virginia?" The Negro's deep voice resonated in the spartan quarters of the old mansion.

She stiffened, recovered, and said, "I shall be fine, Charles."

"Yes'm." He left them alone. Mrs. Gentry kept staring into the other parlor till the rear door slammed shut. The lady steeled herself quickly as she returned her gaze to Zeb. "Beth died at some place called Phantom Hill, far west of Fort Worth . . . wherever that place is. Mister DeVere was kind enough to send us a letter, saying he had buried her in the cemetery at that miserable stagecoach station. I guess I should be thankful for that. Knowing, I mean . . . her fate. Otherwise . . ."

Now she bawled without control, but Zeb had what he wanted. He walked out the door, mounted his mare, and rode out of Vicksburg. He needed to catch up with Ebenezer, Luansy, Petey, and Prescott. He didn't know exactly where Franklin was, but it was in Texas. That's where Ebenezer was going. Turned out, he was bound for that state, too.

Chapter Sixteen

It did Ebenezer's heart a world of good to see Zeb come loping back to the wagon. Hearing that Zeb hadn't caught Ben DeVere, hadn't killed him, and that he'd be traveling as far as Dallas made Ebenezer feel better, too. Mostly, however, Ebenezer was glad to see Zeb Hogan for selfish reasons.

The wagon was parked off the road, letting other wagons pass, while Petey and Luansy squatted in the weeds, looking hopelessly lost. They were on a hilltop, looking down the bluffs at the Mississippi River. Wagons lined down the road to the ferry and stretched a quarter mile behind the Hall Farms & Plantation wagon.

"Where's Prescott?" Zeb asked as he swung stiffly off the mare.

"Gone." Ebenezer shook his head.

"Gone?" Zeb thundered.

"He took off when he heard that Lee had surrendered," Luansy said as she walked toward the two, carrying Petey in her arms, straining at his weight. The boy was fidgeting, wanted to get down, but Luansy didn't want him running around as he was prone to do, not with all the horses, mules, oxen, and wheels churning past them. "Took the money you gave him, Zeb. Said we could go to Dallas if we had a mind to, but he was getting back to his woman."

Petey stopped writhing long enough to say: "He said we could tell that major fellow in Texas that he could go to . . ."

Luansy squeezed her brother tighter.

Zeb choked off a curse.

137

"We're better off without him," Luansy said.

"Yeah, but he knowed where we was going," Zeb said. Suddenly he whirled back to the mare, unfastened his saddlebag, withdrew the wallet, and tossed it to Ebenezer. "How much money do we have left, Ebenezer?"

The young runaway withdrew a few bills and counted. "Sixty-two dollars and thirty-five cents." He returned the money, and handed the wallet back to Zeb. "But I'm not sure this money's good any more, Zeb. It's Confederate currency. And as much as things cost these days, it sure isn't enough to get us across that river. Look at how big it is."

The river was bigger than the St. Croix or anything Zeb had ever seen in Wisconsin. He had seen the Mississippi, but it hadn't looked this wide, this ominous, back then. A couple of ironclad gunboats sailed down the river, which was muddy and deep, maybe a mile or more across. The sailors on the decks looked like specks of lint, and the two freight wagons on the ferry, leaving the Mississippi side of the shore, looked like toys from where he stood. Zeb couldn't recall ever seeing so much water.

"I don't think we could find a log and float across this one, Zeb," Ebenezer said, trying to be funny.

Zeb didn't laugh. After staring at the river for better than a minute, he suddenly smiled, tied his mare up short behind the wagon, then hurriedly climbed into the driver's box. "I bet there's something we can trade for passage in the back of this wagon."

"We can't do that, Zeb," Ebenezer protested. "It's not ours."

"Spoils of war," Zeb said. "You want to argue, or you want to find your family?"

* * * * *

All that day, all that night, all the next morning and afternoon, the ferry moved back and forth across the river. It was late the next afternoon before they finally reached the ferry. By then, they knew they wouldn't need anything to barter. The ferrymen were letting everybody cross for free. "Fine Christian folks," someone said as word came from the river that, with the war all but over, the ferry operators were helping people flee the Union Army, run away from their broken dreams.

Once on the ferry, Ebenezer sat down and stuck his feet in the river. Just so he could tell his family that he'd touched the big river. When Petey saw what he was doing, the boy stuck his bare feet in the river, too, and they both laughed. It felt good.

They crossed to DeSoto, Louisiana, and made it through the marshes that stretched at least a mile from the river's edge. Cotton fields lay in ruins as they traveled west. Gone were the great forests. Here much of the land was cleared, but the bogs they passed stank to high heaven.

The roads were crowded with Negroes and whites, all westbound, most of them helping each other.

Zeb, Ebenezer, and Luansy learned how to float their wagon across the rivers and bayous, strapping big pine logs on the wheels, turning that rickety old wagon into a boat. They would help the wagon in front of them cross, and the folks in the wagon behind them would help them across. Working together, no matter if they were black or white. There wasn't camaraderie. Far from it. Yet all of the travelers knew they needed to help one another, if for no other reason than to get away from the crumbling South as fast as possible.

By the third day, they found themselves traveling with a middle-aged couple, Uncle Bristineau and his wife, who were bound for Shreveport. Ebenezer and Zeb could barely understand a word the Bristineaus said, but found them to be good, hard-working, friendly white people, though their skin was burned dark. The sausages Mrs. Bristineau made were spicy and delicious.

Yet everywhere Ebenezer looked, he saw heartbreak. He had lost count of how many abandoned wagons they had passed on the road, or how many graves they had seen.

A red-headed woman in a soiled, faded calico dress ran along the bar ditch, screaming her child's name, asking everyone she passed if they had seen her little girl, Amelia. Most travelers shook their heads, and kept right on riding west, but Ebenezer, who was driving the wagon, tugged on the lines, and pulled the wagon off to the side of the road. Zeb turned his horse around, and loped back.

"What the devil you doing?" he snapped.

"I aim to help this lady find her lost daughter." Ebenezer set the brake.

"We got no time for such foolishness. Get that wagon back on the road. Hurry, or else we'll lose our place in line."

"Sergeant Ben DeVere can wait, Zeb."

Zeb tensed, but Luansy said, "Please, Zeb."

Ebenezer nodded at the woman, who was already running down the road toward the next wagon, her voice cracking with emotion.

"You can go on, Zeb," Ebenezer said. "You can go to the devil. Or you can help me."

"Please," Luansy said again.

"All right." Zeb turned the mare around, jumped over the ditch, and picked his way through the woods, hunting for the girl, Amelia. Ahead of them, Uncle Bristineau set the brake to his wagon, told his wife he'd be back as soon as he could, and he leaped down, calling out Amelia's name.

They found her on the banks of Bayou Laforche, sitting in mud and rotten leaves. She was throwing twigs into the river, singing a tune. Her mother ran to her, swooped her into her arms, and she couldn't stop kissing her cheeks and thanking Zeb for all his help, though it had been Uncle Bristineau who had found her.

"That girl was lucky," Zeb told Ebenezer as they headed back toward the wagons.

* * * * *

The next morning, they rode past a thick-shouldered white man whipping a slave tied across the rear wheel of a wagon.

"You'll be free," the man yelled, "when you're dead and gone, Joshua! I'm your master. I'll always be your master."

People just rode right on by, not stopping to help. There was nothing they could do. Ebenezer rode on, too, not saying a word, but every time the whip slashed that slave's back, he jerked, angry, ashamed, tormented.

* * * * *

They floated across so much water—the Tensas, Macon, Beouf, Laforche—Luansy joked they would likely have gills before they reached Texas and thick forests returned. A week later, they paid $35 to cross a bridge over the blue Quachita River, and went through the town of Monroe. A new courthouse was being built. Uncle Bristineau explained that the old one had been blown apart by a Federal gunboat a couple of years back. A number of rough-looking men idling outside the courthouse stared at Luansy and Ebenezer as they rode past. Ebenezer wondered if they stared that hard at Uncle Bristineau and his wife when they passed in their wagon.

They traveled six more miles before pulling off the road and making camp that evening. Mrs. Bristineau cooked red beans, rice, and sausage, while Luansy made coffee and cornbread. They went to sleep full and contented.

* * * * *

A savage kick to the ribs woke Ebenezer. He tried to roll out of his blankets, but a boot slammed into his back. For a moment, he thought he was stuck in some nightmare. But then rough hands jerked off the blanket, and a belt lashed across his back and buttocks. Laughter followed.

His hands clawed through the dead leaves and mud as he tried to get away, push himself up, but something cracked against his skull, and his face was planted against the leaves. He tasted blood. A woman screamed. A shotgun roared. Little Petey cried. Ebenezer lunged, rolled, heard a voice drawl, "He's a fast little coot, ain't he?"

Crawling for the wagon, for a weapon, for anything, he felt another boot catch him in the stomach, and he cartwheeled in the air, landing on the stack of logs he and Petey had gathered for the fire. He smelled the wood smoke, but saw nothing except a blaze of orange.

Another scream. Zeb's! These roughnecks were beating Zeb, too. "Leave them be!" Luansy's voice.

Nobody listened to her. Something sharp, like a belt buckle, struck Ebenezer's head. Boots began kicking his legs, his side, his head, and he drifted off into a bottomless pit, thinking that he had been Master Hall's slave all his life, and that Zeb Hogan had been wrong when he told him he was free now that General Lee had surrendered. *I must be Abraham Lincoln's slave, now*, he thought to himself.

Chapter Seventeen

That cracker trash had left behind a shovel. Maybe it had been their idea of a joke.

When Zeb came to, he staggered over to the smoldering ruins of the two wagons. He was sore, cut and bruised all over, but he didn't think any bones had been busted.

Petey clung to Luansy, both of their faces chalky, as the young girl knelt over Ebenezer. She looked up, brushed one hand across her bruised forehead.

Zeb trembled with rage. "How is he?" he managed to croak.

"I don't know. He's alive."

Zeb looked at Petey, normally cheerful, rambunctious, but now petrified. The boy wouldn't even look up at Zeb, just stared at Ebenezer, lying on his back, his face a bloody mess, his body battered. He seemed barely alive.

"Where's Uncle Bristineau?"

Luansy dropped her head, and numbly Zeb turned around, and walked to the edge of camp, where he found the old Cajun slumped over against a sycamore tree, his head smashed so horribly that Zeb could see his brains. On the other side of camp, Zeb found Mrs. Bristineau, her back riddled with buckshot. Zeb couldn't stop the tears. Sobbing, he found that shovel, and started digging two graves.

He was still digging when a train of wagons stopped. It was midmorning by then, and at least a dozen wagons had passed them, the passengers looking straight ahead down the pike, not daring to glance at Zeb, or the others, not even the smoldering remains of the wagons. Nobody had stopped to help, not that Zeb could blame them. How many folks in trouble had they passed along the road? And they had done the same, except that one time. He tried to recall that little girl's name they had found on the riverbank, but her name escaped him. Zeb hadn't wanted to stop to help the mother find her lost child. That had been Ebenezer's doing, and now Ebenezer was lying on the ground, the tar beaten out of him. Could be he was dying.

He looked at the grave he was digging, then leaned against the shovel, crying without control, when a steady hand gripped his shoulder.

A man's deep voice said, "That's all right, son. You go ahead and cry. There's no shame in that. I'll take the shovel."

Zeb wanted to protest, but couldn't. He felt himself being steered to a rotten stump. He sat down, watched this stranger hand the shovel to a big brown-skinned man with a black walrus mustache, and then walk over to Luansy, Petey, and Ebenezer. With picks and shovels, other men came from their wagons, and Zeb forced himself up, dammed the tears, and walked over to help these strangers bury the Bristineaus.

* * * * *

"Glory to God, he ain't dead."

"No. Not yet anyhow. He's comin' to."

The voices sounded like they were in a tunnel. Ebenezer blinked at the two faces, out of focus, and then smelled the smoke from a pipe. Something cool was placed on his forehead, over his nose, and slowly the faces cleared. Luansy grinned, but Ebenezer found no joy in her face. Squatting next to her was a man in a butternut coat, black hat, and a wicked scar that stretched from just underneath one of his brilliant green eyes, through his dark brown beard stubble, flecked with gray, all the way down to the cleft in his chin. The stranger brought a pipe to his mouth.

Someone squeezed Ebenezer's left hand, and he gently turned to see little Petey, who also managed a grin. Ebenezer tried to return the smile, but he never knew one to hurt so badly.

"What happened?" he finally managed to ask.

"You got bushwhacked," the man said.

Ebenezer tried to rise to his feet, but didn't make it far. It felt like somebody had dropped an anvil on his chest and pricked his side with a thousand pear spines. He sank back down with an *oomph*, and closed his eyes to fight off the pain.

"Easy, boy," the man said. "You got six busted ribs . . . a broken nose. You took a beatin' it'd take most fellows a month of Sundays to get over. It's a testament that you aren't dead."

"Where's . . . Zeb?"

He waited to hear that Zeb was dead, but no word came. When Ebenezer's eyes opened, the man with the scar jerked a thumb over to his right. "He's . . ." The man frowned, spit, swallowed.

"He's helping them bury the Bristineaus," Luansy said.

The words stunned Ebenezer more than if she had told him that Zeb was dead. Ebenezer couldn't believe it. Uncle Bristineau was a kindly man, and his wife . . . It just didn't make sense. It wasn't fair. Ebenezer started shaking, sobbing, trying to wake up from this terrible dream.

"Ebenezer."

Through the tears, he saw Luansy's ashen face.

"Zeb's all right," she said. "They jumped us last night. Uncle Bristineau was supposed to be on guard duty, but I guess he fell asleep. They beat up Zeb, but not as bad as they done you. Burned both wagons, after stealing what they could ride off with." She paused, shutting her eyes tightly, shaking her head, trembling, her words now soft. "Stoved in Uncle Bristineau's head. They shot Missus Bristineau when she tried to run away. No call to kill either of them . . . not that way. It was pure cussedness. Took our guns . . . what little money we had left."

"What about you?" Ebenezer asked, though he wasn't sure he wanted to hear the answer.

"I'm all right."

He let out a sigh of relief.

"They didn't bother me. Other than this." She raised her left hand, revealing a cut that had been stitched with horsehair. No matter how many stitches, that wound would leave a terrible scar.

"Who did this?" Ebenezer asked.

"Scavengers," the white man said.

"Southern deserters?" Ebenezer remembered the looks some of those men back in Monroe by the courthouse had given them. He had half a mind to ride back to town and leave it in ashes. Only he couldn't stand up, let alone ride anywhere.

The man shrugged. "Maybe. Could be Yankee deserters. Blue or gray, they ain't nothin' but trash."

Ebenezer looked at the man again. "Who are you?"

The man puffed on his pipe, removed it, and smiled. "Captain Livingston Taneyhill," he said.

* * * * *

"The war ended for me at Corinth," Captain Livingston Taneyhill said. "Oh, what butchery that was."

Zeb shot out, "My brother was in that one, too."

"Yeah?" Captain Taneyhill pushed back his hat. "What outfit?"

For once, Zeb couldn't think up a lie. He recalled James's brief account of the fight, remembered Sergeant Major Engstrand telling stories about the 16th Wisconsin and all the glory they had reaped in what he called some of the most savage fighting he had ever seen.

Zeb swallowed. "Uh . . . the South Carolina Reserves."

"Really." Captain Taneyhill's tone told Zeb that he had been caught in a lie. Yet the captain merely tapped his right shoulder with his left hand. "Took a Yankee ball here," Taneyhill said.

"Still can't raise this arm past my chest. So I went back to Harris County, went back to freighting." He jerked his thumb toward his wagons. "Got a load of sugarcane bound for Jefferson."

"Where's Harris County?" Petey asked.

"South Texas. Down around Houston was where I hung my hat," Taneyhill said. "But I left Houston. Moved my operation to Jefferson."

"Where's that?" Luansy asked.

"Just over the border. Now, where were y'all bound?"

"Dallas," Ebenezer said.

"Franklin," Zeb told him.

Taneyhill reached inside his coat and withdrew his pipe and some tobacco. Ebenezer watched, fascinated, as he managed to tamp tobacco into the pipe's bowl, using only his left hand. He put the pipe in his mouth, fished a lucifer from a pocket, and struck the match against his leggings, then brought the flame to the bowl, drawing on the pipe stem until he was satisfied.

All with one arm, Ebenezer marveled.

"And you?" Captain Taneyhill stared at Luansy Taylor.

"Somewhere," she said softly.

What Zeb found peculiar was that Captain Taneyhill never asked where they came from, what they were doing traveling in such country, what the Bristineaus had been to them.

By the Eternal, Zeb realized, *he ain't even asked us our names.*

Luansy said, "You know that General Lee surrendered?"

Taneyhill's nod was short. "I heard."

At that moment, the black-mustached man walked over to the fire. He wore the fanciest little jacket Zeb had ever seen, black silk, but decorated with red velvet trim and silver buttons. Buttons even went up the side of his pants, which were stuck in leather moccasins, and he wore about the biggest hat likely in the state of Louisiana, with a brace of Navy Colts strapped to his waist.

"*¿Señor Capitán?*" he said.

"*Sí.*"

For a couple of minutes they kept right on talking. It was a pretty language, Zeb thought, though he had no idea what they were saying. Finally the big brown-skinned man bowed slightly, said something else, and turned toward the young travelers.

"This is Amado Chavez y Castaño, my *segundo*," Captain Taneyhill said.

Removing that giant hat from his head, the big man gave a gracious bow, said something else in Spanish, and smiled.

Taneyhill said, "I told Amado that we'll move down the road a couple of miles, get y'all away from this place, and make an early camp." Captain Taneyhill spoke again to Amado, and the man donned his hat, turned on his heels, and headed back to the wagons.

"He's a Mexican, ain't he?" Petey blurted out.

"That he is," Captain Taneyhill said, tapping the pipe on a rock. "Though he claims Spanish blood. Amado has made room in one of the wagons for y'all." His head tilted at Luansy and Petey. "Got room in another wagon for you." This time, he nodded at Ebenezer.

"I can . . ." Ebenezer tried to sit up, but collapsed, and the captain grinned.

"When you've mended some," Taneyhill said, "I might have a job for you. Might be able to get you to Dallas. Pay's five dollars a week and found, but I pay in gold, not Texas script." His green eyes landed on Zeb. "And I might be able to get you to Franklin, though that's a bit off my range, if you don't mind workin' up a sweat."

"I don't," Zeb said.

"Pay's the same. Five dollars in gold a week. You got a problem with that?"

Zeb shook his head.

"Some folks do. Some men I've hired don't find it right that I pay a Mexican or a colored man the same as I pay a white man. Those folks don't work for me very long. The way I see it, I'm payin' good wages for hard work, and I don't care what color the man's skin is. You'll find Mexicans, white men, and a colored man, even a Choctaw Indian, as my muleskinners."

"As long as I get to Franklin, I don't mind at all," Zeb assured him.

Captain Taneyhill smoked his pipe for a moment. "Before you sign on with me, you best get one thing clear," he said after he had removed the pipe. "What happened here ain't nothin'. If we run into trouble in Texas, and we lose, we'll all be deader than that man and woman we just buried."

Amado Chavez y Castaño strode back into camp. This time, he held a rifle in his hands.

"Let's see if you can shoot." Captain Taneyhill pushed himself to his feet, took the rifle, and tossed it to Zeb.

The rifle was a Sharps carbine, .52-caliber, a breechloader that Captain Taneyhill said could be fired six times in a minute. "I've heard some folks claim they could shoot it nine or ten times in a minute, but that sounds more like Texas brag than fact. All I want you to do is put a bullet as close as you can to that piece of paper Amado stuck on that sycamore tree yonder."

"Is it loaded?" Zeb asked.

"My weapons are always loaded," the captain said.

The Sharps felt heavy for a carbine, and the hammer was difficult to pull back to full cock, but Zeb took a deep breath as he found the target, perhaps fifty yards away, and slowly let out the breath. When he squeezed the trigger, that carbine sounded like a mortar round going off in his ear, and it kicked so hard, Zeb figured his shoulder would be bruised come morning. He saw nothing except thick white smoke. Almost immediately, Amado said, "*¡Demonios!*"

Zeb knew he hadn't come close to that paper. He had drilled it plumb center. Butting the stock of the carbine against the ground, he looked up at Captain Taneyhill.

"Where'd you learn to shoot like that?" The captain took the Sharps, handed it to Amado, and told him to reload it.

"Sergeant Major Engstrand said it was a gift," Zeb answered, wanting to rub his shoulder, but not daring to, not in front of Captain Taneyhill. "Said I was a natural."

* * * * *

That was likely the only reason Zeb got away with replacing James in the 16th Wisconsin. When he had showed up at Camp Randall in Madison, a lieutenant, who looked no older than James had been, stared at the paper Zeb had given him—the one Zeb had taken out of James's pocket—and shook his head.

"You are not James Hogan," he said.

Zeb cursed his own bad luck. *First soldier boy I run into happens to have known James.* "I'm his brother," he said. "James taken sick, and died."

"Died?" the officer asked coldly. "Or deserted?" He raised his voice. "Did he send you in his place, boy? Has he turned yellow?"

Zeb whipped up his right hand, would have slapped that miserable excuse of a Union officer then and there, would have ended any chance he had of escaping Madison, when a rough hand grabbed his wrist and jerked him back.

"Easy there, lad," the deep voice said behind him. To the officer, who was taken aback that he had almost been slapped by a kid, the voice said, "Lieutenant, sir, I had the privilege of serving with Private Hogan, and he was no coward, sir. If this boy says the Almighty has called James away, you can bank on it, sir."

"Well, we can't replace Private Hogan with him." The lieutenant pointed a shaky finger at Zeb. "He doesn't look twelve years old."

"I'm . . ." Zeb stopped, felt two massive hands squeezing his shoulders.

"Lieutenant Thorstad," the voice said, "let's see if the lad can shoot before we kick him out of this man's army."

By April, Zeb was wearing a blue uniform, a bit too big, and had won three shooting contests, placed second twice, third once. Sergeant Major Engstrand called him the pride of the 16th Wisconsin, so when the soldiers boarded a train for Prairie du Chien, Zeb was with them. Zeb was with them on the steamers they took down the Mississippi and Tennessee Rivers, and finally he was marching, rifle slung over his shoulder, three hundred and seventy-five miles to Ackworth, Georgia, to get into the war.

Chapter Eighteen

By the time they reached Texas, Ebenezer Chase could walk, sometimes, without wincing. Captain Taneyhill's muleskinners knew that Ebenezer couldn't shoot as well as Zeb Hogan. In fact, he couldn't shoot at all. They learned this when Captain Taneyhill had Ebenezer fire a musket at a paper target Amado Chavez y Castaño had put on a tree at the edge of the woods. When Ebenezer pulled the trigger, the kick of that old musket almost knocked him on his hindquarters.

"Criminy," Taneyhill said, "he missed the entire forest."

Amado sniggered. Standing there, Ebenezer felt ashamed, holding the musket in his arms, feeling his ribs, head, and shoulder throbbing.

"You can't shoot." The captain took the musket, and tossed it to Amado.

Ebenezer could have told him that. The only weapon he had ever fired had been back in Alabama the night the horse rolled over on Zeb, and he didn't believe he had even come close to hitting anyone—thank the Lord.

"What can you do?" the captain asked. The other muleskinners chuckled. Even Taneyhill seemed bemused.

While Ebenezer tried to think of an answer, Zeb Hogan replied, "He can read and write." He spoke defiantly, as if defending the runaway slave, and Ebenezer looked across the campsite at Zeb, standing there as if he would fight every last one of the captain's men.

So help me, Ebenezer thought, *I can't figure that white boy out. Half the time he's about to thrash me, or leave me, and other times he's like the best friend I've ever had. What else could I do? Pick cotton . . . crop tobacco . . . noodle catfish?*

Captain Taneyhill's brilliant green eyes bored through Ebenezer for the longest while before he reached inside his vest pocket, pulled out a big gold watch, and opened the cover, holding it out for Ebenezer to see. "Read the inscription," he said.

Ebenezer looked at the letters. Some of them made no sense, and he knew he couldn't pronounce them right, but he tried his best: "'To Livingston. *Ad augusta per angusta.* Your loving wife, Christina.'"

With a sad smile, Taneyhill snapped the watch's case shut and slid it back into his pocket. "That's pretty good, Ebenezer."

"What's that mean?"

"It's Latin. Supposed to mean . . . 'To high places by narrow roads' . . . or something like that. There's a place in my crew for a young man who can read and write."

"I didn't know you had a wife," Ebenezer said, thinking of Lizzie and Tempie, and suddenly, feeling tears well in his eyes, he blurted out, "I got a wife. And a baby girl. They're in Dallas."

Taneyhill just stared into the woods.

"That's why I've got to get to Dallas," Ebenezer said. "I've got to find them."

Taneyhill blinked, and seemed to shudder.

"You have any children, Captain Taneyhill?" Ebenezer didn't know why he asked that, why he was talking so much, prying into the captain's personal affairs, when the captain hadn't even asked his name—Ebenezer had volunteered that—or what he was doing traveling with two white teenagers and a four-year-old white boy. Ebenezer suspected that he was talking to keep from crying.

"I had two daughters," Captain Taneyhill answered, but without looking at Ebenezer. "Diphtheria claimed them both. And Christina."

Ebenezer's head dropped. *Should have kept my mouth shut.* "That's another reason I left Harris County." Taneyhill took a deep breath, slowly exhaled, and sighed.

"Not much need for reading and writing out here, though, Ebenezer," the captain said, forcing a smile. "But maybe we'll make a muleskinner out of you."

* * * * *

Murphy wagons, Captain Taneyhill called them. He had ridden up to Missouri to buy them. The wagons had high wooden sides. The exterior blue paint was flaked and chipped, the insides were painted red, chains and irons all black, but scarred from heavy use. With a heavy canvas cover, each wagon was about ten feet long and had a tool box in the front, a feed box for the mules in the back, grease and water buckets hanging from the rear axle.

In all, Captain Taneyhill's train comprised sixteen wagons, each loaded with five thousand pounds of sugarcane, double-hitched with a rear caboose. Ten wheels, twelve mules hitched in pairs, with a muleskinner riding what Taneyhill called the left-wheeler, the jack closest to the front left wheel of the lead wagon. The driver held a brakeline and a jerkline, and most of the mule-skinners could, and would, cuss up a storm. Ebenezer had never heard such language. He felt sorry for Petey and Luansy having to listen to the men.

When the muleskinners had to turn a wagon, it was pure disorder. Most of them would give the jerkline a yank, holler out some prime curses, and the mules would start jumping every which way. Somehow, the wagons managed to turn, and the mules would get back into line and head on down the road.

It was truly something to see, though Ebenezer never quite understood how either man, wagon, or mules managed to do those jobs.

"You'll learn," the captain said when he deposited Ebenezer with a gray-bearded Mexican named Gonzales. Ebenezer had figured Captain Taneyhill would put him with the head-shaven Negro named Jerome, but that big man kept to himself, hardly said a word except when he was screaming "gee," "haw," or "yay" at the mules in his team, punctuating those words with the foulest cusses Ebenezer had ever heard.

The Choctaw muleskinner was named Pitchlynn, but everybody called him Pitch. He was short, with a barrel chest and long salt-and-pepper hair that fell to his massive shoulders. His arms looked like oak trunks. The other Mexican muleskinner was Severo, who had a beautiful baritone voice and would sing each night in camp while one of the white muleskinners, a rangy, blond-haired man in his twenties called Riley, sawed a fiddle. Ebenezer couldn't understand any of the lyrics to the songs Severo sang, but they sure were pretty tunes.

The other muleskinners were white—Carter, Sweazy, and Pruden—men who were hard and tended to their mules and kept to themselves, though they appeared to enjoy Severo's singing and Riley's fiddling. Amado wasn't a muleskinner. As Taneyhill's *segundo*, he was the assistant wagon master who rode alongside the wagons or scouted out ahead.

That shoulder wound might have put Livingston Taneyhill out of the Confederate Army, but he ran his train like a general. They were up before dawn, washing down sourdough biscuits and fried salt pork with bitter coffee, on the trail before the sun was up, stopping between 10:00 a.m. and 2:00 p.m. to water the mules, and then driving on till nigh sundown. They covered twelve to fourteen miles a day.

Zeb and Ebenezer had made better time walking. Ebenezer figured that Zeb would want to quit the wagon train since they were traveling so slowly, but after what had happened to Uncle Bristineau and his wife, Zeb might have feared traveling alone. There was power in numbers, and although Captain Taneyhill's train had only ten men, they were ten of the toughest-looking men Ebenezer had ever seen. Each of them carried a rifle, musket, or shotgun near the tool box in the front of the wagon, and wore a brace of pistols tucked inside a sash or holstered on a belt. Sweazy and Pruden also had knifes—Pruden sheathed his in his right boot and it looked practically as big as an Army saber. Gonzales called them Bowies, and said Sweazy and Pruden kept theirs sharp as razors.

* * * * *

"Hop onto the pole mule," Gonzales told Ebenezer one morning.

Ebenezer stared at him with a comical expression, until Gonzales put his hands on his hips and demanded: "*Muy pronto, Señor* Ebenezer, before *Capitán* Taneyhill begins bellowing like the devil."

Tightly bandaged ribs prevented Ebenezer from hopping, but he climbed into the saddle on the left-wheeler, and Gonzales handed him the jerkline, which was strung through harness loops on what Gonzales called the swingers all the way to the near leader, where the line was affixed to the bit. Ebenezer's right hand was sweating, but Gonzales did not seem to notice. He put the brakeline in Ebenezer's other hand.

"Remember what I told you, Ebenezer?" he asked.

Ebenezer feared he had forgotten everything. His mouth felt drier than cured tobacco.

At that moment, Captain Taneyhill's shout sent Ebenezer up straight in the saddle, and he heard himself yelling, "Yay!" To his amazement, the mules started straining, and the double-hitched wagons and caboose behind him began moving, rolling along. He heard the other muleskinners shouting brutal curses, heard the cracks of whips, but he remembered what Gonzales had told him: "Cursing shows a 'skinner's ignorance, and a whip is for oxen, not mules. All you need is a strong voice, and the know-how to handle a jerkline."

Gonzales walked beside Ebenezer, in case the kid got into trouble. When Ebenezer saw Amado up ahead on his high-stepping black horse where the road forked, pointing down the right lane, he glanced at Gonzales, but the Mexican merely smiled.

Wetting his lips, Ebenezer gave the line three quick jerks, and yelled—"Gee!"—and watched the chaos. Some of the swingers jumped over the tongue in one direction, the leaders in the other, and the wagon turned easily to the right. Ebenezer shot a frightened glance behind him, but the two wagons and trailing caboose turned easily, and when he swung around to look ahead, he caught a glimpse of Amado nodding his head with approval, grinning like a beaver.

"Yay!" Ebenezer shouted. The mules jumped back into position, and they were going straight.

Three short jerks and "gee" meant turn right. A steady pull and "haw" meant turn left. "Yay" meant keep going straight. Sounded easy, but it was anything but. Ebenezer had seen six-mule teams pulling wagons loaded with cotton or tobacco back at Hall Plantation in South Carolina, but this team had twelve mules, pulling two wagons and a caboose, and he was leading Captain Taneyhill's train.

Gonzales kept walking alongside, encouraging him, and when Ebenezer got into trouble, the Mexican would help Ebenezer get out of it. The mules tended to mind Gonzales's voice a lot better than they did Ebenezer's, though he would proudly admit that he did better on his first day as a muleskinner than he had ever dreamed he could do. By the time the train pulled into Jefferson, however, Ebenezer's nerves were shattered.

Chapter Nineteen

With its thick growths of piney woods, and rich black-land cotton plantations, East Texas reminded Ebenezer Chase a lot of Florence, South Carolina. Yet whereas Florence was a railroad town, Jefferson was a river port, and that's where Captain Taneyhill led his train.

Side-wheelers and stern-wheelers lined the wharves, some of the stacks coughing out thick black smoke as the steamboats prepared to shove off and head down Big Cypress Bayou, which was big, deep, and black. Never had Ebenezer seen so many boats, but Gonzales shrugged and said, "That is nothing. You should have seen this city before the war. Yankees control the Mississippi, and that has stopped much of the traffic up the Red River and across Caddo Lake to Big Cypress Bayou."

As the mules pulled the wagons down busy streets, Ebenezer was struck by the realization that Jefferson hadn't been touched by this war. Maybe that's why the roads had been full with so many travelers leaving Mississippi and Louisiana. Texas must have seemed like a godsend to many of those poor folks.

To Ebenezer, Jefferson looked like a boom city, especially when he recalled the destruction he and Zeb had seen in Columbia, Atlanta, Meridian, Vicksburg. He tried to block out the images of the battlefield graves they had passed, or the cemetery where their journey began back in Florence. Here, there was no sign of war. Women, dressed in the finest clothing, walked down boardwalks, and men in silk hats and broadcloth coats smoked long cigars as they idled outside of the businesses.

Yes, there were slaves. Ebenezer had seen them in the fields they had passed, planting cotton and corn, or plowing new rows. In Jefferson, they unloaded the ships on the docks, sweating as they strained to move bulky, five-hundred-pound cotton bales. Others hammered horseshoes in the stables, sat in fancy carriages waiting for their masters to finish their business, or walked behind the ladies, carrying brown packages full of merchandise, never lifting their eyes.

Maybe the war isn't over, Ebenezer thought. *Maybe we'll never be free. Maybe Mister Lincoln fought that war just to keep the Union together. Maybe some slave-man will find me, bring me back to Master Hall, and this time Missus Hall won't be able to save me from Mister Anderson's whip.* He tried to stop such thoughts and forget the images of the black men and women of Jefferson, Texas. Slaves. All of them slaves.

Tried, but couldn't. Not completely.

Big brick warehouses lined the wharves, and Ebenezer saw the black letters against whitewash that spelled out the building they were bound for.

TANEYHILL FREIGHTING CO.
ESTABLISHED 1853

Gonzales told him to stop, and Ebenezer tugged on the brake-line, and yelled at the mules, "Whoa!"

"Keep the brake taut," Gonzales said. "The mules will want to follow the others."

Behind him, Captain Taneyhill was already giving orders. "Sweazy, Pitch, take your loads over to the Rebecca's Wake. Captain Hollister will be wantin' to shove off quickly. Jerome, get yours over to Dekalb's. Tell Frank we'll settle up later."

The door underneath the TANEYHILL FREIGHTING CO. sign opened, and an older gentleman in a white shirt, loosened tie, and sleeve garters stepped outside, tamping tobacco into a fancy ivory pipe.

The wagons skinned by Sweazy, Pitch, and Jerome rumbled by, and just as Gonzales had warned, Ebenezer's mules wanted to follow, but he kept saying, "Whoa!" Pruden bellowed as his mules wanted to keep moving, but both muleskinners managed to keep the wagons in place.

"*Bueno*," Gonzales said. "You may dismount now."

As he slid out of the saddle, Ebenezer's legs felt wobbly on the ground again.

Captain Taneyhill rode up. "Rest of you men, get the wagons into the warehouse. All except yours, Severo, and yours, Gon— Ebenezer. Yours are bound for Dallas. Help Gonzales unhitch the mules. Ebenezer, get them to the corrals."

Chaos returned as the other mules pulled out, taking the wagons into the warehouse as the big brown doors were pulled open. Men, women, and children, white, black, and brown, stopped on the other side of the street to watch the show.

A man in front of the office door had his pipe going. "Hello, Liv," he said to Taneyhill, and gestured at Ebenezer with his pipe stem before sticking it back in his mouth. "Who's the new 'skinner?" The pipe didn't stay in his mouth long, because Luansy and Petey were climbing out of a wagon and onto the boardwalk while Zeb eased his bay gelding to the hitching rail, cradling that Sharps rifle across the pommel, waiting for instructions.

Ebenezer admired the way Zeb rode. Looked like he was born in a saddle, and only a few weeks had passed since he had swung onto his first horse.

Staring for a minute, the man with the pipe regained his senses, and grinned widely. "You starting up an orphanage, Liv?"

The captain slid from the saddle and handed the reins to Amado, who kicked his horse into a trot and disappeared around a corner.

"Chas McCampbell," Taneyhill said, "meet Zeb Hogan and Ebenezer Chase." Ebenezer looked up from over a mule's harness, and nodded, but McCampbell ignored him, staring at Luansy as the captain continued the introductions. "This is Luansy and Petey Taylor. They ran into some trouble east of Monroe."

McCampbell's head shook, but his smile never failed. "And you just had to help."

"They're earnin' their keep," Taneyhill said, rubbing his bad shoulder. "Zeb here's about as good a rifle shot as Sweazy."

"They run into trouble. How about you?"

"Not this time."

"No Yankees?"

"Didn't see any soldiers, blue or gray."

McCampbell smiled at Petey. "What's the boy do? Or her?" he added, glancing again at Luansy.

Zeb didn't like how McCampbell looked over Luansy.

"Like I said, Chas," the captain said, "they had trouble."

McCampbell shook his head. "You're a good Samaritan, Liv." He turned and finally gave Ebenezer a moment's consideration. "Thought you didn't hold to slavery."

"I don't. I hired them. Ebenezer's got the makin's of a good muleskinner."

McCampbell tapped his pipe against the red brick wall. "You'll get a sheriff serving you with a writ, Liv, you start harboring runaway slaves. It's bad for business."

Captain Taneyhill climbed up the steps to the boardwalk, and gave McCampbell a hard stare. "Maybe you ain't heard, Chas, but Lee surrendered."

The pipe returned to the man's mouth, but he kept talking. "Kirby Smith ain't. Not yet, and we Texians ain't never gonna bend to no damnyankee rule. And maybe you ain't heard the news, Liv. That Abolitionist zealot, Abe Lincoln, he's dead."

* * * * *

For the rest of the day, Ebenezer felt as if someone had whacked him alongside the head with a sledge-hammer. He moved around in a daze, sick, worried, wondering what Mr. Lincoln's death meant for his kind. He and Gonzales got the mules to the corral, then wandered back to the warehouse to help the others unload the wagons and then load them up again with sacks of flour, gallons of molasses, and crates and crates of shoes and boots. There must be a big cobbler operation in this town, Ebenezer decided. Captain Taneyhill ordered them to be real careful with a dozen bolts of calico cloth. Cloth was hard to come by in Dallas, he said, and he would make a handsome profit on that fabric. Two wagons were loaded with farm equipment.

Hard work it was. The weather had warmed, the day remained humid, and Zeb and Ebenezer were sweating fiercely by the time they finished shortly after dusk.

"What happens now?" Zeb asked.

"The four wagons of sugarcane and these others, they will go to Dallas," Gonzales replied.

"When will we leave?" Ebenezer asked.

"*¿Quién sabe?* The day after tomorrow? Perhaps longer. It is up to *Señor* Taneyhill."

"How long will it take us to get there? To Dallas, I mean."

"Fifteen, sixteen days."

Ebenezer nodded. In a little more than two weeks, he could be with Lizzie and Tempie, but he didn't know how to feel about that now, not with Mr. Lincoln killed. He wasn't even sure he'd be able to find his family, or, if he did, what he could do? What if slavery wasn't over?

Amado came over, spoke in brisk Spanish to Gonzales, then turned to Zeb and Ebenezer. "You two," he said. "*Vámonos.*"

The boys dragged their feet out of the warehouse and down the streets. People looked at Amado with silent respect, or maybe fear, and they eyed Zeb curiously. They barely gave Ebenezer any consideration.

On Delta Street they turned and walked a few more blocks before coming to a big wooden house, a single-story painted yellow with red shutters, four towering columns, a covered porch lined with rose bushes that had already greened up. Three red-brick chimneys climbed out of the wood-shingled roof, and two bois d'arc trees in the front yard.

They climbed the steps onto the porch. Ebenezer and Zeb felt shocked when Amado walked in the front door without knocking, motioning for the two boys to take a seat in the parlor. They obeyed, and the *segundo* walked down the hall, calling out something in Spanish.

It was Captain Taneyhill's house. Ebenezer knew that because he saw the captain's belted revolver, hat, and coat hanging on the coat rack in the foyer. Although the outside of the house was fine and rich-looking, the inside was rather Spartan. A saddle was draped over a rocking chair, and the only picture on the wall was a portrait of a red-haired lady in a fancy dress whose eyes seemed to follow Zeb no matter where he wandered in the parlor.

"You reckon that's the captain's dead wife?" Zeb asked.

"I'm not going to ask him," Ebenezer said.

Hearing footsteps, the two lads turned, waiting. Zeb practically shot out of the sofa when he saw who it was, the Sharps carbine falling off his lap and onto the rug. He swept off his hat, staring with his mouth wide open. Ebenezer's mouth dropped open as well.

Chapter Twenty

She took their breath away.

Zeb had always figured that Luansy Taylor was a right handsome girl, but never had he seen her so dolled up, wearing a visiting dress of blue cotton, with white satin trim on the sleeves and collar and a false-fronted white vest. She had taken a bath—he could still smell the rose-scented soap on her—and her hair was not only combed, but also curled. Her lips, which had always appeared so rough and chapped, were rosy against her fair skin.

"How do I look?" Petey, at Luansy's side, blurted out, but Zeb couldn't take his eyes off the girl, whose face started blushing.

"You look real good," Ebenezer said.

"What you think, Zeb?"

Zeb made himself turn from Luansy, and nodded at Petey. Luansy's little brother had also bathed, and Zeb barely recognized him without dirt caked to his face. The four-year-old wore front-fall trousers the color of nutmeg, an osnaburg work shirt, untucked, and brogans.

"Lu-Lu made me take a bath." Petey sneered. "I didn't wanna. Captain Taneyhill brung me these clothes. Brung Lu hers, too. She had to take a bath, too. I don't think she minded it. She kept hummin' while she was a-soakin'."

"You both look nice," Zeb said, and looked back at Luansy. He knew he didn't look nice. He had ripped a shirt sleeve loading wagons, and his hair remained matted and damp from sweating like a hog in that warehouse. He felt downright filthy. Kept waiting for the captain to show up and demand that he get in a

165

tub of water. He couldn't remember the last time he had actually bathed. Floating across those streams and rivers didn't count.

More footsteps sounded down the hall.

Captain Taneyhill, his face shaved clean now, his hair cut, slicked back, and combed, wearing a fine green frock coat, striped britches tucked inside shiny black boots, stopped in the hallway. Amado Chavez y Castaño stood at his side.

* * * * *

"The *Jimplecute* doesn't have any news about the assassination." Folding the newspaper, Captain Taneyhill set it on a table next to a bottle of whiskey and a tumbler filled with amber liquid. "From what Chas McCampbell told me, though, Lincoln was shot at a theatre in Washington City."

They sat on the front porch, bois d'arc trees swaying in the evening breeze.

Captain Taneyhill took a sip of whiskey and, facing Ebenezer, said, "I don't know what this means, Ebenezer. To you. To your people." He looked past Ebenezer and down Delta Street. "To Texas or the South." His good hand found the tumbler of whiskey, and he polished it off. "You still want to go to Dallas?"

"Yes, sir," Ebenezer said. "I've got to."

The captain's head bobbed slightly. "You'll go with him, Zeb?"

Zeb nodded. Dallas, he had learned, was on the way to Franklin.

"All right." Taneyhill filled his glass with more whiskey. "We'll leave Wednesday at first light."

That told Zeb nothing. He didn't know what day it was, hadn't for a long, long time.

"I have contracts to deliver freight to Dallas, and Franklin intrigues me, Zeb. I don't want you to think I'm as good a Samaritan as Chas McCampbell thinks I am. This is business for me. There's salt for the takin' near Franklin, and it's through country I've never seen. I've always had a touch of the wanderlust. Still, I could make a handsome profit deliverin' goods to Franklin, maybe as far west as Mesilla in New Mexico Territory, load the wagons up with salt, come back here. But that's a two-month journey, probably more, to Franklin, and it's rough country. Water's scarce. Comanches and bandits aren't."

"As long as I get to Franklin, I don't . . ."

"That's just it, Zeb. You might not get to Franklin. You might get killed."

"Maybe. Maybe not. I've made it this far."

"Why? What's so almighty important in Franklin?" He took a big gulp of the whiskey. "I know Ebenezer's reasons for getting to Dallas. Good reasons, too. What are yours?"

Zeb met the captain's stare. "I thought you said out West, people minded their own affairs."

Taneyhill lowered the whiskey. "You work for me . . . it is my affair."

"He wants to kill a man." Zeb, Taneyhill, and Ebenezer turned to see Luansy standing in the doorway, staring through the screen door. She didn't look so beautiful. She looked mad as all get-out. "Sergeant Ben DeVere."

"Sergeant?" the captain asked.

Zeb cleared his throat. "He ain't no soldier no more."

"How about you?" The captain's green eyes turned fierce.

Zeb had lied to so many folks, it came natural. It often felt as if he were spouting out the gospel, yet there just was no way in blazes he could ever lie to Captain Taneyhill. He couldn't find any words, not even to speak the truth.

"Zeb," Taneyhill said easily, "I know you wore the blue. Engstrand, that sergeant major you spoke of, that's a Yankee name." The captain sighed. "And I don't know too many Southerners, not in this day and age, who'd be travelin' across

Louisiana with a young runaway slave, and a couple of kids. I think you know me well enough to know that I won't turn you in to the provost marshal, Union or Confederate."

"Tell him, Zeb," Luansy pleaded.

So Zeb did.

* * * * *

They all gathered around the table, even Amado, the *segundo*, in the big dining room later that evening, and when a plump, graying Mexican lady named Consuela brought in a massive ham from the detached kitchen, Zeb's mouth started watering. He had never seen so much food: pecan-laced biscuits, sweet potatoes, rice, goober peas, plus cream for coffee or tea, and apple cobbler cooling off in the pie safe. He felt ready to make up for practically starving to death at Andersonville and Florence, and the nigh thousand miles Ebenezer and he had traveled since then.

"It ain't even Thanksgiving!" Petey blurted out, reaching for one of the biscuits, only to have his hand swatted by his sister. He jerked it back, rubbing it, and then, in a calmer voice, asked, "You celebratin' the end of the war, Capt'n Taneyhill?"

"Lincoln's dead," the captain said firmly, shaking his head. "I don't know what that means. General Kirby Smith and his boys haven't surrendered. Nor has that Cherokee Confederate, Stand Watie, up in the Indian Nations." He pushed back in his seat and looked across the table at Ebenezer. "Right now, as far as Texas is concerned, your wife and daughter are still slaves, with an owner in Dallas. Now, I don't hold with slavery . . ."

"Then why did you fight in the war?" Luansy's voice and eyes seemed colder than ice.

Taneyhill looked over at her. Gently he asked, "Did your folks own slaves?"

"No," she said. "They were all around us, though."

"Yet you said your brother was fightin' for the Confederacy. I'm a Texian, Luansy. I was fightin' for my home, same as your brother."

Offering a smile, he continued. "Ebenezer's bound and determined to go to Dallas. Zeb still says he has to make Franklin. What about you? And your little brother?"

Her lips started trembling, and she bit the bottom one to stop, giving Zeb a quick look, then staring at her little brother who was fidgeting in his chair, his boiler about to blow, wanting to know why everyone was talking and not eating the food before it turned cold.

"You mean . . . ?" Luansy began.

"You can stay here. We got a fine subscription school in town. Got us a crackerjack teacher named Waldeck."

"Can I think about it?" Luansy asked.

"Most certainly. Now let's eat."

"It's about time!" snapped Petey.

* * * * *

Zeb stood on the porch, talking to Captain Taneyhill about nothing important, just anything, enjoying the singing of crickets, the warm breeze rustling the leaves. A steamboat whistled somewhere on the bayou, and the faint sound of music from one of the saloons carried across the evening air.

"They started to build a railroad," Taneyhill was saying, "but only got five miles of track laid before the war stopped construction. So there still is no railroad in this part of the country. Which means freighting business is good, especially since the Yankees control most of the rivers and have blocked the Texas ports in the Gulf of Mexico."

Amado Chavez y Castaño finished his whiskey, and spoke in Spanish. The captain nodded, told Amado good night, and the big *segundo* donned his hat, saying, "*Buenas noches,* Zeb." The Mexican strode down the steps, turned on Delta Street, and walked back toward town, whistling.

Now alone with the captain, Zeb knew Taneyhill would say something. He knew what it would be about, too.

"You think Ben DeVere's worth it?" Taneyhill asked.

"Sergeant Major Engstrand thought so."

"He's dead. You ain't. Got a lot of years left. How many battles you ever take part in, Zeb?"

"A couple," Zeb said.

"Kill anybody?"

Zeb didn't answer.

"It weighs on a person . . . killin' a man. You take away his
life, but you also take away a good part, the better part, of yours."

"You ever killed anybody?" Zeb asked.

Bluntly Taneyhill answered, "Five." He poured the last bit
of whiskey from the bottle into his tumbler. "That ain't countin'
in the war. In war, sometimes, you never know, though I warrant I slayed a few at Corinth before they damned near killed
me. Two of the five I'm sure I killed were Comanches. Now,
you ask Chas McCampbell." The captain sipped his whiskey.
"Chas'd tell you Indians, especially Comanch', don't count, but
they were men, fightin' for their way of life, and I took that
away from them. The other three were bandits . . . two on the
Sabine River, another down around Travis County, tryin' to
take my wagons, tryin' to take my life, and the lives of my men.
Scum of the earth, white trash, brigands. Now all five of those
men . . ." Here he stopped, sniggered, and finished his whiskey.
"*Men*," he said bitterly. "One of them Comanches wasn't older
than you. But all five of them would have killed me if they'd
gotten the chance, and they wouldn't have lost any sleep. I'm
not sorry I killed them. I sure ain't tradin' places with them. But
I'll tell you this, Zeb . . . and it's fact . . . hardly a night goes by
that I don't picture those five men's faces." He stood up, and
walked to the edge of the porch, leaning against the railing,
staring up at the moon. "You think about that, Zeb. You think
about if Ben DeVere's worth killin'."

The front door opened, and Luansy Taylor stepped out. She had
a throw over her shoulders, even though the night remained warm.

The captain turned, waited, but Luansy just stared, not saying anything. Still, Captain Taneyhill knew what she wanted, so he picked up his hat, put it on his head, stuck the empty bottle underneath his arm, and grabbed the glass. "Don't stay up too late," he said, and went inside.

Chapter Twenty-One

"Ebenezer. Ebenezer, wake up."

Ebenezer softly snored in the trundle bed as Zeb shook his shoulder. Zeb had turned up the lamp and kept jostling the runaway slave, whose eyes slowly opened. Shaking his head, he mumbled, "Zeb . . . what . . . what time is it?"

"I don't know. You awake?"

"Noooo." It came out as a groan. Ebenezer tried to roll over, tried to put a pillow over his head, but Zeb knocked the pillow away, and shook him harder.

"Ebenezer, I gotta ask you something."

"Can't it wait? I'm plumb tuckered out, Zeb. We did a lot of work . . ."

"Ebenezer, what's it like?" Zeb sank onto the floor, leaned his head against the footboard of the big bed. "Being with a girl, a woman?"

Shadows danced on the wallpaper. The flame in the lamp flickered as a breeze blew through the cracked window.

Grumbling, Ebenezer tossed off the covers, and sat up in the bed. He stared at Zeb. "What are you talking about?"

Zeb shrugged. "You know . . ." was all he managed to get out.

Ebenezer let out a half sigh, half laugh. "Are you in love, Zeb Hogan?"

"I don't know. She's staying."

"Miss Luansy?"

"Uh-huh. She told me tonight. Then she started crying on my shoulder. She said she feared she might never see me again.

173

But she said she had to stay. Couldn't bring Petey with her, chasing after me, trying to stop me from . . . Well, the captain's offering her a job, and both of them the chance to get an education. I reckon you know how important it is to read and write."

"I'm not that good at it."

"Better'n me. I always figured it was just a waste of time. What good was it to read? Write? I could shoot better, or at least as good as anyone in the 16th Wisconsin Infantry. I could march. I made it all the way to Jefferson, Texas, from the Florence Stockade. My folks never held no faith in schooling. Said it was a waste of time. We was so poor, and I was so stupid, I didn't know no better. Now, I think my ma and pa kept me and James out of school 'cause they didn't want us to be better than they was. That's how they looked at it, I think."

"That ain't . . . that isn't right," Ebenezer said. "Parents should want their children to be better than they were. That's what I want for my little Tempie. I'd like her to know what it feels like to be free, to always have been free. She's too young to ever know she was born into slavery. That's . . ."

Silence. They watched the shadows.

Zeb laughed, and looked at Ebenezer. "Don't think we ever talked like this. On our journey, I mean."

Ebenezer smiled. "Half the time we were arguing."

"Or fighting."

The slave nodded. "Or that."

Zeb rubbed his jaw. "You punch pretty good."

Ebenezer laughed.

Silence. The shadows kept dancing.

"I said I could teach you," Ebenezer said at last. "Your letters and all."

"I remember."

"Or . . . well . . . I bet Captain Taneyhill, he'd send you to that subscription school, too. Smart as you are, brave as you are, you'd be reading and writing in no time, Zeb."

"I can't. I got to find . . . got to finish . . ." Zeb's head shook. "It's my duty. It's about my honor."

For the first time since Zeb had known him, Ebenezer Chase cursed. Climbing out of the trundle bed, turning, staring down at Zeb, Ebenezer cussed Zeb for a fool. Ebenezer's shadow was a giant against the wall. "Duty! Honor!" Ebenezer spit out those words angrily. "They're nothing but words to you, Zeb. You don't even know what they mean."

Zeb met his stare, but could say nothing.

"Captain Taneyhill's a good man. He's given you a job, pays you good money. You got a girl who loves you, though . . . Lord help me . . . I don't know what she sees in you. And you're gonna throw all that away. For what? To kill a man. To kill yourself in the process."

No longer could Zeb watch those glaring eyes, so he focused on his brogans. *Criminy, ain't even my shoes. They was Luansy's pa's.* The wind rustled through the trees, and he heard Ebenezer's heavy breathing and, through the walls, over in the next room, Luansy Taylor's soft sobs. He could picture her crying into her pillow, trying not to wake little Petey. His stomach twisted. Just a couple of hours ago, they had been sitting on the front-porch swing, her head on his shoulder, his arm around her. Zeb was telling Luansy that everything would be all right, that he'd come back, after he found Ben DeVere in Franklin, that he had to see this thing through, that he had come too far, that he wouldn't hold it against her if she never wanted to see him again, but he just couldn't quit. Sergeant Major Engstrand had been like a father to him.

Luansy had just sat there, the swing barely moving, shaking her head, saying: "Of course, I'll wait for you, Zeb. I'll wait forever . . ."

What if Captain Taneyhill's right? Zeb found himself wondering. *What if I get killed, long before I ever catch up to Ben DeVere? What if Ben DeVere kills me? Or what if the law don't see things the way I do? What if I shoot down Ben DeVere, but the law hangs me for murder?*

He could envision Luansy Taylor wearing black for the rest of her life, waiting on Zeb Hogan . . . forever . . .

His mind raced back to the Florence Stockade, and he pictured old Dave Gardenhire telling him: *You're about as mule-headed a boy as I've ever known.* Gardenhire had been right. Zeb knew that. He also knew he couldn't quit. He found his resolve, and looked at Ebenezer Chase, and told him the same thing he had told Captain Taneyhill, the same he had just told Luansy. "This is something I gotta do."

With another curse, Ebenezer stormed out of the bedroom, slamming the door shut, stomping out to the front porch, leaving Zeb alone with those shadows dancing against the wall.

* * * * *

Two days later, the Taneyhill train pulled out of Jefferson. Zeb never knew leaving could be so hard. He had never regretted pulling up stakes and lighting out from Madison, leaving behind his mother and father, but walking out of the captain's house that morning, shaking hands with little Petey, and hugging and kissing Luansy before they walked down to the warehouses with Ebenezer tore at his heart, left his insides numb.

He had a job to do. Needed to keep telling himself that.

First was getting to Dallas.

* * * * *

Three days out of Jefferson, they came to a dogtrot cabin tucked in a little clearing about fifty yards off the Dallas road. A woman in a homespun dress raced out of the front door, waving a white rag over her head, hollering something insensible. Captain Taneyhill and Amado spurred their horses and rode down the trail to meet her. Zeb stayed by the lead wagon and kept the Sharps rifle ready, looking in the woods, trying to spot any ambushers. After a brief conversation, the woman's shoulders sagged, and she turned and hurried back to her cabin, while the captain and Amado rode back to the train.

"What'd she want?" Sweazy asked from atop his pole mule.

The captain shook his head. "She thought we were Yankees. She was begging us not to burn down her home."

They rode on.

"That's crazy," Pruden said and spat out a river of tobacco juice.

"No, it ain't," Zeb said, but only Ebenezer heard, and Ebenezer kept quiet. He knew what Zeb was thinking. They had seen Columbia, Atlanta, Meridian. Pruden hadn't.

They rode on.

* * * * *

No bandits waylaid them. They hardly saw anyone else during those two long weeks to Dallas. They pulled into the city, which had a population of about two thousand—most of those, Zeb guessed, rough-looking gents idling outside of the grog shops—and headed straight for warehouses along the Trinity River.

Ebenezer didn't want to be unloading the wagons, but he didn't complain, didn't shirk his duty, just went right on sweating and straining. Zeb wondered if he would be so patient once they reached Franklin, when he got as close to Ben DeVere as Ebenezer was to his family. After a couple hours of back-breaking work, Captain Taneyhill rode his big bay gelding into the warehouse.

"Ebenezer!" he called.

Ebenezer finished helping Zeb and Gonzales lift a McCormick's Reliable self-raking reaper out of the wagon and onto the dirt. Slowly the black teen looked up at the captain.

"Come along," the captain said, "I've found where Clyde Hall lives. You might as well come, too, Zeb."

* * * * *

From Commerce Street, they left the warehouse, Zeb and the captain riding slowly and Ebenezer walking behind. Three blocks up, they turned left onto Jefferson Street, went down past Main and Elm. Ebenezer kept calling off the street names from the signs on the corners, like he was trying to remember how to get to wherever they were going. At Calhoun Street, they turned right and rode up a few more blocks before the captain reined in and swung down off his horse in front of a big white house.

To Zeb, it looked to be built of solid marble, with fine columns lining the front porch.

They tied their horses to a hitching post out front as a buggy rode down the street, then walked up a stone path to the house, climbed the steps. When the captain turned a white porcelain knob, a bell rang somewhere inside the house. After a long while, they heard footsteps, and finally the door swung open.

Ebenezer expected a Negro to open the door, knowing that Major Clyde Hall had many slaves, but it was a dumpy-looking man in a plaid sack suit, cravat undone, shirt front darkened with sweat, with a half-empty tumbler of whiskey in his right hand who opened the door. He peered at his visitors through bloodshot eyes.

"Well," the man said, straightening and running his free hand through what remained of the hair on his head. "Mister Livingston Taneyhill, what brings you to my humble abode?"

"Hello, Clyde."

"That's Major Hall to you, sir," Hall said stiffly.

The captain just laughed. "Major. And I'm only a captain."

"That's right, sir. I outrank you."

"Yeah, but the funny thing is the boys of Harris County elected me captain when we joined up to fight. You named yourself major, and never even got close to a Yank."

Hall drained his glass. "If you wish to conduct business, Taneyhill, I have an office on Pacific Avenue. How'd you find where I live?"

"I asked. And this isn't about freighting. I bring news. Well, Ebenezer, here . . . he does."

Ebenezer shuffled his feet. "Good afternoon, Major, sir."

"What do you want, boy?"

"Well, sir, we met up with Mister Prescott in Mississippi. We traveled with him a spell."

The glass almost slipped out of Hall's hand. "Where is Charles Prescott? Where is the wagon of . . .?"

"He ran back home, Major, sir . . . when he learned that General Lee had surrendered. Afterwards, bandits waylaid us somewheres in Louisiana. If it wasn't for Capt'n Taneyhill here, sir, we'd never have made it."

Major Hall considered Ebenezer for a moment. "The wagon?" he asked.

"Bandits . . . scavengers . . . attacked us. Stole our horses, went through the wagon. Burned it. And they killed . . ." Ebenezer couldn't finish.

Clyde Hall muttered an oath. "That worthless, cowardly little Prescott." His eyes found Taneyhill, but quickly returned to Ebenezer. "Wait a confounded minute. I know you. You're my sister-in-law's houseboy, her pet darky."

Ebenezer cleared his throat. "I'm looking for Lizzie and Tempie, sir."

The major, well in his cups, didn't appear to have heard. "No, I can't believe Oliver would have sold you," he mumbled to himself more than to Ebenezer.

Ebenezer's fists clenched so tightly, his arms began to shake.

"You have his wife and daughter," Captain Taneyhill said. "I'd like to buy them from you."

Hall's mouth fell open, and he looked at the three uninvited guests. After a minute, he laughed. "You?" He snorted. "Falling off your Abolitionist wagon, Livingston?"

"I never was an Abolitionist, Clyde. I just never saw any point in owning another man, woman, or child."

"You fought on the wrong side, my friend."

"At least I fought."

Hall bristled, if only for a moment, before he stepped inside the door, waving his guests to follow. The house lay in shambles, though not from the kind of ruin Zeb and Ebenezer had seen in other cities. This was just dirty, stinking, dusty.

Drunkenly Hall staggered to the parlor, grabbed a decanter, filled his glass, spilling a healthy dose, and collapsed in a chair by a floor-to-ceiling window. "I am drunk," Clyde Hall announced, although the trio already knew that. "I have been drunk since I learned of Appomattox Courthouse."

"Lizzie Chase," Captain Taneyhill reminded him. "And her daughter, Tempie. Where are they?"

"Confound it, man, do you see any charcoals here? A few of them ran off when they learned Lee had surrendered. Another nefarious scoundrel, a colored brigand, absconded with several . . . promising them freedom. The local constabulary and some rangers have been pursuing them. I told Undersheriff Stricklyn that he could bring my slaves back dead, for all I care. Even with Lincoln assassinated, the South . . . it is finished."

"Where's my wife and child?" Ebenezer shouted, and he stepped forward, ready to thrash the drunkard. He probably would have, had Zeb not grabbed him from behind, pinning back his arms. Ebenezer grimaced, his ribs aching, but Zeb didn't let go, wouldn't let Ebenezer strike a white man, not a rich one like Clyde Hall, not in a city that had hanged and whipped a bunch of slaves just five years back. Ebenezer might have been hurting, but he refused to give up. He didn't stop until Captain Taneyhill told him to. Only then did Zeb let go.

"That's right," Hall said, as if he remembered. "You were mighty upset when Oliver sold me that little baby. Yes, now I remember. Lizzie was a handsome woman. Could keep a man cozy a night."

Zeb grabbed Ebenezer again. This time Ebenezer didn't listen to the captain's orders, or Zeb's pleas. Finally Captain Taneyhill had to push Ebenezer against the wall. A map fell off its hanger, slipping to the floor. Hall just laughed.

"Where are they?" Ebenezer roared.

Taneyhill held Ebenezer's left arm with his one good arm. Zeb used both hands to grip Ebenezer's right.

"Where's my wife? Where's my child?"

Hall finished his whiskey, and shook his head. He was still laughing when he answered. "Boy, they're both dead."

Chapter Twenty-Two

Once, back at Hall Plantation in Florence County on a September afternoon, Ebenezer had fallen off a wagon out by the tobacco barn, landing on his back so hard that all the air had left his lungs. He had gasped, trying to get oxygen, staring up at the panicked faces of the slaves standing over him, none of them knowing what to do. Another time, a jenny named Eleanor had slammed a hoof into his back when he wasn't looking, and the pain became so intense that he wanted to cry out, but couldn't. He had just stood there at the corral, mouth open, waiting to scream.

Which is how Ebenezer Chase felt in Major Hall's parlor.

His mouth hung open, and again the pain became intense, too deep and horrific to cry out. *The major's lying*, he tried to convince himself, but suddenly the major stopped laughing, and the drunkard began sobbing, blubbering like Ebenezer thought he should have been doing.

"Yellow fever," he heard Major Hall say. "Last October . . . late in the season. The outbreak . . . claimed thirteen lives . . . including . . . my . . . wife . . . Annie Mae. If only I'd . . . been here . . ."

The major might have said more. Probably he did. Ebenezer just couldn't hear. Couldn't hear a thing. The chandelier and the wainscoting started spinning around like they were caught in a tornado. A hand touched his shoulder, and Ebenezer knew Zeb Hogan was speaking to him, but Zeb's words made no sense, didn't mean a thing, and then there was a scream. Ebenezer's.

Finally he had found his voice. The chandelier and the wainscoting turned black, and Ebenezer slipped into that welcome darkness.

* * * * *

"Ebenezer?"

His eyelids fluttered, and Zeb Hogan's face slowly came into focus. Zeb's eyes looked red, as if he had been crying. Ebenezer tried to tell himself that this had been a dream, but Zeb broke the illusion.

"I'm plumb sorry, Ebenezer. I . . . well . . . I ain't got the words to say . . ."

Zeb's head hung down, shaking sideways. Behind him rose the yellowing canvas tarp of one of Captain Taneyhill's Murphy wagons.

"What happened?" a far-off voice asked. Ebenezer recognized the voice as his own.

"You fainted back at that walking whiskey keg's house. We brung you back here."

"Where?"

"Wagon yard. We're spending the night. Lighting out at daybreak tomorrow." Zeb sniffed. His next words came out with urgency as he looked at Ebenezer. "It ain't fair. It just ain't right. It . . ."

"Nobody ever said life was fair, Zeb. Or right." Ebenezer pushed himself to a sitting position, and the pain hit, like it finally hit him that time Eleanor kicked him so hard, like the time when he had slipped off the wagon and knocked the air out of his lungs. He saw sweet little Tempie and poor young Lizzie, and he knew that he would never see them again, not in this world, that they were dead, had died long before he had ever run off from Hall Plantation. Ebenezer started bawling, crying so hard he felt his whole body shaking. Wheezing, choking out sobs, he experienced a pain worse than he had ever felt. He felt Zeb's strong hands pull him close, hold him so tightly, and then he heard Zeb's moans, knew that Zeb was crying, too.

The muleskinners and the captain—and other wayfarers spending the night in the wagon yard—watched, but none said a word, nobody made any jokes, nobody even bothered to offer a prayer. They just let Zeb and Ebenezer cry it out.

Eventually Ebenezer sucked in a lungful of air, held it a spell, and slowly exhaled. Zeb released his hold, took the time to wipe his eyes with his grimy shirt sleeves. His lips kept trembling, but he managed to ask: "You all right?"

"Yeah," Ebenezer said. "It hurts, though."

"Hurt when James died," Zeb said. "Hurt like blazes. Same when Sergeant Major Engstrand died, maybe even a bit worse, him being like a pa to me. You don't ever really get over it, but it gets . . . well . . . the pain won't hurt this much always."

It's one thing to lose a brother, a friend, Ebenezer thought, *but it's an entirely different pain to lose a wife and daughter.* Still, Ebenezer gave Zeb a steady nod, wiped the snot hanging from his nose, rubbed away the tears. "Thanks, Zeb," he said.

Zeb shook his head as if to say he hadn't done anything, but he had. He most certainly had. He had been there for Ebenezer. Ebenezer hadn't realized what a friend he had in Zeb Hogan. They had been at odds for most of the journey, tolerating each other, depending on one another, often despising the other. No, they had never been real friendly, even after saving each other's bacon a time or two, but Ebenezer guessed that you don't come through all they had come through without forming some type of bond. He wasn't sure if Zeb considered him a friend, but Ebenezer knew he would never have as good a friend as Zeb Hogan.

Spurs jingled and, smelling the hay and dust of the wagon yard, Ebenezer and Zeb looked up to find Captain Taneyhill walking across the yard from a campfire, holding his hat at his side.

He knelt in front of the two boys. "Y'all feel like eatin'?" the captain asked.

Ebenezer shook his head, and Zeb said, "We ain't real hungry right now, Captain."

"You'll need your strength," he said.

"Maybe in a bit," Ebenezer said, just to say something.

Taneyhill placed the hat on his head, pushed up the brim. "Amado's takin' half the wagons back to Jefferson in the morn," he said. "Loaded with cotton. I'll be leadin' the other wagons to Franklin, and across the border to El Paso." The captain looked grim. "Ebenezer, you'll be goin' with Amado."

"No," he said, and thought to add, "sir."

Zeb gave the runaway slave a curious look.

The captain stared hard at Ebenezer for the longest while. "The wagons I'm takin' are loaded with gunpowder. It ain't gonna be an easy trip."

"I'm going on. Zeb . . ." Ebenezer let the words die. *Me and Zeb come this far*, he thought. *He could have abandoned me countless times, and I reckon I've floated my stick alongside his all this way. Besides, Zeb might need my help when he finally meets Sergeant Ben DeVere.* Then another thought struck him, rocked him: *There's nothing for me in Jefferson. Nothing for me . . . anywhere.*

The captain sank to sit on the ground, his legs tucked inside each other. He pushed his hat back. "There's a munitions factory in Dallas, been manufacturin' gunpowder and the likes for the Confederate Army," he said, "and for some of the rangerin' bands posted around Fort Belknap when the Comanch' and Kiowa would start actin' up."

"Like Selma," Ebenezer said, and the captain stared with a blank expression.

"They was making powder at Selma, Alabama," Zeb explained. "Or so me and Ebenezer heard. Making it from ladies' pee."

"What?" For the first time, Taneyhill looked shocked. He turned his head while Zeb explained about the ladies of Selma donating their chamber-lye to the war effort.

"Well," the captain continued, "I don't know about that, but the mayor and the owner of the factory have decided they don't want this gunpowder to fall into Yankee hands. They'd rather have it go to Maximilian."

"Who's he?" Zeb asked.

"Emperor of Mexico. He's got his hands full fightin' a bunch of rebels down south."

"Shucks," Zeb said. "Seems to me that Texas ought to be supplying them Mexican rebels with that powder. Seems to me you would think this Maximilian fellow is a lot like Abe Lincoln."

The captain managed to stop the smile creasing his face. "Well, he ain't. But the fact is Maximilian isn't popular with his people. Not popular with a lot of folks. The United States government won't recognize him. Maybe that's why a lot of Confederates have been saying they'll cross the border and fight for him, though I don't care much for him, either. So if . . . and that's a big if . . . if we make it to Franklin, cross the border, and meet Maximilian's emissaries, there's a good chance we'll have a rough go gettin' those wagons delivered to his troops."

"We're coming with you," Zeb and Ebenezer announced in unison. Zeb kept talking. "Nothing's keeping me from settling up with Ben DeVere."

"Comanches might. Bandits might." Taneyhill shook his head. "What I'm tryin' to get through those thick noggins of yours is that there's better than a fair to middlin' chance that we'll be bushwhacked for that gunpowder long before we ever reach Franklin. I never knew anybody in Dallas who could keep a secret, especially that verbose mayor. Way I figure it, word's out what we're haulin', and Comancheros, gunrunners, and just about every b'hoy from the Nations to the Nueces Strip will be after it. If we get to Mexico, then we've got the *Juaristas* . . . those are the Mexican rebels wantin' Maximilian's head on a platter . . . to worry about."

"Then why do it?" Ebenezer asked. "Especially if you don't like this emperor fellow, either?"

The captain shrugged. "They're payin' me good money to try."

Chapter Twenty-Three

Texas turned hard. Everything about the country got tough: the land, what grew on it, what slithered across it, and what flew overhead across a big, blue sky. Long gone were the forests and swamps of the South, and Zeb grew to miss those long-leaf pines. Out here, it seemed, the only thing passing for trees were scrawny old cedars here and there, more along the river bottoms—when there was a river, and that was rare—and pesky mesquite. Mostly only cactus grew out of the chalky hills. Even the water was hard. Sometimes it tasted like pure brine, but more than likely it went down like iron.

By the Eternal, Zeb thought when they were two days out of Fort Worth, *never thought I'd feel this . . . not after all them rivers we crossed in Carolina, Georgia, and all . . . but, criminy, I miss all that water.*

Ten days later, they reached Fort Belknap, where they filled water barrels and canteens. After that, they saw only a big emptiness as they followed the trail John Butterfield had laid out for the Overland Mail Company before the war broke out. Since then, the US government had moved the trail out of the South, but Captain Taneyhill said the old trail was still used by some Texian entrepreneurs and the jackass mail.

Zeb had to take the captain's word on that. He hadn't seen anybody, other than members of the wagon train, since leaving Fort Belknap. Not even Indians, and he had a hankering to see a warrior.

Typically Zeb rode either on the point, usually alongside Captain Taneyhill, or brought up the rear, riding some distance behind the wagons skinned by Sweazy, Pruden, Severo, and Gonzales, with Ebenezer assisting the latter.

Ten miles a day proved lucky. Eleven or twelve was unheard of. Eight became good. They averaged six. Captain Taneyhill took no chances, not with all that gunpowder. They kept the cook fire away from the wagons, and after they ate supper, they would move on another mile or two before making camp.

"Best way to travel through Injun country," Sweazy told Zeb.

Zeb didn't mind playing things safe, though it irked him. Slow as they were traveling, he felt he would never get to Franklin. Sergeant Ben DeVere might have flown the coop by the time they reached that town.

* * * * *

Scanning the horizon, standing in the stirrups on a ridge top, Zeb let out a whistle, and Captain Taneyhill loped his horse over to the youngster.

Eagerly Zeb pointed up the trail, yelling: "Comanch'! Maybe Kiowa!" He fumbled with the Sharps.

"Easy does it," Taneyhill said, studying the riders.

"But they's Indians."

"You won't see a Kiowa or Comanch' unless they want you to spot them," Taneyhill said. "As for me, I got no particular interest in seeing one on this here trip. Those are white men."

"Bandits?"

"Rebs."

Slowly Zeb relaxed. A few minutes later, he could make out their gray shell jackets and brown hats. Still, it had been so long since he had seen Secesh, he practically gawked at the seven riders. By the time the Rebels began climbing the ridge top, the wagons had caught up with the captain and Zeb.

"Keep that Sharps handy, Zeb," Taneyhill whispered. "Just in case." Turning in the saddle, the captain motioned at the mule-skinners to relax, but be ready.

The leader, a sergeant with a gray goatee, held up his right hand, and the six Rebs behind him reined up. The sergeant kicked his bay horse—so skinny her ribs looked to be about to poke free—into a walk, and he trotted up to the captain and Zeb.

"You heard any word about General Johnston? Or Smith?" the Confederate asked.

"I haven't, Sergeant," Captain Taneyhill said, "but the war's over. You've heard about Lee, I take it."

"Yeah." The word came out like a curse. The sergeant turned in the saddle, waved his men forward. As they rode up, he faced the captain. "We were down south, near Brownsville. Turned back the Yanks at Palmito Hill." He shifted to ask one of his men: "When was that, Marcus?"

"They had us whupped on the twelfth," a raw-boned kid, who looked younger than Zeb, announced proudly. "Then Rip Ford come along with us the next day, and we beat the devil out of them."

That was May 12 and 13. General Lee had surrendered to Grant on April 9. "What a waste," Zeb heard himself say.

The sergeant shook his head. "It was the Yankees' fault. We had us a truce, but the Yanks broke it. They just wanted some jubilate, the vainglorious fools. Colonel Ford figured the Bluebelly leader desired to get in one more fight before the war had ended. After that little ruction, we heard the news about Lee. I still . . . it's just . . . I can't believe it."

"Believe it." Captain Taneyhill spoke with authority, and the sergeant and the dusty, weary, bleary-eyed soldiers seemed to sit a little straighter in the saddle. "The war's over."

"Most certainly it's over for them dead Yanks we left at Palmito Hill, and the hundred or so we took prisoner," the rider with an eye patch said, and the pockmarked man riding beside him laughed. The others didn't find humor in his remark. Nor did Captain Taneyhill.

"Colonel Ford, he led us back to Brownsville after the battle, not that it was much of an affair," the Rebel leader said. "Some of the boys talked to him, said we'd done our duty, that the war was pret' much over, that maybe it was time for us to go home. Colonel Ford, he just nodded his head, said he wouldn't stop us. So me and the boys decided to come on up this way."

"Back home," the raw-boned boy said, and tears welled in his eyes.

"Home." The sergeant choked out the word.

"No news from General Smith?" the boy asked.

Captain Taneyhill's head shook.

"Then there's still hope," the one with the eye patch remarked. "If Smith and Johnston can combine their forces, we'll lick the Yanks yet."

"It's over," Captain Taneyhill said. "Smith and Johnston likely have surrendered by now. Go home. We lost. The time for fightin' is over. Now's time to start rebuildin'."

"Yeah," the sergeant said.

"Y'all seen anything on the trail?" Taneyhill asked.

"No, sir," the sergeant replied. "Just a church at Phantom Hill. Figure that one out, eh. How about y'all?"

The captain shook his head. "We've seen only one stagecoach, heading east, since we left Belknap. No Indian sign. Been smooth since we left Dallas."

"It'll be good to see Gainesville again." The sergeant saluted the captain, and rode on, followed by his men.

* * * * *

Three days passed, but the country stayed the same. They rode underneath a mesa, the wind blowing hot, the sky cloudless. The sun baked the riders, mosquitoes pestered them, buzzing by their ears, biting their necks.

The captain had sent Zeb back behind the train, and he had fallen maybe a quarter mile behind Pruden's double-hitched wagons. His left hand slammed the back of his sweaty neck, missing a mosquito, when there came a loud crack.

It was a sound Zeb had heard often. It came from an Enfield rifle, and none of Captain Taneyhill's men carried Enfields. He kicked the roan into a lope, hanging onto the Sharps and reins, bouncing in the saddle as he put the horse into a gallop. Another report echoed across the valley, then another. Urging the roan to run harder, giving the gelding plenty of rein, Zeb somehow managed to pull the Sharps' hammer to full cock.

His mouth turned dry as he crested a little hill. Flames consumed Pruden's wagon tops, his two lead mules lay dead in the traces, and Pruden was sprinting to where Sweazy was forming the other wagons into what might pass for a circle. Pruden had cut loose the remaining mules, and they were loping down the road, not bothering to stop in the fort Sweazy was organizing.

The road narrowed as the roan carried Zeb down the hill toward the burning wagons. Those bushwhackers, whoever they were, had picked a good spot. They had stopped Pruden's wagons at a narrow spot in the road, pretty much blocking any chance the other wagons had of retreating.

Holding his breath, Zeb guided his horse toward the burning wagons. Heat from the flames singed his hair. His right boot scraped against the rocky wall, but he managed to get past. He had to get past—*before* all that gunpowder blew up. A bullet zipped past his ear as he saw Gonzales waving at him, urging him on. Dust kicked up a few rods in front of Zeb, but he never heard that shot. Gonzales stopped waving, and lifted his rifle. Smoke belched from the barrel, obscuring his face, then came a deafening roar behind Zeb. Heat blasted his back, and Zeb found himself flying over the roan's head as the little gelding stumbled.

He landed with a thud, felt the Sharps boom underneath him. Rolling over, Zeb used the Sharps as a crutch to push himself to his feet, thinking it a wonder that he hadn't blown his head off with his own rifle. The roan limped away, and Zeb staggered toward Gonzales. His hat was gone. His ears rang. His knees burned from scrapes and tears, and he tasted sweat, blood, and dirt. He made it a couple of steps when a second blast knocked him off his feet, but he came up again, quicker this time, pushing forward through the smoke and dust as he watched Gonzales ram a rod down the barrel of his rifle, cap the nipple, bring the stock to his shoulder, and squeeze the trigger. A bullet whizzed past Zeb, and he recognized the sound he had heard much too often, the sound of a bullet striking flesh. Behind him, a man groaned, and Zeb shot a glance over his shoulder to find a black man dropping to his knees, falling on his side. Zeb looked back and dived, crawling under the caboose of Gonzales's wagon, coming up inside the perimeter of the circle. Gonzales had already reloaded his rifle, and Zeb began readying the Sharps.

"Zeb! Zeb! Up here!" Sweazy yelled.

Zeb could barely hear him, with his ringing ears. Words, noises all sounded like they were coming from a tunnel. He finished loading the Sharps, started running toward Sweazy, who was turning around, screaming. A figure shot ahead, leaped over the wagon tongue, started running up the road. Severo was pulling the mules into the center of the circle. Pruden let out a curse, and cut loose with his revolver.

"That fool kid!" Sweazy yelled again.

Out of breath, Zeb looked around and could see Ebenezer running up the road. Running toward Captain Taneyhill, who was pinned underneath his dead horse.

"He ain't got no gun!" Sweazy cried as two men rode right for Ebenezer and the captain.

Zeb raised the Sharps. The closest rider was a colored man, too, but that wasn't not what Zeb saw. He saw a Rebel soldier, and he recalled the first time he had seen the elephant, back in Georgia.

* * * * *

The gray line moved forward, and Sergeant Major Engstrand ordered: "Fire!" Zeb brought up his rifle, drew a bead on a Johnny

Reb. Musketry roared around him. A bullet slammed into Private Larson's throat, and he fell beside Zeb, gagging, blood spurting, him choking, drowning. Zeb glanced at the dying soldier, made himself look away, heard Sergeant Major Engstrand yelling. Zeb tried to find another charging enemy soldier in his sights . . .

After the fight, after they had driven back the Confederates, Zeb knelt in the trench, cleaning his rifle, and when he stopped, then he started shaking.

Sergeant Major Engstrand put his hand on Zeb's shoulder, and whispered, "Tough day, eh, laddie?"

"Sergeant . . ." Zeb held out the rifle for Engstrand to inspect. "I never fired a shot. Not the whole time."

"I know," he said.

Zeb figured Engstrand would be furious. Zeb's inaction could have cost them the battle. He wouldn't have been surprised had Engstrand ordered Zeb court-martialed, shot for cowardice. Instead, Sergeant Major Engstrand pulled Zeb close.

"Aye, I know. It's a hard thing, Zeb, to kill another man. And it should be a hard thing. It should always be hard."

* * * * *

The gray-coat soldier disappeared, and Zeb again saw the black rider, coming down hard for Ebenezer and Captain Taneyhill. Zeb aimed low, the way he had been taught to do by Sergeant Major Engstrand. He squeezed the trigger, stepped aside, calmly reloaded. Both horse and rider went down, the horse rolling up, clambering to its feet, wandering off, the rider lying facedown, shaking his head, dazed, just a few rods behind the captain and Ebenezer.

As the second rider leaped over the captain's dead horse— the hoofs of the dun-colored beast almost colliding with Captain Taneyhill's head—he tugged on the reins, swung around, and brought up a six-shooter. A puff of dust was raised off the horseman's vest at the same time the stock of the Sharps slammed into his shoulder, and the rider, who looked to be a Mexican, toppled from the saddle as the horse bolted down the pike.

Zeb was again reloading the Sharps as he watched Ebenezer pull the captain from underneath the dead horse. Taneyhill rose unsteadily, put his good arm around Ebenezer's shoulder. They staggered forward.

"Come on, Ebenezer!" Zeb shouted. "For God's sake, hurry!"

Yet he knew it was hopeless.

Other riders galloped out of the brush to intercept them.

"They'll never make it," Sweazy said.

Zeb thought: *And there's nothing I can do to save them.*

Chapter Twenty-Four

Fright gripped Ebenezer, almost paralyzed him.
More than a dozen riders had cut off Ebenezer and Captain Taneyhill a good forty yards from the wagons. Some of those men aimed rifles at Ebenezer and the captain, while the others cut loose with a cannonade of musketry that kept Zeb, Pruden, Gonzales, Sweazy, and Severo pinned down.

Ebenezer Chase waited to die. *Odd*, he thought, *I never figured I'd get killed by my own kind. Thought it would be a white man . . .*

Most of the riders were black, although a couple were Mexican. Two of the Negro riders swung off their mounts, one of them shoving a revolver in his sash, barking an order at the prisoners, but Ebenezer couldn't hear anything above the deafening roar of rifles. Horses danced around nervously, white smoke filled the sky, and the bitter smell of sulphur tore at his nostrils.

The man who had yelled, a broad-shouldered Negro missing his right ear, cuffed Ebenezer across the cheek with a gloved backhand, felling Ebenezer to his knees. His partner, a Mexican in an embroidered shirt, was busy shoving the captain, belly down, on the Mexican's horse, then swung up and kicked the chestnut gelding into a lope. Missing Ear jerked Ebenezer to his feet, shouted again. This time Ebenezer heard him.

"Get on, or I leave you here to feed the ravens!"

He slammed Ebenezer against the bay horse. Blood spilled out of Ebenezer's nose and busted lips, and he felt himself being thrown roughly onto the horse like a sack of oats, or perhaps a corpse, which Ebenezer soon expected to become. Missing

197

Ear mounted behind Ebenezer, raked spurs across the bay, and Ebenezer bounced around on the saddle, kept in place only by a firm hand pressing against his back. After rounding the bend in the road and moving through some brush, Ebenezer was flung onto the hard ground. His head ached. He struggled for breath. The sound of the battle slowly died.

"Ebenezer?"

It was the captain's voice. Ebenezer looked up, saw the blue sky, turned to the left, and found Captain Taneyhill sitting up. Blood leaked from wicked cuts on the captain's forehead and cheek, and his right arm dangled uselessly, his sleeve slick with blood that kept spreading, dripping from a hole in his shoulder, down his arm and off his fingertips. *The same place where he'd been wounded at Corinth!* Taneyhill's features revealed incredible pain, but somehow he managed a smile.

"Reckon I won't be seein' any new country, after all." He bit his lip, shook his head, kept talking. "That was a brave thing you did, Ebenezer . . . runnin' out to fetch me. Should have looked after yourself, though."

"I couldn't do that, Captain."

Taneyhill's head bobbed. "Well, I'm proud of you."

"Shut up!" a voice thundered, and Taneyhill and Ebenezer watched the gathering of horsemen. They came from all directions—blacks, Mexicans, and three white men wearing the dirty blue jackets and the lighter blue pants of the Union soldiers. Foragers. Scavengers. Bushwhackers. Murderers. All the names fit.

"Emil," another voice—deeper, more authoritative—sounded behind the wall of mounted ruffians. "You and Carlito keep peppering them with pot shots. Just be careful not to hit those wagons. We've already lost a ton of powder."

The horses parted, and a giant black man rode through on a prancing white horse. His hair was white, close-cropped, and he sported a big mustache, carried a brace of revolvers on his hips and a big rifle in huge hands. He wore no hat, though a long, yellow scarf hung around his neck against a fancy blue bib-front shirt. Seeing the captain and Ebenezer, he guided the beautiful horse toward the prisoners and pulled on the reins. Two men, one colored, the other Mexican, took the reins as he dismounted while working the lever on a fancy rifle he carried, sending an empty brass cartridge spinning into the air. The man made a beeline for the captain and Ebenezer.

"Your boys are pretty good shots." Hard black eyes locked on Captain Taneyhill. "Killed two of my men, wounded four more, and I don't have that many to spare."

"Likely," the captain said, "you'll lose more if you don't skedaddle."

The big man laughed, swinging the rifle barrel till it rested maybe an inch from Taneyhill's nose.

"That gunpowder won't do you no good . . . dead."

Ebenezer let out a heavy sigh, perhaps even a moan, remembering Captain Taneyhill's warning that bandits likely knew of the load, and would ambush them long before they ever made it to Mexico. The big Negro leader didn't even consider Ebenezer, just kept his rifle trained on Captain Taneyhill.

The captain didn't blink, kept right on staring at the big man.

"Don't," Ebenezer said softly, and the big man's massive head slowly turned.

"You like being a slave, boy?" he asked.

"He's no slave," Captain Taneyhill said. "I pay him . . ."

"Shut up!" the white-haired Negro said. "I'm talking to the boy."

His voice triggered some dormant memory, and Ebenezer stared up into those eyes, not answering, and felt himself nervously playing with the red button ring on his pinky. As the big man looked closely at Ebenezer's quilt vest, then at the button ring, the wrinkles around his eyes tightened, and he lowered the rifle.

"Ebenezer?" he asked.

"I . . ." Ebenezer shook his head. It couldn't be, but the voice was his. Back at Hall Plantation in South Carolina, Uncle Cain had always kept his head shaved, and Ebenezer had never seen him with a mustache, certainly had never seen him wearing heavy Dragoon revolvers in fancy tooled holsters and carrying a repeating rifle. Ebenezer looked at the Negro's left hand, saw the two missing fingers, the ones he had lost to a snapping turtle while noodling for catfish.

"Uncle Cain?" he said.

Quickly Cain Riddell tossed the rifle to a wiry Negro standing a few feet away, reached down, and jerked Ebenezer up and into a tight hug. Almost as quickly, he shoved Ebenezer an arm's distance away, eying him up and down, grinning widely. "What is you doing in Texas, boy? How'd you . . . ?" His eyes brightened even more, and he shook his head. "Tempie and Lizzie. You comes for them, eh?"

His head dropped. "They're dead, Uncle Cain." The words were barely audible.

"Dead?" Cain's voice boomed like thunder.

"Died of yellow fever in Dallas . . ." Ebenezer's voice wavered. "In October." He shook his head. "I came for them." He looked his uncle in the eye. "Remember you told me about that white couple on Lynches River . . . Tres Hudgens and his wife? I run off, found them. Run off with a soldier who'd escaped from the prison camp in Florence. He's . . ." Ebenezer decided not to tell Cain that Zeb Hogan was with the captain's wagons. "Wanted to get to Lizzie, to see my baby again, but . . ." His head fell once more.

"You come more than a thousand miles to find your wife and daughter," Uncle Cain said, marveling over the statement. Suddenly he roared, "Do you hear that, men? This here is Ebenezer Chase. He run off from Hall Plantation, same as me. This boy was like a son to me. And now, here we are. This is Providence's doing, boys. We'll celebrate once we've finished our business here."

Not one of his men said anything. They just stared. Off in the near distance, Ebenezer heard the muffled reports of rifles. Uncle

Cain's sharpshooters were doing his bidding, keeping Zeb and the others pinned down.

"Uncle Cain," he blurted out, "Captain Taneyhill here . . . he's a good man. Saved my life. Please don't hurt him. Or his 'skinners. Please stop what you're doing. The war's over. The captain . . . He's . . ."

Uncle Cain did the strangest thing. He laughed, pulled Ebenezer close to his chest, almost crushed Ebenezer's back with those strong arms. "Boy, did Major Hall tell you Tempie and your wife were dead?" Like he hadn't even heard Ebenezer's pleas to spare the captain.

At first, Ebenezer could only nod. Finally he said, "His wife died, too."

"His wife . . . sure . . . and good riddance. But not Tempie, not Lizzie. I freed them, Ebenezer. They're in my camp a few miles south of Phantom Hill. Major Hall, he lied to you, boy. That's just like that conniving, miserable white stinking son-of . . ."

"Cain!"

Cain Riddell turned toward one of the men in the blue coats, a tall man with a red goatee and the left side of his face blackened and disfigured from gunpowder that had gotten underneath the skin. "Smoke from them two wagons we blew up is bound to draw attention," the man said. "If we're gonna get the rest of that load, we better start working on it."

Uncle Cain extended his arms, and the Negro holding his rifle tossed it back to him. Cain caught it, and held it out for Ebenezer's inspection. "Ever seen one of these, Ebenezer?"

He shook his head. Cain's words had left Ebenezer in shock. Question after question raced through his mind. *Could Tempie and Lizzie still be alive? Can I trust Uncle Cain? Is he right? Why would Major Hall have lied?* Was it, as his Uncle Cain had said, Providence that he had met him more than a thousand miles from South Carolina? Ebenezer remembered that time in Louisiana, when he had spied Prescott's wagon, bound for Dallas. *Fate . . .*

divine intervention . . . just plain luck? The hand of God? Or the devil's bidding? Tempie . . . Lizzie . . . alive?

No, he couldn't believe what his uncle had said, couldn't even believe that he, Ebenezer Chase, was here, in Texas, talking to him. Couldn't quite fathom what he'd become. An outlaw. A renegade. Yet Ebenezer started to remember other things that he had heard at Major Hall's house in Dallas. Most of the slaves had run off after hearing of Lee's surrender, the major had said. But what else? Slowly the words sounded in his brain: *Another nefarious scoundrel, a colored brigand, absconded with several, promising them freedom. The local constabulary and some rangers have been pursuing them . . .*

"It's a Henry repeater," Uncle Cain was saying. "Shoots a .44-caliber rimfire. Sixteen shots. All you gots to do is work this lever." He did, sending another brass cartridge, this one unfired, arcing into the air and into the dust behind him. "Aim, and pull the trigger. The Rebs said the Henry could be loaded on Sunday and shot all week, ain't that right, Tanner?"

The scarred white man grunted something.

Just as quickly Uncle Cain Riddell tossed the rifle to Ebenezer, who almost dropped it. The rifle was heavy, awkward, a silver plate attached to the brown stock, the brass frame reflecting the sunlight, the long, black barrel warm from being fired. Fired, most likely, at the captain, Ebenezer's friends, and Ebenezer himself. His arms started shaking. A few of the outlaws put their hands on their guns, some of them watching Ebenezer, others eyeing Cain Riddell with suspicion.

Riddell laughed again. "Keep this man covered, Ebenezer." Riddell pointed a huge finger at Captain Taneyhill. "If he moves, kill him. Just point that Henry at his head, and squeeze the trigger." His stare hardened. "You thinks you can do that, boy?"

The rifle felt like an anvil in Ebenezer's arms. He tried to shake his head.

"White men owned you all your life, Ebenezer," Riddell said. "They sold your wife, your daughter, took them away from you. You don't owe that man"—he practically spit on Captain Taneyhill—"nothing!"

Ebenezer's knees started to buckle.

"This will be over soon, Ebenezer," Riddell said. "Then I'll takes you to see your wife, your daughter." Smiling. "She's a tigress, that baby of yourn. How long has it been since you've seen her?"

His lips parted, but yet Ebenezer couldn't say anything.

"I've freed slaves, Ebenezer. Made men out of them. We'll sells this powder to the Comanches. They hate the white man as much as I do. We'll be rich, Ebenezer. You can buy your wife and daughter all the things they should have had to begin with. We'll ride away from here free, Ebenezer. Free!"

"Or you can die with your boss man," Tanner said with a sneer.

"Shut up, Tanner," Riddell said. His right hand rested on Ebenezer's shoulder, giving that reassuring squeeze the old man had always given Ebenezer and other young slaves back on the plantation. "You's free, Ebenezer. Do what you will."

With that, he turned, walked away, leaving Ebenezer with the Henry rifle and Captain Taneyhill.

Slowly Ebenezer turned the barrel toward the captain, but couldn't look at him, at least not in the eyes.

Chapter Twenty-Five

"Here comes somebody," Sweazy said.

Zeb pulled back the Sharps' hammer, drawing a bead on one of the bold-as-brass riders easing down the road.

"Do not shoot, Zeb," Gonzales whispered. "They carry a flag of truce."

"I see it." Zeb didn't, however, lower the barrel, or the hammer.

The sun, low in the west and behind the riders, made it hard to make out any of the riders, yet finally it became clear that the lead rider was Captain Taneyhill. As they drew near, Zeb could tell that the captain looked as if he had been trampled. Three men rode behind Taneyhill, and all the horses stopped about twenty-five yards from the wagons.

Slowly Taneyhill slipped off the saddle. His right arm looked broken, bloody. One black man dismounted, also, pointing a fancy rifle at the captain's head.

"*Madre mía*," Gonzales said. "That is . . . Ebenezer Chase."

"*Demonio*," Severo whispered.

This time, Zeb lowered the rifle. His stomach felt queasy. It couldn't be, but yes, there they were. Captain Taneyhill stood in the center of the road, with Ebenezer at his side, training a Henry rifle at the captain's head. Another rider, a burly black man with white hair, no hat, and a walrus mustache, held a rifle with a white bandanna tied to the barrel, and rode forward a few rods.

"We gots your boss!" His voice boomed with authority. "You wants him back. We wants what's left of your wagons. Let's trade."

205

Sweazy's voice startled Zeb. "Send Captain Taneyhill in. We'll let you have the wagons."

The black man on the white horse cackled. "No, I don't think I trust you. Y'all just hightail it back toward Belknap. We'll take the wagons, send your captain along after you."

"How could we trust you?" Sweazy asked.

The man laughed. "Gentlemen, please . . . ask anybody about Cain Riddell, and they'll tell you that I'm an honorable man."

"Yeah!" Sweazy yelled. "I've heard all about Cain Riddell. Blackheart. Black bas—"

"Watch your tongue, muleskinner!" Cain Riddell thundered. "You's likely heard that Cain Riddell ain't a man to be trifled with."

Cain . . . That jogged something in Zeb's memory, but he couldn't place the name, except the Bible story.

"Rangers are looking for you," Sweazy said. "So is a posse out of Dallas."

Riddell bowed his head, shaking it, and crossed himself. "Alas, that posse found us last week. Unfortunately for them. Now you give me those wagons," Riddell said, "or I start cutting off your captain's fingers. You call the tune, *amigo.*"

Suddenly the captain started yelling, "Boys, blow up those wagons! Don't let these swine get that gunpowder! Blow it up, get out of here. They won't let me live no matter what you do! Blow it . . ."

Zeb couldn't believe what happened next. Ebenezer Chase swung the barrel, which clipped the captain behind his ear, knocked him to the knees. A man behind Riddell slid off his horse, jerked the captain up, threw him on his horse, led him away. Quickly Zeb recovered, bringing the Sharps back up, putting the rider in his sights, before switching to the big man with the white hair.

"You listen to your captain," Riddell was saying, "and you'll all be dead."

"Just do like Uncle Cain says!" It was Ebenezer talking now, and Zeb swung the carbine, found Ebenezer Chase's ratty old quilt vest in his sights. The Sharps began trembling in Zeb's hands.

Uncle Cain . . . Now Zeb remembered. Ebenezer had spoken of him. Talked right highly of him. Hadn't he been a slave back on that same plantation as Ebenezer? Had Ebenezer been lying to Zeb all this time? Was this his plan? No, it didn't make a lick of sense. Zeb's head shook. He closed his eyes, opened them, tried to keep that carbine from shaking, tried to keep the tears out of his eyes, and kept the gun barrel aimed at Ebenezer Chase.

"I'll give you ten minutes," Cain Riddell said. "Then I'll start cutting Mister Taneyhill's fingers off his right hand."

Ebenezer mounted his horse. Zeb followed him with the Sharps.

"We could kill them," Pruden said.

Bile rose in Zeb's throat.

"No," Sweazy said. "They're still under a white flag. Besides, they'd kill us, and the captain. They have us outnumbered. Could blow us all to perdition if they wanted to."

"I cannot believe Ebenezer Chase is one of them," Gonzales said.

"Darky turncoat," Pruden said.

"Shut up!" Zeb snapped. "Ebenezer ain't . . ." He couldn't finish. Couldn't forget what he had just heard. Or seen.

The bushwhackers, Ebenezer, and Taneyhill were out of sight now.

"Cannot be far away," Severo said.

"Likely just around the bend," Pruden said.

"How many men?" Sweazy asked.

Gonzales shrugged. "*¿Quién sabe?*"

"Dozen would be my guess," Pruden said. "Maybe more."

"Ebenezer," Sweazy said, "he had one of them quick-shooting rifles. So did a couple others I saw."

"Henry lever-actions," Pruden agreed. "Spotted a Spencer amongst them blackguards, too. They not only got us outnumbered, they got us outgunned."

Severo crossed himself. Sweazy let out a little curse.

When Zeb stood, he butted the Sharps on the ground. "Let's give them the wagons," he said.

Chapter Twenty-Six

*F*orgive me, Lord, for hitting the captain like that, but I had to.
If I hadn't, one of Uncle Cain's highwaymen might have killed
him, then they would have killed Zeb . . . Gonzales . . . I had to do
that. Don't you see? Had to give Captain Taneyhill and Zeb, all the
others, a chance. It was the only way.

When Ebenezer had finished mouthing the prayer, Captain
Taneyhill was rubbing the knot behind his ear where Ebenezer
had struck him with the Henry's barrel. They were back to the
camp, Ebenezer guarding the captain, Cain Riddell arguing with
the scar-faced man named Tanner.

Suddenly a Mexican rider on a bay horse loped into camp,
waving a pale sombrero over his head, screaming, "They leave!
The muleskinners run from the wagons! On foot!"

Captain Taneyhill stopped rubbing his head.

Riddell clapped his hands, beaming. "Excellent."

Tanner barked an order. "Ride those men down. Kill every
last one of them."

"No!" Riddell shouted. "Let them go."

"Riddell . . ." Tanner began, but the old Negro cut him off.

"We need to get those wagons out of here first, Tanner, and
head north to the Nations. You said it yourself about that smoke
drawing attention. Those 'skinners can't hurt us, and it's a long
way to civilization." Turning, he said urgently, "The mules?"

The Mexican pointed over the ridge. "They turned them
loose. Some wander toward us. Others toward the burning
wagons that block the road. Some into the brush."

"Emil!" Riddell gestured at a black man with a brown porkpie hat. "Get to those wagons." He pointed at the Mexican on horseback. "Carlito, you and your boys rounds up those mules. *¡Vamanos! Muy pronto.*"

"What about him?" Tanner gave Captain Taneyhill a menacing stare.

"You stays here, Ebenezer," Riddell said as he mounted the big white horse. "Kill him if he moves. Shoot him down as a white man would do you or any man of color."

Ebenezer felt confusion all around him. The sun was starting to tip behind the mesa. Choking dust rose as men mounted their horses, whipped them into gallops. Ebenezer threw Captain Taneyhill a quick glance, then looked at the silver plate on the rifle's stock. For the first time, he read the words:

In deep appreciation to Leonard J. Stricklyn
From the people of Dallas County, Texas
June 21, 1863

Stricklyn. Major Hall had mentioned him. He was the undersheriff, had led the posse after . . . Cain Riddell. Ebenezer watched Riddell ride through the brush, remembered what he had yelled at Sweazy just a few minutes ago. Something about the posse having caught up with them. *Unfortunately* . . .

Riddell had killed them. Murdered them.

Ebenezer looked around to determine if Cain Riddell and his renegades had left him alone with the captain. He swung around, hoping, but . . . no . . . three men . . . a Mexican and two Negroes . . . remained in camp. One of them was looking at the trailing dust, the other two at Captain Taneyhill and Ebenezer.

"Ebenezer?"

Ebenezer turned to the captain.

"Work the lever on that rifle," he said.

"Huh?" Looking at the Henry in his hands.

"The lever. Cock it."

Ebenezer eyed Taneyhill with suspicion, then ratcheted the lever down and up. The heavy metallic clicks sounded incredibly loud.

Captain Taneyhill did the strangest thing. He smiled. "As I expected," he said.

"What?"

"It's empty."

Then Ebenezer remembered that, when he had seen Riddell twice work the lever, a cartridge had been ejected, one empty, the other unfired. He looked at the dirt, spotted the live shell. Swallowing, he inched his way to the bullet, picked it up.

"Quick, now, Ebenezer," the captain said. "It's a little awkward to load one of those, but we'll need that one shot."

He had said *we*. An intense relief washed over Ebenezer. *He trusts me, knows I'm not a turncoat.*

"Turn the lever locking latch." Taneyhill pointed at the rifle.

Ebenezer found the latch, turned it, and the lever went down maybe a half inch. "Push the lever," Taneyhill said. "Then feed that shell into the tubular magazine. There. Under the barrel. No, rim first, Ebenezer. Rim first. Good, lad. Good. Keep that rifle pointed away from you. There you go. Now, angle it just a tad, let the cartridge slide a bit. All right, now rotate the barrel back into . . ."

A murderous explosion rocked him forward, and Riddell's three men let out a yell and headed for the wagons. Ebenezer's ears rang again, and when he looked up, Captain Taneyhill was pushing himself to a seated position.

Shaking his head, Ebenezer straightened himself. The captain cleared his own head, pointed at the rifle, whispered, "Jack the hammer." Ebenezer did as instructed. "All right," the captain said. "It's loaded. But Cain Riddell doesn't know that."

Thick white smoke rose into the darkening sky. "What happened?" Ebenezer asked.

Captain Taneyhill chuckled. "Good lads," he said. "They followed my instructions."

The wagons! They had blown up all that gunpowder and, given the time it had taken, Ebenezer decided they had likely caught and killed a number of Cain Riddell's men. Ebenezer began sweating furiously.

Moments later, a bay horse burst through the brush, its saddle swinging underneath its belly, the horse's eyes wild with fright. The bay kept right on running. Another Negro rode into camp next, blood streaming from his mouth and nose. Others stumbled through the brush, one of the Mexicans crossing himself, shaking his head when one of the men left behind asked him something.

Finally Cain Riddell loped through the brush, swung from his horse, and began barking orders: "Get mounted! Those 'skinners blew up every last wagon."

"Where is Emil?" one of the black men asked.

"Scattered from here to the Brazos River!" Riddell yelled. "Tanner was right. Should have knowed better. We'll ride down every last one of those . . ."

A bullet killed the magnificent white stallion. Riddell whirled. Another shot came. Ebenezer turned. Captain Taneyhill struggled to his feet. A Mexican clutched his side and dropped to the ground. A puff of smoke rose from the brush, and another one of the bandits fell.

"Come on, boys!" Taneyhill yelled, waving his hat over his head. "Give 'em what-for!"

Ebenezer blinked back surprise as Zeb Hogan stepped forward, knelt, brought the Sharps rifle to his shoulder, and pulled the trigger. The gun roared, and another man pitched from his saddle, fell writhing on the ground, blood pouring from his thigh. Then Ebenezer saw Severo, swinging his rifle like an axe, the savage sound of impact carrying over the din of battle. Severo dropped a white forager with the blow, reached down, grabbed a Henry rifle, began firing. Sweazy leaped out of the brush, knocking a Mexican from the saddle, slashed with his knife, snatched up the dead man's rifle . . .

"You lying, stinking, miserable white . . ." Riddell drew one of the heavy Dragoon revolvers from his holster and made a beeline for Captain Taneyhill. "I'll see you dead if it's the last thing I do."

Ebenezer remembered the Henry rifle he held. Stepping in front of Captain Taneyhill, blocking him from Riddell, he swung the barrel, pointing it at Cain Riddell as the outlaw leader made his way toward then. Riddell didn't even seem to notice the young black boy with the repeating rifle.

"Uncle Cain," Ebenezer begged, "please, stop."

Spotting Ebenezer, Riddell chuckled, but kept right on walking. "Go ahead, Ebenezer, shoot me. Kill your Uncle Cain."

Ebenezer's finger tightened on the trigger.

"You always was nothing more than a Sambo. House darky. Missus Hall's pet. You ain't got the guts. You think I'd trust you . . ."

"Cain!" Tanner galloped into their midst. Riddell spun around, spotted the scarred white man on his horse, aiming a pistol down at him. "You got my brother blown to bits. I knew I never should have sided with some ignorant charcoal fool." The pistol belched smoke and flame. Riddell fell on his back, his gun spinning underneath a mesquite. The horse reared, Tanner steadied it, then saw Captain Taneyhill. Saw Ebenezer. Thumbed back the hammer.

Ebenezer had just started to bring the rifle up when something pushed him from behind. He caught a glimpse of a hand jerking the rifle from his grip. Tanner's revolver roared. Something buzzed over Ebenezer's head. He hit the ground, rolled over, watched Taneyhill bracing the stock against his left thigh, his right arm still hanging uselessly, lifting the barrel. He saw it all happening as if in a dream, as if time was stretching, moving all so slowly.

Tanner's horse rearing.

The gunman cocking his revolver.

The Henry booming.

The horse pitching to its side, spilling Tanner from the saddle.

Captain Taneyhill bringing the empty rifle up in his good arm, cutting loose with a savage Rebel yell, charging Tanner as the bushwhacker rose to his knees, snapping a shot, cocking the pistol.

Another shot boomed behind Ebenezer, and Tanner's chest blossomed crimson as he fell on his back, shuddered once, then lay still.

Turning, Ebenezer saw Cain Riddell on his side, his right arm extended, holding the other Dragoon pistol. The revolver slipped from his fingers, and he slumped over, letting out a small moan.

* * * * *

The next thing Ebenezer knew, he was cradling Riddell's head in his lap, tears streaming down his face, asking him, "Why, Uncle Cain? Why . . . ?"

"My choice, Ebenezer," he said. "Free man's gots a right to choose his . . ." His eyes shut. He trembled. "Make your own choices, boy. Make the right one."

A shadow crossed his face. Captain Taneyhill stood over him, holding the revolver he had taken off Tanner's dead body. The sound of gunfire died down. Most of Cain Riddell's men were dead or hightailing it out of there, wounded.

"That Henry . . ." Riddell said. "You told the boy . . ."

The captain's head bobbed slowly.

Grinning, Riddell faced Ebenezer again. "You woulda shot me . . . Ebenezer?"

His head shook, but Cain Riddell knew Ebenezer was lying.

"That's all right," he said. "You done good, boy. There's a preacher man at Phantom Hill. Bury me there." Riddell reached over, gripped Ebenezer's hand. "I ain't nothing but a runaway, Ebenezer, nothing more'n a swamp runner, but you's free. Now, find our camp, you . . ."

He never finished.

Chapter Twenty-Seven

Once, Phantom Hill had been an Army post, but no more. Lately it had been used as a stagecoach stop, which explained why the corrals were so solid among a city of crumbling adobe walls. It didn't explain the whitewashed church, standing out among the stone and earthen-colored buildings. The building hadn't always been a place of worship, just one of the adobes the Army had built, which somebody had turned into a church.

It would serve the purpose.

Zeb Hogan and the others would be busy this day, digging graves. Had it been left to Zeb, Cain Riddell would be rotting with the others they had buried in a shallow, single grave back alongside the trail. Sweazy felt the same. So did Pruden. But Captain Taneyhill and Ebenezer reminded them that Cain Riddell—Uncle Cain to Ebenezer—had likely saved the captain's life, and that an outlaw, even one as bad as Riddell, deserved to have his last wish granted, and he had asked to be buried here.

The muleskinners had gathered what stock they could find. Several of the mules, many of the bandits' horses, and a great number of men had been killed when the wagons had blown up. Pruden had wanted to go after the bandits that had gotten away, but Sweazy had said to let them go. They had to set the captain's busted arm, get that shoulder back in its socket, and, most importantly, dig the bullet out of his shoulder before the wound became infected. They had to figure how they could get back to Jefferson.

Captain Taneyhill had ordered Sweazy on a scouting mission southwest. To check on Riddell's camp, just in case the bandit hadn't been lying, that he had women and children there. The rest of the group headed to Phantom Hill. They had to bury Cain Riddell. More importantly, they had to bury Miguel Gonzales. They had paid a price for that assault on Riddell's men.

Zeb wondered if it had been worth it.

"I'll fetch the preacher," Captain Taneyhill, his arm in a sling, said after the bodies of Riddell and Gonzales had been carried to the Phantom Hill cemetery. When the blanket fell off the old Mexican's face, Zeb reached down to cover it, but Ebenezer beat him to it. Tears rolled down Ebenezer's cheeks, and he looked up at Zeb, shaking his head.

"It's my fault," he said.

"No, it ain't," Zeb responded.

"I never was one of the gang," Ebenezer said.

"I knowed that, too. Reckon I taught you good." Zeb forced a smile.

Ebenezer looked perplexed.

"How to lie," Zeb explained.

Ebenezer smiled, but only briefly, before he frowned again. "Uncle Cain, he was the real liar," he said. "Told me my wife and daughter were still alive. Gave me an empty rifle. He would have killed me and the captain."

"You saved the captain's life," Zeb reminded him.

"No." Ebenezer's head shook. "Not really."

A horse whinnied, and Zeb looked past the runaway slave's shoulder, saw people coming into the old fort's grounds. Most of them walked slowly, looking scared, as if they didn't know what to do, which way to go, what to expect. Women, mostly. Negro women and some children. A white man rode behind them, and Zeb recognized the rider as Sweazy.

"Hey," Zeb said softly, slowly lifting his arm, pointing. He wasn't certain, didn't want to raise Ebenezer's hopes.

Ebenezer spun, looked, took a step, stopped. His heart pounded. He had to catch his breath, searching the faces of the women, some middle-aged, a few with white hair, and a couple of younger ones in their late teens or early twenties. One of the latter carried a child.

"God!" The word shot out of Ebenezer's throat, part prayer, part exclamation. His knees started to buckle, but he recovered, and shouted out a name: "Lizzie!" Suddenly he was dashing toward them, and the young woman, holding a toddler tightly against her breasts, was running to meet him, screaming out Ebenezer's name.

When they embraced, tears started to fill Zeb's eyes. He looked at the shovel in his hand, wondering if he should start digging or go over to his friend, meet Ebenezer's family. *No,* he told himself, *give them time alone.* That's what Pruden and Sweazy were doing. Zeb felt himself smiling, until a voice from behind chilled him.

"I am not a Catholic priest, but I will do the best I can, Mister Taneyhill. I have not yet been ordained, just felt the calling."

Zeb Hogan would have known that voice anywhere. He whirled, mouth hanging open, dropping the shovel, his eyes hardening. The little runt in the black broadcloth suit looked up at Zeb, blinking away his own surprise.

"Private Hogan?" Sergeant Ben DeVere asked.

* * * * *

"After Beth died of cholera here," DeVere said, "I drank myself into oblivion. Like I always did. When I sobered up, I realized I couldn't go on as I'd been going. I'm probably the last man on earth you'd ever think would feel the call to spread the gospel, to help others." DeVere shook his head.

Zeb kept quiet.

"I was never a fit soldier, Zebulon. Dare I say, I was a coward. Yet the love of God has filled my heart now. After I'd passed out, after I had missed Beth's own funeral, I woke to find somebody had left me a Bible, put it in my hands. I read it, filled with the love of God, of Jesus Christ. I knew this was where I must be, helping wayfarers, helping, saving myself. Yet I owe you an apology. I owe all of Wisconsin, all of the Union Army, an apology. They let you out of the Florence Stockade in February, right?"

They walked through the little cemetery, Ben DeVere acting as if they were long-lost friends, Zeb despising himself for letting the traitorous sergeant think that. Zeb hated himself for not having killed DeVere when he had first seen him.

Finally Zeb found his voice. "They didn't let me out. I escaped. It was after Sergeant Major Engstrand died."

Shaking his head, Ben DeVere stopped walking and started to cry. "Engstrand was a good man. Better than I'd ever hope to be." A curious look appeared on DeVere's face, and he stopped sobbing just long enough to ask, "When did . . . you escape?"

"February. Couple of weeks, I reckon, before Sherman burned Columbia. I been running ever since, chasing . . ." Zeb couldn't finish, though, looking at DeVere's weak face, watching tears spill down his cheeks. The man was crying for Sergeant Major Engstrand.

"Forgive me, lad. May God have mercy on me. I am . . ." As the tears stopped, DeVere sighed. "You poor lad. Had you stayed at the Stockade, you would have been paroled. The Rebs turned them loose . . . likely just after your escape."

Those words almost knocked Zeb to the ground. "How'd you know that?" he asked.

"'Twas in one of the newspapers a traveler left me. Brigadier Winder, the prison commander, the man I hold responsible for those wretched conditions we . . . no, you . . . had to deal with in the Stockade, died of a heart attack in Florence. After his death, Colonel Forno closed the Stockade, shipped the prisoners to North Carolina . . . to be paroled." DeVere stopped talking, and pointed. "Here. Here is Beth's . . ." Yet he couldn't finish. Taking a number of steps forward, clutching his Bible, he fell to his knees, sobbing again, praying for his dead true love, for his own miserable soul.

Zeb looked at the little cross, saw the name scratched into one of the timbers, studied the cacti blooming like regular flowers on her grave. Most of the graves here were sunken, without markers, but not Miss Elizabeth Gentry's. The wind blew. Zeb heard the sound of Ben DeVere's sobs, the sound of the spades striking earth as men dug the new graves in the post cemetery.

Two graves, Zeb thought. *We ought to be digging three.* His hands balled into fists. He had vowed to kill the man, but he kept thinking of something Sergeant Major Engstrand had told him, after that first battle in Georgia.

It's a hard thing, Zeb, to kill another man. And it should be a hard thing. It should always be hard.

Captain Taneyhill's more recent words, too, echoed in Zeb's ears. *It weighs on a person, killin' a man. You take away his life, but you also take away a good part, the better part, of yours.*

Images of the men shot the day before flashed through his mind. Likely Zeb had killed some of them. He had spent most of last night shaking, throwing up, sick at all that he had done. Not that he was sorry, just sick. Like the captain once said, he sure didn't wish to trade places with the men he had killed.

Slowly Ben DeVere rose, mumbled an apology, fished a handkerchief from his coat pocket, and mopped the tears off his cheeks. "Well," he said, "I suppose it is time for the first funeral. Come, Zebulon. Let us pay our final respects to *Señor* Gonzales and, yes, even that blackheart, Cain Riddell."

* * * * *

It was June 19, 1865. While Zeb Hogan and the others stood there on a hot, windy day in West Texas, a Federal general named Gordon Granger read General Order No. 3 from a balcony in Galveston:

"The people of Texas are informed that, in accordance with a proclamation from the Executive of the United States, all slaves are free. This involves an absolute equality of personal rights and rights of property between former masters and slaves . . ."

From then on, men and women of color in Texas would celebrate June 19 as their holiday. Juneteenth, they would call it.

The people gathered for a double funeral at Phantom Hill, of course, knew nothing about what was going on more than four hundred miles away. They just watched the Reverend Ben DeVere and listened to his words.

He preached a good funeral. Said some fitting, comforting words over Miguel Gonzales's grave, and did the same for Cain Riddell. Afterward, the captain paid the Reverend Ben DeVere a little bit of money. The preacher thanked him, and turned to leave. He did not look at, or speak to, Zeb Hogan.

The wind blew hard, warm. It was spring, practically summer. Ben DeVere kept walking, head down, never glancing back.

"Well?"

Zeb looked over at Captain Taneyhill. Beside him stood a beaming Ebenezer Chase, holding his little Tempie in his left arm, his right hand gripping his wife's hand.

Zeb turned and briefly watched Sergeant Ben DeVere walk to the little whitewashed adobe building, Bible in hand. The man Zeb had traveled more than one thousand miles, south by southwest, through war-ravaged Southern states, across the savage plains of Texas to kill.

A lot of country Zeb had traveled. He had grown up, too. A boy when he escaped the Florence Stockade, with some boyish notion of duty. Ebenezer had been right. Duty . . . honor. They had been just words to Zeb Hogan. He hadn't truly known what they meant. Now he knew.

Zeb had a duty, to God, to Luansy, Ebenezer, and Captain Taneyhill, but mostly to himself. He had to honor himself, too. Once he had been a Union soldier, and he could not disgrace that uniform by murdering a man, a pathetic shell of a man, but a man of God. A man who had begged for forgiveness.

"Well?" the captain asked again.

Zeb shrugged. "Can't kill no preacher," he said.

Ebenezer smiled. "You couldn't have killed him anyway. I know you too well, Zeb Hogan."

Without answering, Zeb headed for the mules.

Ebenezer Chase was right. He usually was.

THE END

About the Author

Johnny D. Boggs has worked cattle, shot rapids in a canoe, hiked across mountains and deserts, traipsed around ghost towns, and spent hours poring over microfilm in library archives—all in the name of finding a good story. He's also one of the few Western writers to have won four Spur Awards from Western Writers of America (for his novels *Camp Ford*, in 2006, *Doubtful Cañon*, in 2008, and *Hard Winter* in 2010, and his short story, "A Piano at Dead Man's Crossing," in 2002) and the Western Heritage Wrangler Award from the National Cowboy and Western Heritage Museum (for his novel *Spark on the Prairie: The Trial of the Kiowa Chiefs*, in 2004). A native of South Carolina, Boggs spent almost fifteen years in Texas as a journalist at the *Dallas Times Herald* and *Fort Worth Star-Telegram* before moving to New Mexico in 1998 to concentrate full time on his novels. Author of dozens of published short stories, he has also written for more than fifty newspapers and magazines, and is a frequent contributor to *Boys' Life*, *New Mexico Magazine*, *Persimmon Hill*, and *True West*. His Western novels cover a wide range. *The Lonesome Chisholm Trail* (Five Star Westerns, 2000) is an authentic cattle-drive story, while *Lonely Trumpet* (Five Star Westerns, 2002) is an historical novel about the first black graduate of West Point. *The Despoilers* (Five Star Westerns, 2002) and *Ghost Legion* (Five Star Westerns, 2005) are set in the Carolina backcountry during the Revolutionary War. *The Big Fifty* (Five Star Westerns, 2003) chronicles the slaughter of buffalo on the southern plains in the 1870s, while *East of the Border* (Five Star Westerns, 2004) is a comedy about the theatrical offerings of Buffalo Bill Cody, Wild Bill Hickok, and Texas Jack Omohundro, and *Camp Ford* (Five Star Westerns, 2005) tells about a Civil War baseball game between Union prisoners of war and Confederate guards. "Boggs's narrative voice captures the old-fashioned style of the past," *Publishers Weekly* said, and *Booklist* called him "among the best Western writers at work today." Boggs lives with his wife Lisa and son Jack in Santa Fe. His website is www.johnnydboggs.com.